The Last Confessions of Sylvia P.

The Last Confessions of Sylvia P.

A NOVEL

Lee Kravetz

HARPER
An Imprint of HarperCollins*Publishers*

This book is a work of fiction. References to real people, events, establishments, organizations, or locales are intended only to provide a sense of authenticity, and are used fictitiously. All other characters, and all incidents and dialogue, are drawn from the author's imagination and are not to be construed as real.

HarperCollins books may be purchased for educational, business, or sales promotional use. For information, please email the Special Markets Department at SPsales@harpercollins.com.

FIRST EDITION

Library of Congress Cataloging-in-Publication Data has been applied for.

ISBN 978-0-06-313999-2

22 23 24 25 26 LSC 10 9 8 7 6 5 4 3 2 1

FOR JANIS

FIRST STANZA

The Name

Every poem is a moment. It makes no promises.

—Boston Rhodes, "Polaris"

1

Estee, 2019

The safe holdings room at the St. Ambrose Auction House has no windows, two late-nineteenth-century oil paintings on the back wall, a small wooden table, and privacy, the most valuable item in the archive. As a master curator for the house, I introduce myself to Elton and Jay Jay, the Dyce brothers. Elton, wearing a gray street jacket, blue jeans, and a T-shirt that reads *FREE BEER, IT'S WHAT'S FOR BREAKFAST,* asks, "What's a master curator?" Think of my role as not merely that of a broker, but as a kind of archaeologist, a purveyor of restoration, a butler to history, though my essential utility is that of a caretaker, performing one's calling with decorum and formality.

"Pellegrino?"

Yes, the water's free.

They accept.

"My specialty is rare books," I say, and Jay Jay says he wants to know about the most impressive object the auction house has ever sold. St. Ambrose has moved paintings, atlases, and sculptures, all impressive, all special.

"What I mean is," Jay Jay says, "what's the most you've ever sold an item for?" I can tell that underneath his baggy pants, spotless white high-tops, and Bruins jersey, Jay Jay is toned, like a convicted felon is toned, like a bored junkyard flunky with a set of barbells is toned.

Several years ago, a Gutenberg Bible in my care sold for twenty-one million dollars. As I say this, the Dyce brothers share a kind of dazed, defenseless awe, and Jay Jay asks, who buys a Bible for twenty-one million dollars? As long as objects come up for auction, there will always be those willing to own them, no matter the cost. Collectors, investors, people for whom money is no object. Rather, it is the sellers who come from different places, different backgrounds, different means.

"So I'm thinking we came to the right woman, then," Elton says. "I mean, if it's good enough for Gutenberg."

Elton Dyce used to own a bar on Dorchester Avenue. It went under after his divorce—his second, he says. Afterward, he joined up with his brother's business, buying and flipping houses, many of them dilapidated and in disrepair. The ones in foreclosure are often abandoned, meaning Elton and Jay Jay are left razing rooms and hauling furniture to Dennison Consignment or selling sofas and dining room sets on eBay. The house on Napoleon Street, an old Victorian, was empty when they purchased it through a probate sale. The Dyce brothers take turns telling me about the sagging old Victorian with the peeling paint, the drooping wraparound covered porch, the dripping radiators, the cracked ceiling plaster. "Anyway, when we get around to inspecting the attic, I find this," Elton says, nodding to Jay Jay.

Jay Jay reaches inside a duffel bag at his feet and lifts out a metal container. He places it on the table between all of us.

For a master curator, is there anything more perfect than coming face-to-face with a closed box? For instance, a seller once showed me a shoebox containing a first-edition copy of Victor Hugo's *Cromwell*. Within a safety deposit box, I found a well-preserved *Book of Hours* bordered in illustrations of bright yellow lemons and caterpillars. In a cardboard storage box, I identified a copy of *Julius Caesar* dating back to the seventeenth century, its pages brown and chipped as though made out of thin sheets of clay. It has been this way from the beginning, when I first spied a dark case high up on a closet shelf in my home, reached my arms, stretched my fingers, brought it down to the floor, and opened it to find a black Corona typewriter—my mother's—with its three rows of round keys, each one yellow, off-yellow, yellowish white with cracked coverings. The typewriter's frame, the corner of the frame, specifically the left corner of the frame, was dented, mangled really.

What I'm saying is, objects, like boxes, carry multitudes. What I'm saying is, often when people bring their objects to a master curator for initial appraisal, I still experience a moment of anticipation, of pause, before engaging with it. It's these revelatory intangibles that still keep me going. What I'm saying is, this is the case with Elton and Jay Jay and the object they've brought me today, a grayish-brown container with two flimsy handles on its sides. Keeping it shut is the job of a small, round lock. Fingerprints break its coating of dust. At this point, the box can hold anything. It just might hold everything.

The box looks as though one of the Dyce brothers has taken a flathead screwdriver and pried apart the lock mechanism. "We're hoping you can tell us what these are," Elton says, raising the lid.

In my sweater pockets, my hands will always find a pair of cloth gloves. I pull them on before removing three college-ruled notebooks one at a time from the lockbox. Separating the notebooks, I lay them side by side on the table. The cover of the black notebook is torn and partially falling off its metal spiral. The blue cover of the second notebook is mostly intact. Written in black ink across the top of the third notebook's green cover are the letters *V* and *L*.

Jay Jay says that in the house-flipping business, when it comes to seeking and locating hidden gems, he and his brother are like truffle pigs with their noses in the dirt. They know promise when they smell it. "They're just journals. But . . . I don't know—I mean, they look old, right?"

"Also, the way the box was wedged up there in the attic," Elton adds, "it looked like someone put it way back there on purpose."

"Like it was hidden," Jay Jay says.

In my time as a master curator, I've learned the difference between recovered objects and discovered objects. One is lost. The other is buried, like a secret, like evidence. And yet all objects that transcend time endure a process of burial, a period of hidden preservation. That is, deceit is part of their makeup.

"Anyways," Jay Jay says, "later, we were watching *Antiques Roadshow*, and Elton gets this idea that maybe the notebooks we found are worth something."

Ah yes, the PBS challenge that has found me appraising more replicas, counterfeits, cheap re-creations, and tchotchkes mistaken for antiquity than I care to remember. Who doesn't like a mystery, or to hang their aspirations on the *what if*? At sixty-five years old, I myself have never grown tired of the promise. I try to let these prospectors down easy. I'll tell them I'm sorry, but these objects are not what they hoped they'd be. A master curator is part psychologist and part parent nursing a child's bruised feelings. Every so often, however, an object appears—a statuette in a forgotten set of drawers, a piece of jewelry in the pocket of old clothing, a Fabergé crystal vase in the back of a cupboard. At this point, for all sellers the thrill of discovery narrows to a singular point: the question of value. They want to know how much their object is worth, how much their object will go for at auction, how much their object will change their lives. That proposition—the *how much*—is as integral a quality as an object's rarity, age, and condition. The role of a master curator therefore is also part banker, part assessor, and part doctor delivering her prognosis.

I run two fingers across the *V* and the *L* drawn in heavy ink on the green cover. Making the shape of an okay sign, I take a corner and open the notebook. The pages are filled with handwriting, small, neat, vivid, and tender. The letters are a mix of block print and cursive. Each word is angled and rendered with consideration like fine stitching—

I reach the end of the first sentence and stop reading. I double back, and it is only after I've studied the opening again that I move on to the second line and the third. The pad of my finger traces them like routes along a map, the foreign becoming the oddly familiar.

Elton, catching the color I feel rising in my cheeks, says, "So? What is it?"

I turn and read through more pages. "Well," I say eventually, clearing my throat, "it appears as though someone has deliberately transcribed *The Bell Jar.*"

Jay Jay's expression is lodged somewhere between mild interest and dull curiosity. He scratches his belly under his jersey. "What the fuck's a bell jar?"

I know *The Bell Jar,* as a work of classic fiction from the mid–twentieth century, does not exactly fall in line with the more archaic works of my own critical catalog, otherwise procured chronicling the inventory of the Académie des Beaux-Arts, the archives of the Spanish National Library, or even the St. Ambrose Auction House. Still, as a book, *The Bell Jar* is instantly recognizable to those well versed in works of American literature. It is safe to say that the Dyce brothers are not. They are no more readers than they are antique book collectors. "It's a novel," I say, "a pseudo-memoir really, written roughly fifty-five years ago," and Jay Jay raises his hand, interrupts me, says why would a person transcribe a whole book? He says that it seems like a real waste of time, and Elton suggests it could be some kid's school project. Either way, I can tell that the thought of the object being anything less than an authentic manuscript of historical, and therefore high-monetary, value is bringing Jay Jay down.

I lean over the table, returning to the open notebook. The text is full of scratched-out words, and variations of words, and words circled and underlined. To me, it reveals a kind of process.

In my mind, two gears click into place. Quickly, I flip back to the front cover. I touch my fingers again to the letters *V* and *L*. The oddly familiar becomes the irrefutable.

"Victoria Lucas," I whisper to myself.

Elton turns the bill of his cap backward. "Victoria who?"

I raise my eyes from the notebook. "Victoria Lucas. It's a pseudonym."

Jay Jay looks bewildered, as though I am speaking in another language. "That means it's a pen name," Elton says flatly, and Jay Jay, wounded, says, "I get what a pseudonym is, dipshit. I'm asking, whose pseudonym is it?"

"Sylvia Plath's," I say.

The safe holdings room grows quiet around us. After a long moment, Jay Jay says, "Okay, I'll bite. Who's Sylvia Plath?"

1

Boston Rhodes, 1958

My Dearest Professor Lowell,

I've moved in and out of the realm of confession so many times. Only now, at the end, have I found my strength. For your kindnesses, and because you were there and don't yet realize what you saw, no one deserves the truth more. You see, I fear you've bought into a false history. I want to set you straight; I want to tell you my part.

You once said, we poets are detectives, that we are to call attention to the details ordinary people see every day and overlook, to carve out secrets as one uses a spoon to gut oysters. With this letter it's my hope that I can set things right. I will point your eyes to the details you have overlooked.

There was intent. There was motive. There was a weapon.

The first time I met you, you were a mess of a man. Do you remember?

I tracked you to an address on Beacon Street, a brownstone across from a deli, an old synagogue, and Tang's Tobacco where I used to fetch Crüwell-Tabak for my father. Up four flights of steps, I entered a crowded apartment full of ornate wood moldings, high white plaster ceilings, and Persian carpets. Candles stuck into green wax-crusted wine bottles cast a dismal light. Meticulous oil paintings, mostly of schooners, covered the walls. The Dansette record player maintained an unbroken stream of jazz as I staked out a corner of the living room and unbuttoned my winter jacket. That's when I first spied you, leaning against the stone hearth. Your expression suggested you were either wearing the most uncomfortable shoes or managing a toothache. Your clothes, a ragged coat, woolen pants, a rumpled button-down shirt, and natty red scarf, intimated a man who was tormented by profound devils.

The first reader at that night's gathering of the New England Poetry Club was a woman who approached the microphone at the top of the living room wearing a black Inverness cape. She was small and witchlike, but the most unusual thing about her had to be a beaver-hair tricorn hat upon her head. From a small book in a voice that was somehow both flat and feverish, she read a poem she called "The Paper Nautilus." After her, a man with a thick dark beard and wire-framed glasses read a marvelous poem he called "Hearts Needle." I watched, and I listened, and I pictured myself in front of a large group of people like this someday.

When it was time for the next poet to read, you made your way to the makeshift stage. You were met with a deluge of applause louder than anyone had received thus far. Regarding the audience with eyes both dazed and serious, your mouth cast a touch askew, you adjusted your glasses and fumbled through a handful of loose pages.

You'd scarcely uttered your first lines when a heckler barked, "Utter dreck!"

But you, the professional, the icon, the poet hero, paid the heckler no mind. You read on, even as the insults persisted.

"Horrid! Toothless!"

All that noise, I saw, was coming from a small white-haired man seated in a leather chair at the back of the room. He looked like a lion lounging lazily on his rocky throne. Sloping newspaper-colored brows sprang up in all directions. A skein of smoke negotiated its way up from the cigarette in his fingers as he groaned, sighed, and spewed his invective.

"Puerile raffle!"

The whole room sprang to your defense. The crowd shouted down the old man in a manner that subdued him for a period, but when no one else seemed to be paying him any mind, I watched him bring the tip of his cigarette to the corner of a sheaf he'd brought with him that night. I sat there frozen as his pages started to burn, and it took someone else shouting "Fire!" and panic and smoke filling the apartment before my limbs regained their power. With a kind of lackadaisical gleam, the old man let the burning paper drop to the surface of a side table, where it collected more pages for fuel and burst into an inferno.

The first reader, the woman in the tricorn hat, rushed over fanning at the fire to put it out. Instead, flames jumped from the side table to the cuff of the old man's jacket, and he leapt to his feet as fire gobbled up his right arm.

When I was a girl, I witnessed my mother rush to the aid of my oldest sister, who was choking on a hunk of bread. Fortified with comparable speed, I now barreled through the gathering. Snatching a glass along the way, I doused the smoldering papers. They curled into slowly closing fists. Then I turned my efforts to the old man, and after I beat back the flames from his arm, he addressed me as though I was the most beautiful thing he'd ever seen.

"I suppose," he said breathlessly, "there's some poetry to dying by the page."

"Robert Frost's a bastard!" said the guy mixing drinks at the bar in the den. The gathering of the New England Poetry Club was still clearing of smoke.

Beside me, your hand navigated the display of bottles on the counter, an exhibition of ales, whiskeys, rums, brandies, and an ewer of *baijiu* wrapped in rice paper and cinched with a satin ribbon. As you settled on Old Fitzgerald—the good stuff—you said, "Jealous fucking Jahweh!"

I was baffled. "*The* Robert Frost? But . . . why would he do that?"

"Light himself on fire?" You took an empty glass and poured yourself a drink. "Professional rivalry. It's a pisser, slipping into irrelevancy. Do me a favor. Next time, don't be so quick to put him out."

I saw my opening and introduced myself to you. "Professor Lowell, Agatha White." I then added, "Poet." I'd recently come to understand that poetry was going to be essential to my life. The realization, I explained, was thrilling but also confusing. When I'd thought I was going to be a housewife or mother, I'd felt ambivalent and unsure. Eventually, I decided the only way forward for me was to pilot a scholarly path and set myself on this pursuit. "To put it plainly, I want to join your workshop. If I'm going to be the greatest poet in history, I'm going to need the greatest teacher. Anyway, the shrew at the registrar's office told me the workshop's reserved for advanced poets, which I take to mean *published* poets. But how am I supposed to get published if no one's ever heard of me? You see my dilemma."

"And you thought it was a good idea to ambush me at a public reading?"

"The first rule of sales, according to my father, is never go through an intermediary. Face-to-face, close the deal."

I opened my pocketbook and passed you a typed page. The title, "Polaris," was typed across the top. Inked in the margins, I'd notated handwritten sound patterns and rhyme schemes.

"I feel this offers a good deal of wonderful, if underdeveloped, creative potential."

Drinking from your glass, you read from the page, and gave equal consideration to both.

"It's good, isn't it?"

After a moment, you said, "It moves with ease and is filled with experience, like good prose. You stick to truth and simple expression of difficult feelings. It's the line of poetry I'm most interested in myself. It's confessional and personal and poetic in its un-poetic-ness."

I wanted to be in your workshop more than anything, I said. I'd bring my own chair. I'd sit in a corner. I needed an authentic critic with a sense for quality work; I needed you, Professor Lowell. If only you'd give me a chance, I'd show you that I was the least amateur writer in your whole miserable classroom.

I followed you to your car. Outside, we entered a form of silence only knowable to secluded corners of old towns on winter nights. The restaurants were dark. The streets were gloomy canals of cold cars and dirty snow heaps. You got into your Chrysler with its snow-dusted windshield, started the engine, and rolled down your window. "You're green, but there's at least two solid lines in each stanza." You tried to hand my poem back to me. I refused to take it. You'd have had to drive over my foot to leave without giving me an answer. So you gave me an answer.

If your first lesson to me was on the dangers of professional rivalries, lesson two was this: I wasn't a real poet. Not yet.

The classroom at the second floor of the college was just big enough for twelve students around the Formica table. You made me prove my worthiness to sit among the other eleven. With that used-up look of yours, you—sour, disinterested, at times mildly intrigued, though mostly contemptuous—read my pieces aloud. Here, I came to know just how poorly I wrote sonnets. In your voice, my words came off strained, each choice I'd made so obvious and purposeful it lost any organic urgency.

I struggled to understand what you meant when you spoke about the eternal rivalries, how there exists a tension between words and meaning, and how poetry is a competition between logic and sound, a war in which meaning and the dream state face off. For one to win, it must stuff out the other. "Poetry's purpose is singular, to celebrate the troubled relation of the word to what it represents. It's a rivalry between the two, and the poet unites them!"

One evening, just as the workshop ended, you and I shared a moment. Do you remember? You placed the copy of my old poem, "Polaris," in front of me.

"What's it mean?"

I'd written "Polaris" about my father and his three daughters who loved him so. We were his young women, cultured in social graces, mannered in deportment and etiquette, models of the best in society, money, and education. Whenever we saw our chance, we presented ourselves to him, this man of importance. We were in endless competition with one another over top marks, volunteer hours at the Mayweather Convalescence Home, the fairest complexion, the most precise punctuality. The object of the game was to capture the light in our father's eyes. It was a bright but unreachable light. At stake was nothing less than his affection. He appreciated young women who knew a perfectly appointed table, who attended to their weekly hair wash and setting, who didn't fidget. My marks were lacking. I didn't volunteer anywhere unless my mother forced me to. The others had their fair skin, while I had my grandfather's Eastern European complexion, which was darker and dappled with freckles. And yes, I was often late, and yes, I fidgeted, chewing on my nails and smacking my chewing gum. Not that I didn't try to make my father proud. I just came up short.

"So, the poem's about you," you said, "but I don't see you anywhere in it." Then you eviscerated the poem. The one or two lines you'd liked the night we met hardly stood up against the force of your gale. "Reading this poem, I don't know how you feel or what you think. It's *safe*." You made the word "safe" sound like you'd swallowed a mouthful of horseshit.

I wasn't sure what to say. I looked at my fingers. "It's just a poem . . ."

"Every poem is a revolt. Anything less isn't worth my time."

I felt ashamed. I wasn't going to bring a poem like this to workshop again. In fact, I wasn't going to come back to the workshop at all.

You snapped up my hands. Yours were warm and firm.

"I also believe your instincts are better than any of the poets I've ever had in this room. Polaris. The North Star. It's your destination, Agatha. A poetry revolution is coming. You're a part of it," you said. "In fact, I do believe you have it in you to lead the whole thing."

I promised myself I'd never write another benign word, that I'd bare my soul in every line as though I were baring it only to you—you, who'd asked to see me and my ugly core. From then on, mastering the confession of poetry was my one longing. Accordingly, I became your star pupil.

And that's how it might have stayed had The Name not arrived in your workshop one rainy Tuesday afternoon and ruined it all.

Of course, everybody in your workshop knew who Sylvia Plath was. The presence of the famed poet sent a charge through the room that inexorably changed the dynamic, tenor, and chemistry of the practicum.

By the way, Professor Lowell, do you know that your face is perpetually contemplative? It's possibly the most symmetrical face I've ever known, not quite handsome but attractive in its serene confidence. Yet on the day Sylvia arrived here, I saw the architecture of your bones change shape. What were you thinking in these moments? I wonder. What intoxicating thought was potent enough to crack that stone façade, or for that matter, shatter the order and etiquette of the workshop you'd so ingrained into us? When you had us make space for Sylvia at the table, Maxine in our workshop was more than happy to get up and bring in a folding chair from another classroom. That's right: while I'd fought hard these many months to earn a place among you all, the table just gave Sylvia a seat. And instead of launching into your lecture while perpetually pacing the room, as was your usual way, you addressed the workshop from the head of the table, directly beside our interloper.

Another thing you never let workshop participants do was read our own work aloud. You preferred to pick one of our poems and recite it, first to yourself, and then for our benefit in a low, sometimes frightening, rendition. It was the way we did things. You reserved your judgment and allowed the workshop to settle on its own before offering forth your critique. But on that day, you fingered the pages of Sylvia's folio. You chose a poem from it, handed it to Sylvia, and in your soft, dangerous voice you said, "Please read this for us."

Sylvia stood, the legs of her chair leaving the discolored rug and scraping against the hardwood floor. She was thirty years old if I had to guess, and outfitted stylishly in a red dress and red French shoes and red matte lips. She had Lauren Bacall's aloof expression of cool observation, her face powdered to lighten the pigeon-feather gray under her eyes.

"'Tale of a Tub,'" she said.

She lowered the page to her side and began to recite by memory verse after verse, her tone vital and vibrant, her gaze unblinking. By the fourth stanza, your workshop had inhaled like a big pink lung.

> "'. . . We take the plunge; under water our limbs
> waver, faintly green, shuddering away
> from the genuine color of skin; can our dreams
> ever blur the intransigent lines which draw
> the shape that shuts us in? . . .'"

It was an unusual poem about an equally unusual subject. *A bathtub?* Yet the workshop clung onto each syllable of Sylvia's recitation.

"Succinct!" the workshop said.

"Perfect!" the workshop said.

"Clearly the work of a Major Voice," you said, praising the poem from the start. And why not? She was so confident, so self-possessed, so self-assured, as though she were the only person in the room that afternoon.

Oh, but darling, I was there, too, was I not?

Sure, Sylvia Plath was well published, but she was no Adrienne Rich. She was certainly prettier than Adrienne Rich, though, that trodden handbag. Was the preferential treatment you offered Sylvia necessary? Did you want to fuck her? *Were you fucking her?* The swiftness with which Sylvia ingratiated herself, combined with your immediate admiration and appreciation of her work, indicated so. For a poem to earn your praise and achieve your designation of Major Voice required of its author months of psychic pummeling under your tutelage. To have Sylvia's work appear before you, fully formed and praiseworthy, boggled the mind.

Here she was, breezing into your workshop. No one questioned the merit of her bravado when, on her second day with us, she compared the poem of our own Sam Albert, which was more experimental than his usual fare, to Herbert—as though Sylvia were fluent in the works of the seventeenth-century poet! Unlike Sylvia, when I first started in the workshop, I knew my place. For the first time in my blusterous, magpie life I'd shut my mouth and listened as you lectured on the "don'ts" of writing poetry: *Don't* do anything bizarre or distracting with composition. *Don't* just throw in a bunch of historical references and confusing and contextualized voices in different registers or tongues. *Don't* throw in metaphors before we even know what the poem is about. Then there were the "nots": We're *not* modernists! We're *not* writing the Bible! We're *not* preservers of a culture in decline! The "ares" followed: We *are* literalists! We *are* mirrors! We *are* conveyors of emotion! We *are* detectives! "Above all else," you'd said, "we write poetry within an asylum from reason."

I'd struggled to understand what you'd meant by this: How did one write within an asylum from reason? But now that Sylvia Plath was here and commanding the workshop's attention, I knew I needed to figure this out quickly. Carving out time between keeping up with the home and putting my daughter down for naps, I set up a workstation on the dining room table with my typewriter, a row of sharpened pencils, and a rhyming dictionary. Here, I tried in earnest to write within an asylum from reason. Eventually, I figured out that you had meant *write without constraints*!

I left my feeble first attempt on my husband's desk for Kildare to read, but my new poem just sat in his study, untouched. Disappointed but undeterred, I placed the poem on his pillow instead. When he came to bed that night, I pretended to be asleep until I could hold in my excitement no more.

"Well?" I pounced.

"Well . . ." said my husband, reading the poem.

"Who do you think will publish me first?"

Kildare looked a little shaken. "Agatha, you can't publish this."

"Of course I can."

The poem was called "A Visit to Dr. No." The piece delivered its speaker, a young woman, to a private clinic in a soap-colored row house. In the waiting room, the speaker's hands were clammy. A sick anticipation had entrenched itself. She found distraction by picking through magazines in a basket. Gracing an ad were two women, one wearing a graduation cap and gown, the other extending her hands toward the sky, the sun flashing off of her diamond engagement ring. The speaker scoffed at the ad, which read: "What was a diploma compared to that precious sparkling ring?" A man, who appeared as a "ghost-white ship" retrieved the speaker, led her to a bedroom-turned-clinic, gloomy and wood-paneled. She undressed and climbed onto a metal table. Opening her legs for her, the man inserted a rubber tube, "red as a soda fountain straw," and packed her insides with cotton balls. The poem ended with a promise of hemorrhaging and fever and freedom.

"It's a poem about . . ."

"Abortion," I said.

Kildare stammered. "It's, it's . . ."

"Too brilliant?"

"Too personal!" he gasped. "They'll think it's about you."

Nobody was going to think it was about me, but Kildare said people would assume, which made me mad. Then he grew worried.

"Is it about you?"

I did not dignify that with an answer. While the content of such confessional poetry belongs to the confessor, the confessor shall never be a part of the poem. So said you, Professor Lowell. In workshop, you called this the Invisible Hand of the Poet. The poem speaks for itself!

"Professor Lowell says we must write poetry within an asylum from reason. Why not write about life's most personal experiences?" Maybe Kildare would have preferred the mundane "Stopping by Woods on a Snowy Evening," or better yet, *The Cat in the Hat*!

Kildare switched off the lamp. After a while in the dark, he said, "Then again, what do I know about poetry?"

I huffed. "Exactly! What do you know?"

In the biggest test yet of my cocksure bearing, I submitted "A Visit to Dr. No" to you and the workshop. You propped a boot up on the windowsill and began to read my piece aloud. Your voice bellowed like a *djembe* drum, hard and swift and audacious.

You remember, don't you? How the whole workshop sat in silence, stunned by how far I'd come. You called "A Visit to Dr. No" the work of a Major Voice. I'd finally written something worthy of the designation.

After workshop, Maxine said she absolutely loved the poem, that it was unlike anything she'd ever read before, so dark and raw and real.

Noting the name on the byline, she said, "Who's Boston Rhodes?"

"That's what I'm calling myself."

"What happened to Agatha?"

Kildare had said using a pen name was the only way he'd permit me to publish. These confessions seemed important to me at the moment, but someday I might not want my daughter reading about my journeys into masturbation, abortion, and lust.

My grandfather's name was Mason Rhodes, but because of his money and his influence, most people had known him as Emperor Boston, the king of a city on the river between three blue mountain peaks. These days, most people just remembered him for Emperor Fine Fabrics, but at one time the Rhodes family owned the wealthiest international ports along the Boston Bay. We'd seen the fog roll into the glassy, dark sea for generations, so I guess Emperor Boston was entitled to his clout.

"Professor Lowell says confessional poetry can't be true unless it's all true," Maxine said.

But protecting people from the truth was the only way Kildare was going to allow me to keep writing, producing, and attempting to publish. I was going to make a name for myself, even if it was the name Boston Rhodes—she who utilizes her Major Voice, her true voice, her venom voice, which cuts to the marrow of the truth.

Several weeks later, I learned that *Ladies' Home Journal* chose "A Visit to Dr. No" for publication. George Starbuck said, "Guess this means you'll be joining the Ring."

I didn't think George, with his narrow shoulders and thinning brown hair, liked me. In the workshop, he seemed to garner a bit too much satisfaction poking holes in my work. At the same time, I'd also noticed a sympathetic tone to his critiques that fully expressed itself in the subtle gestures of his not-insignificant brows.

"The Ring?"

"It's just a friendly little competition among some of the members in the workshop."

The rules of the Ring were straightforward. At any given time, the Ring crowned the student who landed the most publications of his or her work. Content mattered, but so did the caliber of the magazine.

The Ring, I learned, gathered after the workshop at the Ritz-Carlton bar. Why here and not some cheaper bar stool? Because each of us was nothing if not aspirational. Because the Ritz-Carlton made us feel like royalty. Because at the Ritz-Carlton, we celebrated our ascension into the jurisdiction of *the literary* by surrounding ourselves with opulence. Because at the Ritz-Carlton, we were celebrating one another, and our poetry, in a manner we were sure the rest of the world eventually would as well.

Another thing that you were always going on about, Professor, was the belief that we were going to birth a revolution and usher into the twentieth century a great poetry movement comparable to that of Chaucer's or Shakespeare's. How many times did you tell us poetry was dying on the vine by failing to connect with people? ("We are literalists! We are mirrors! We are conveyors of emotion! We are detectives!") At the Ritz-Carlton, Maxine, Sam, George, and I believed we each had an obligation to reestablish a connection through raw and dangerous poetry. If there was going to be a poetry revolution, it was going to start in this low-lit and lavish den with the four of us at the helm.

Here is the scene: The Ritz-Carlton, in every season, was a slow-burn autumn evening. We entered the lobby, a toe's dip into a realm of a thousand champagne-colored lights and bouquets of craning tulips by the truckload. Our table was in a secluded part of the club, away from the horseshoe bar with its spear of crystal shards dangling from the ceiling. We ordered from waiters in uniforms buttoned up to their Adam's apples, and who donned small hats and satin gloves. I usually sat between Maxine and George, the three of us pressed into a plush red-leather booth. Sam often complained that he never finished his first drink before George was selling him on his second.

I'd quickly come to understand my ranking among the Ring. Maxine told me the *New Yorker* had already published her, twice if you counted a criticism she'd written. George had half a dozen publications. Sam had five published poems, but they'd gone to *Harper's* and the *Saturday Review of Literature*, which carried real weight. Since joining the Ring, I'd only gotten three poems in print, but they were strong publications that, according to our subjective scale, put me on solid footing with George and Sam. Maxine was publishing the most frequently, and I wondered how I was ever going to surpass her. Rumor was, Maxine had been a runner-up for the esteemed Radcliffe prize, which would have been tops. I'd given considerable thought to applying for the Radcliffe prize myself. Winning that would most certainly put me in the lead.

Here I was, with Maxine holding my hand on the mirror-top table, and George on my other side, his arm around my waist and holding me close to him, and Sam sipping his drink across from me. This was quite possibly the most content scene of my entire life, infused with the promise of a future full of possibility.

But then Maxine learned who Sylvia's husband was, and suddenly she wanted to invite Sylvia into the Ring, too. "She's married to *Ted Hughes*!" Maxine's wide gesture sent martini spilling down her wrist and under her sleeve. As much as we knew about Sylvia Plath prior to her rude arrival, the name Ted Hughes carried far more weight. Cavorting with Sylvia brought us close to the poet behind the famed collection *The Hawk in the Rain*.

"Can you believe it? In our workshop!"

I didn't see what the fuss was all about. It wasn't as though Ted Hughes had enrolled in your workshop, just his wife, the poor thing. To me, there was nothing sadder than the spouse of a world-renowned poet. Watching your husband become a critical darling was bound to be hard for anyone who fashioned herself even a halfway decent artist.

"Just imagine being a fly on the wall in his life!"

Yes, a fly. A tiny, pesky, buzzy little insect.

Maxine blathered on: "I bet Sylvia could use some friends of her own. It can't be easy living under someone else's shadow all the time."

Hoping to put a swift end to the conversation, I removed myself from it and went to the bar. In the time that it took me to order another drink in an opalescent glass and return to our table, Maxine had roped George and Sam into her campaign.

"That's a fine idea!" George was saying. "I quite enjoyed her 'Tale of a Tub.'"

Maxine said, "Oh, it's just a terrific little poem, isn't it?"

"She can't just join the competition in the middle of it," I said.

George frowned. "Why on earth not?"

Clearly things were getting tense, so I softened my tone and produced a conciliatory smile. I touched George's wrist and pouted at Sam.

"I'm only saying, the wife of Ted Hughes doesn't have to knock very hard to get any magazine to open its doors for her. I don't think it's fair to any of us, really."

"You're just worried about losing your lead," Sam said, looking at me with a rather sad expression.

"I don't have a lead," I reminded him.

"Oh, that's right," Sam said.

"Well," George said, looking at me, "we'll just have to beat Sylvia Plath the old-fashioned way, won't we? When I look at Boston Rhodes here, I see someone who's up for the challenge."

George had no idea.

3

Ruth, 1953

OCTOBER 1—

Freud once said that analysis is a cure through love, yet when it comes to the patient known colloquially as the Mad Poet, affection is hard to come by. Hence, treatment remains an unsolvable puzzle.

He has been a patient at McLean three times in as many years. An educated man, some sort of poet savant, and very much a lunatic, he resides in the ward of Men's Belknap. Dr. Beuscher has passed the patient off to me, as though to say, *I've had my fill; let's see what you can do.*

A volatile introduction to the Mad Poet today as I came into the common room. The patient was a hulking man working up a frightening head of steam. He gripped his pants and tore them down, and next, off came his shirt. The orderlies proceeded to give chase, with the patient yelping and shrieking and finally tiring between the parlor and the entrance hall, where I put a robe around him and walked him back to his room.

"My name is Dr. Barnhouse. I'm to be your doctor."

"I've never met a doctor I'd like to fuck." He made a face. "Come to think of it, I've never met a lady psychiatrist before, either."

"That's because there aren't any. Not in Massachusetts; not in all of New England as far as I know." That I am the only one in this hospital makes me a bit of a lone wolf. After two months among them, the male doctors still do not understand quite how to address me. The nurses continue to distrust me, too. They hush when I enter rooms. Their cigarettes hit the ashtrays. Early on, Nurse Edme told me it was going to take some time, as the nurses aren't used to having a mother hen around.

Regrettably, the patient's episodes of lucidity remain brief. He rambles without fences in curling soliloquies of tangential and enlightened word storms. Traditional analysis and electroshock therapy under the care of Dr. Beuscher thus far have worked little. These cumulative treatment failures have produced in me a desire to attempt alternative techniques outside of traditional psychoanalytic theory.

As of this writing, I have begun interspersing tinctures of Benzedrine and opium, depending on the cycle of the patient's moods, which I administer using a calibrated glass dropper to his tongue. Nurse Edme has taken exception to the experimental treatment. At times, however, the road map to healing must take us through unconventional territory.

Her true concern, I believe, is Superintendent Frisch. The man has never supported my appointment to the hospital. He would most certainly not approve of my philosophy. At my interview before a panel of administrators and doctors all gathered within the Proctor House last summer, I stated for the record that, were the hospital to hire me, I was not going to be changing bedpans or bedsheets, nor was I to tolerate a questioning of my methods. I must be allowed to work using tools and techniques at my discretion, I'd said. My results were going to speak for themselves. Superintendent Frisch, in a tweed jacket and bow tie, and with Brylcreem in his hair, regarded me with a stony gaze. "McLean Hospital is a bastion of psychoanalysis and tradition, Dr. Barnhouse." Then he addressed his colleagues. "This institution doesn't need maverick doctors." So imagine my disbelief when Dr. Beuscher, having shown me out of the drawing room, shook my hand and offered me the job. He said I was the finest candidate for the position. I cautioned him, I did not tolerate falsehoods, even those designed to soften hard truths. I am no fool. McLean is short-staffed and underfunded, and I am cheaper than a male psychiatrist.

With a dutiful "Yes, Dr. Barnhouse," Nurse Edme has made her final thoughts on the matter of the patient's new treatment plan clear, though it is what she *doesn't* say that I discern clearest of all: *I hope you know what you're doing.*

OCTOBER 15—

A success! In the second week of the patient's revised regimen, he has shown a boost in energy, a stabilization of mood, and a renewed sense of well-being. His skin has become a plump peach hue. The lurching lunacy of his temperament has disappeared. Where once he was climbing the walls, today Nurse Edme is preparing the man's discharge papers. "It worked!" she belted, as though I'd performed some kind of miracle.

The only miracle I see is that, thanks to this small triumph, the nurses have begun to trust me, greeting me and looking me in the eye as they pass. While I make strides among them, from a distance Superintendent Frisch observes my approach with a cool unfriendliness when he visits the ward each day. His two large Dalmatians flank his sides. Upon handing me the patient's release papers, the superintendent, bestowed with a generous but strange sort of smile, said, "Impressive work, Dr. Barnhouse. Though I can't say the ends justify the means."

Really, he would have us all stick to archaic psychoanalysis!

In the patient's final session, he spoke at length about the works of W. B. Yeats and the plays of Samuel Beckett and Eugène Ionesco, much as he has taken to doing of late with his mind finally clear. He really is quite an articulate and thoughtful soul. He was anxious about his emancipation and said that he was going to miss our time together.

"As Yeats's unrequited love once told him, 'Tomorrow I leave you with nothing but memories and ghosts.'"

OCTOBER 30—

I used to play Sinatra records on the Admiral for my daughter. Tiffany and I would sing along with them. I can still hear her voice. Her favorite song was "Sunflower."

She's a sunflower, she's my sunflower, and I know we'll never part.
She's a sunflower, she's my one flower, she's the flower of my heart.

The song has been on my mind, entrenched there as it were, since Superintendent Frisch transferred me from Men's Belknap to the ward of Codman Manor. He has proven himself to be a bitter and vindictive man, as small in character as he is in stature. Dr. Beuscher told me the women's minimum risk ward is far less taxing, but we are both aware that the superintendent has just moved me out of his way. Out of sight is out of mind, and out of trouble.

Nevertheless, I do find this mansion to be quite beautiful. There is a greeting room and a grand staircase that branches off into large hallways. Past parlors and reading rooms veneered in ceiling beams and paisley-patterned wallpaper, the ward gives one the impression of being inside the hull of a large and luxurious ship. First thing, I took on the task of introducing myself to the women of Codman Manor: patients young and old; the helpless and the abandoned; those shuffling through the ward's corridors with vacant cow-like stares; the women wandering within a deluge of detached bewilderment; women who move like sparrows bouncing between fountain pools.

As I moved along the first-floor corridor, I detected a doleful whistling coming from one of the patient rooms. It was only as I neared room nineteen that my ear deciphered the tune—"Sunflower."

Glimpsing a girl no older than twenty, I saw that my whistler was curled into a rocking chair. The toes of her slippers poked out of a red wool blanket. Her hair was chopped short, pelt-like and patchy. Another woman was in the room with her, I noticed. Dressed in pearls, white gloves, and a wide-brimmed structured hat, the other woman was, in fact, fussing over a vase of sunflowers. The girl in the rocking chair seemed to hold no more strength than those cut stems.

When I got around to asking Nurse Edme the name of the patient in room nineteen, she said, "Who, Miss Plath? Why, she's only the most infamous girl in New England."

NOVEMBER 1—

Nurse Edme tells me that Codman Manor has had its share of celebrity over the years. It has been the temporary home to the daughter of a president, a prominent beauty queen, and a famous stage actor. Comparatively, the patient in room nineteen really is more infamous than famous.

Miss Plath is the twenty-two-year-old who recently disappeared. She is also the girl who police found after a statewide manhunt for missing persons that landed her photograph in every newspaper in New England.

"Her first poem was about the ocean at Point Shirley. She was eight years old. From the moment she showed it to me, I knew—*knew*—my daughter was destined for a promising future," said Miss Plath's mother,

Aurelia, as we sat in the receiving hall following her daily visit to Codman Manor. Aurelia was a picture of austerity and seemingly carved from Italian marble. "Suffice it to say, many others have since recognized my daughter's potential for greatness over the years."

Such potential, she explained, had gotten her daughter a college scholarship and, last summer, a prestigious Manhattan internship at *Mademoiselle*.

"But Sylvia came back from it . . . *changed*."

"Changed how?"

"She'd grown . . . well, I guess you'd call it depressed. And there was something else, too."

Aurelia took a spiral notebook out of her purse. Scrawled across the top in blue ink were the words *JUNIOR YEAR*.

She handed it to me. "Go ahead, open it."

I turned through the pages of neat script. As I neared the end of the notebook, however, the handwriting, like Aurelia's daughter, *changed*. It devolved. The letters melted. By the last page, the words were nothing but weak scratch marks.

"After this summer, Sylvia couldn't write anymore. She couldn't read, either. Have you ever heard of such a thing? A writer who can't hold a pencil or study a book?"

Soon after, she said, her daughter had vanished from the house. Foot patrols and search parties spread into hills. Police dragged Morses Pond, and bloodhounds marched through the thickets off Route 16. On the third day of the search, the sheriff, following a quiet, distressed moaning sound, pulled apart a woodpile leaning against the house's breezeway. In the cobwebbed crawl space, he spied the sleeve of a white peasant blouse, the hem of a green dirndl skirt, and a bottle of Nembutal absent fifty pills.

Aurelia was now crying, as if to ask me why her daughter had done such a horrible thing to her. I believed Aurelia's tears, though they weren't tears of grief, just self-pity, and this angered me. Aurelia's daughter wasn't lost. They'd found her, albeit half-dead in a crawl space, but still very much alive.

NOVEMBER 2—

In Codman Manor, every encounter is a first encounter, depending on the day and the patient's mood or state of mind. Few introductions throw me, but meeting Aurelia's daughter today, I was unprepared for her appearance.

I came upon the patient as she was getting her bath. The young Miss Plath was sitting in the bathtub with her knees pressed against her chin. The flesh around her left eye was a plum color, swollen and weeping as though she'd gone a round or two with Beau Jack. A nurse wrung a daub of green liquid soap from a bottle. Miss Plath squeezed her good eye shut, willing the touch of the washcloth away.

Later in her private room, Miss Plath fully dressed and wrapped again in her blanket, I asked her about college, about the classes she liked and disliked, and about the girls she went to school with. She commented on the length of my eyelashes, and then on how, of all the people who have come to visit her here, the only one she wanted to see but hadn't was a boy named Dick Norton, bedbound himself with tuberculosis in a sanatorium in Saranac Lake. I asked if Dick Norton was her boyfriend. "Oh, I have lots of boyfriends," she vaunted. "The strong smell of masculinity creates the ideal medium to exist in."

"How do you manage to turn them away?"

"It's not so difficult. I tell them I've become a communist, or that I no longer associate with wealthy boys. The best one, if you want to know, is I've come down with a case of tuberculosis. But Dickie, he really does have tuberculosis, poor thing."

"Do you mind if I smoke?"

"Knock yourself out. I like the smell. So, are you officially my doctor?"

I told Miss Plath that I was. She seemed pleased by this.

"A lot of doctors keep visiting me. I was getting nervous. They like to talk a lot, don't they?"

I struck a match against a tiny box. "They'll talk you to sleep."

"Oh, I don't need sleep. If you want to know, I once stayed awake for fourteen whole days."

"If you don't need to sleep, then why did you swallow a bottle of sleeping pills?"

Miss Plath peered at me, puzzled. "To kill myself, obviously." She brought the tips of two fingers to the swollen gash of her eye. "But I couldn't. The life force in me was so strong, it counteracted the sleeping pills."

I was intrigued. "Tell me about your life force."

"Well, everyone has a life force, Dr. Barnhouse. Mine's just especially strong."

I told her I was glad that her life force was so strong. She shrugged, as though I had just said the most irrational thing on earth.

"I'll just have to try harder to end it next time. Do you think a drop from a second-floor window will do it? Or jumping from the Longfellow Bridge?"

As I considered her earnestness, Miss Plath laughed.

"You're a pretty lady and all. A regular Myrna Loy. But I'm not gonna let you help me."

We will just have to see about that.

NOVEMBER 7—

Of late, I am besieged by memories and ghosts—Tiffany in her bed, under her blanket, soothed and engaged by my orations. In these reveries, I am reading to my daughter: *Poems for the Children's Hour, Verses* from the American Track Society, *Now We Are Six* by A. A. Milne.

I snuff these moments like a cigarette to the heel of my shoe, but to little avail.

Most certainly, these visions come to me because I have taken to daily readings with the patient in room nineteen. It was with shades of the Mad Poet in my mind that I recently visited Mr. Butler in the hospital library. It's a small chamber bedecked in wood with a gothic chantry-like window. There is a section of used, veined paperbacks, a collection of John Steinbeck, J. R.R. Tolkien, and Daphne du Maurier novels. Large portions are donations from the Massachusetts Department of Correction. Mr. Butler, a patient and the keeper of the books, is less a competent librarian than a compulsive organizer. I asked him if the library carried books of verse or perhaps the plays of Ionesco or Beckett. Mr. Butler said no, but then one morning I discovered a note waiting for me on my desk. "Yeats, Millay, and Frost are here," it read, as though the poets were currently residents of McLean Hospital, which I supposed they are, on loan from the public library in Mission Hill.

That afternoon, I found Miss Plath seated in the music room. Twisting tissue into pellets in her lap, she was an artist's study in arches—the slope of a neck, the bend of her wrists, the curve of her heels lifting out from her slippers. "I thought you might like something other than the scandal pages for a change." I offered her a book, Bible black with gold lettering on the cover. She glanced at the title, *The Wanderings of Oisin*, and pushed it away.

In retrospect, Yeats was a poor first choice, as the patient lost focus, and so at our next session, I got to Edna St. Vincent Millay's *Second April*.

"I saw Millay read once," Miss Plath said. "She wore a gold-colored dress. For a long time I wanted to follow in her footsteps, maybe even attend Barnard and Vassar like she did. Millay suffered a nervous breakdown, too, if you want to know." Later, reading from *Stones from a Glass House*, Miss Plath groaned. "I hate Phyllis McGinley! She'd have us all get married and become housewives! Joyce! Please don't come back until you've gotten Joyce!"

So today, I brought her *Finnegans Wake*, only to find that she'd requested of me a halting, distorted, impossible-to-follow juggernaut of a novel. My conclusion is that the patient in room nineteen remains determined to ride out her time here rather than engage or let me in.

NOVEMBER 10—

On this day, a change in my approach.

"No more James Joyce. No more Yeats or Millay. Just you." I placed my pencil and clipboard in her hands. "Write me a poem."

Miss Plath came back at me befuddled. "I told you, I find it impossible to write even a single word."

I retrieved the clipboard and pencil back from her. "I'll take dictation, then."

"I can't just come up with a poem on the spot. Haven't you heard of inspiration?"

"What inspired you before?"

"Before?"

"Yes, before you came to McLean Hospital."

"You mean before I was brought to an asylum against my will? Frankly, nothing that matters here."

"I want you to write about this place."

Miss Plath sneered. "No one writes about *this place*."

I asked her why not.

"Who's interested in my own domestic tragedy?"

"We all have trials."

"I don't think I'll ever write again, if you want to know."

"So you never become a writer. What *will* you be?"

"Dead." She said this flatly.

I positioned the clipboard again in her lap. "Care to put that in writing?"

"I think I'm done with you."

I placed my pencil in Miss Plath's hand and closed her fingers around it.

"Write your name, and we will be finished."

She refused, and so I repeated my demand. She choked on her outrage. Her one purple lidded eye was frozen in place, the other blazing. "You're a brute!"

I repeated: "Write your name."

"Write *your* name!"

The pencil sailed across the room, smacked against the dresser, and bounced on the floor.

Miss Plath's campaign of resistance continued long after I retreated from her room. She is passionate, but oh, how stubborn!

This evening, I found her in her bed, a thin blanket pulled up to her nose. She'd piled the library books I'd brought her this week on her nightstand. *Finnegans Wake* was open on top, and she'd blacked out pages upon pages of words with the soft-leaded pencil.

When I looked up from this discovery, her one good eye was staring at my staggered expression. "If they want to charge me, they know where to find me."

NOVEMBER 11—

An astonishing and terrible sleep last night! Memories and ghosts defaced my slumber just as Miss Plath has defaced *Finnegans Wake*.

It's Tiffany . . . always Tiffany . . . I am haunted.

Once again, I found my asylum in the emancipation of opium upon my tongue. Relief and rest came to me. After all this time, these self-induced lethargies remain the only method that quiets the echo chamber of my head and restores my natural rhythms.

As my shameful remedy unraveled my consciousness, my final

thoughts came to me, only in Miss Plath's voice, not my own. "If they want to charge me, they know where to find me." But in my mind, she was not saying "charge me" anymore. She was saying "*change* me."

I woke this morning in my hospital dormitory room with the bottle of tincture of opium still in my hand. I held it up to the sunlight streaming in through the thin curtain. My head worked backward, tracking my recall of the night, whereupon I retrieved a fully formed revelation that the opium sleep delivered to me!

To protect the library books from further defacement, I'd placed them on a half shelf by my bedside. I brought *Finnegans Wake* to the desk. Turning quickly through the pages, lest the thought that came to me in the night blow away like a dream, I noted all of the words Miss Plath had blacked out with her pencil.

Presently, I saw that she had, in fact, missed some letters.

Or purposely left letters behind, unmarked by pencil lead . . .

An errant *W*. A stray *E*. A skipped-over *T*, and so on.

On a notepad, I jotted down the untouched letters in long rows.

From somewhere down the hall, I heard the nurses leaving for breakfast as I finished laying out the haphazard letters. Only, I had begun to see that they weren't haphazard after all. I circled a "WE." Then a "TAKE." And a "THE." When I'd finished, I found myself staring at the groupings. I pressed my back into my chair, which moaned softly, and in disbelief I reread the words I'd deciphered.

WE TAKE THE PLUNGE

UNDER WATER OUR LIMBS WAVER, FAINTLY GREEN, SHUDDERING AWAY

FROM THE GENUINE COLOR OF SKIN

CAN OUR DREAMS EVER BLUR THE INTRANSIGENT LINES WHICH DRAW

THE SHAPE THAT SHUTS US IN?

SECOND STANZA

The Listening Game

Show me the difference between confession and poetry,
and I will respond by showing you my ugliest sins.

—Boston Rhodes, in conversation

4

Estee, 2019

Taking a long view of the history of counterfeit items coming to auction, one rises to the top of my mind. The year, 1901. An administrator at the Kunsthistorisches Museum commissions several hapless students from the University of Vienna to create replicas of ten Bruegel paintings and sketches. Over the years, he replaces the authentic works in his museum with the copies. By the time that the museum discovers the deception, ten great objects of antiquity are long-lost.

Throughout the twentieth century, rumors of sightings float through the art world, stories really. Then, in 1981, a print of *The Beekeepers* in pen and ink comes up for sale at the Lempertz auction. The anonymous seller claims it is one of the recovered Bruegel ten. The auction house brings in an authenticator conversant with Bruegel's style, who determines that *The Beekeepers* is, in fact, another counterfeit.

Today, Moses Quimby isn't convinced that the Plath notebooks are authentic, either. He thumbs his mustache as we walk. Halls branch from the lobby of St. Ambrose to offices and a library and two small galleries. If such an item as the original handwritten draft of *The Bell Jar* truly exists, why would it reside in a lockbox in an attic in South Boston?

"You know these sorts of counterfeits come up all the time."

"I have no reason to believe the manuscript isn't legitimate," I say.

This is not entirely true, though. A cursory archival search shows no record of Sylvia Plath writing *The Bell Jar* in three notebooks. Nor is there an account of a handwritten draft of *The Bell Jar* in Sylvia Plath's personal journals.

Quimby is half-distracted, looking at his phone and clicking through his messages. I need to fill him in because I only have the notebooks for three days before the Dyce brothers take the items to Sotheby's.

"The Dyce brothers? The guys with those stupid real estate commercials?" Quimby wants to know if they are as wormy in person as they are in their advertisements.

"If it is real, it would be an unprecedented addition to our twentieth-century slate," I say.

"*The Bell Jar*." Quimby says this with distaste, and I wonder how much of Sylvia Plath Quimby has read. Though I don't remember exactly when I read *The Bell Jar*, I am hard-pressed to recall a time when I have not known the story of Esther Greenwood dreaming of becoming a writer, struggling with identity and norms in a mental hospital after spending a manic summer in New York City. "Even if it is real, I just can't see how it's relevant for our audience."

Relevant? For master curators, an object's relevance is irrelevant. Has the struggle to selfhood ever disappeared? Has our human tendency to focus on our personal inadequacies ever gone out of vogue? Have the blades of Plath's words gone dull over the decades, or do they still draw blood? Not long ago, Quimby and I would not have been having this conversation. Midfifties with graying temples, Quimby styles himself in suits and ties and with dignity and a touch of smugness. He comes from money, and marketing, and an expensive business school. Last year, when a painting of characters from *South Park* sold for ten million dollars at Christie's, Quimby grew convinced that St. Ambrose was missing out on a huge market potential. Impulsively, he refocused St. Ambrose's offerings to the buying power of millennials, a generation he knows nothing about. Then again, neither do I.

Enter Scarlett: twenty-two, long drape of dark hair, pencil skirts, perfume seemingly curated to imprint on Quimby's olfactory stimuli, and who, before Quimby installed her as St. Ambrose's first online sales director, modeled luxury handbags on Newbury Street. Thanks to Scarlett, suddenly St. Ambrose caters to rich young buyers in hoodies who prefer to bid through our new online portal. St. Ambrose has moved away from its standard slates, opting instead for lithographs by Christo, Banksy stunts, and Xerox prints that Scarlett calls "irony art"—as if Scarlett knows the definition of the word "irony." Meanwhile, Quimby, naturally contrarian, has found in Scarlett an audience and validation.

We step into the elevator together, and as the doors slide shut, Quimby looks at me with a bogus display of warmth. Bogus, because he's not a warm man. But the silence and sudden close quarters of an elevator bring about an uncomfortable intimacy. "Is Istanbul still the top contender?" he asks, moving away from the subject of *The Bell Jar*. Braving my retirement among the cities where I curated in the early years of my profession continues to have its special appeal. I have many options to choose from, among them Paris, Berlin, St. Petersburg, and Madrid. I've recently added Beirut and Cape Town to the catalog of possibilities. "Yes, Cape Town is lovely," he says. To be clear, until very recently, retirement was not a consideration I visited in earnest. Yet, an idea, like a celestial body, eventually takes on its own atmosphere and weight. More and more, I feel that I both belong among the antiquities at St. Ambrose and that I do not. "You should consider Buenos Aires. Trust me. Europe is like stale coffee. Buenos Aires has the Malba. And the beaches. You'd do well there."

"Buenos Aires, all right," I say, remembering how, in *The Bell Jar*, Esther Greenwood puts up with eccentric men, men with interesting names like Socrates and Attilla, rich intellects and boys from famous families who play tennis and are perfectly tan but are also too short or too ugly or too bald. Though she hates the idea of serving these men,

Esther Greenwood laughs at their jokes and acts polite. So I will capitulate, and I will engage Moses Quimby in small talk if it makes him feel better, because I know, like all master curators know, like Esther Greenwood knows, that sometimes giving someone what they want is the only move we have in this game of listening and pivoting and dancing.

In the lower level of St. Ambrose, Quimby and I walk a short passageway lined on both sides with doors. I stop at the room marked SAFE HOLDINGS, dial a code into a keypad on the wall, and yank on a handle. Inside, I unlock one of the wooden file cabinets and bring out the lockbox. At the table, Quimby scrutinizes the three notebooks. The pages make the sound of dry leaves crackling as he turns them. "Times are changing, Estee. Nobody's interested in buying the personal library of Charles Dickens or thirteenth-century paleographic texts. The public market desires pieces it can connect with. People want local now. An artist's province matters as much as an object's provenance."

"Sylvia Plath was from Massachusetts," I say.

"You know what I'm saying. Nobody's bidding on literary incunables. People are looking for timely. There's nothing timely about Sylvia Plath."

I have learned over the years that as difficult as it is to argue with Quimby, it is even more difficult to bring an argument to him. I continue to try, nonetheless. "Mr. Quimby, if this is a genuine work of Sylvia Plath's, who better to sell it than us?"

"It's not worth taking it on, even if it is genuine. What'll it fetch? A couple thousand? The authentication costs alone will eat up our profit."

"If it is authentic, I can't imagine St. Ambrose letting this go to another house, can you?"

Quimby peels off his white cotton glove and sighs.

"Here's what I'm gonna do. First, I'll let you carry out your due diligence. Meanwhile, I'll perform mine."

By that, I know Quimby means he will ask Scarlett about the generational appeal of *The Bell Jar* and of Sylvia Plath. He has no ability to judge his instincts anymore. If I can prove the notebooks are Sylvia Plath's, and Quimby is satisfied with their relevance to modern buyers, then he'll consider—*consider*—adding the objects to the upcoming slate.

About that phony Bruegel sketch: several months after the Federal Criminal Police are finished with the object, the counterfeit is returned to the Lempertz Auction House and put on display as an artifact of intrigue. At the age of thirty-two at the time, I am curating the special collections for the Berlin city library when I am granted special permission to visit *The Beekeepers*. In a brightly lit room full of tall windows, I examine the rendering of four hooded men in a field. They are thieving honey from clay hives. Their hands are unprotected from the bees. Their faces are hidden behind basket-woven masks. I find the quality to be most impressive. What a remarkable job the architect of this fake has done! The counterfeiter has gone so far as to re-create the document on parchment from the sixteenth century. Doubt, it seems, is the only quality that gave the object away, for anyone who has followed the story of the Bruegel ten knows it is improbable that, after all this time, one would show up on the open market. That it arrived with no history of where it has been, and no explanation for how it got to auction, continues to elicit more than a little suspicion. Parsimony: the simplest explanation is that it must be a counterfeit.

Though to this very day, I ask myself, what if we all got it wrong? What if the only evidence that the rendering wasn't real was rational thinking coupled with the belief that it simply had to be a fake?

With the Plath notebooks, I hope to eradicate any such uncertainty by bringing in an expert of my own. Despite my specialty in manuscripts, I require a connoisseur of Sylvia Plath and her work. I open my laptop and start an Internet search, the trailhead of all twenty-first-century journeys. The website of Boston University brings me to a professor of literature named Nicolas Jacob. A thorough look at his papers on Sylvia Plath, his four books on Sylvia Plath, and his graduate dissertation on Sylvia Plath, and I believe I have found my assessor.

Nicolas Jacob is curt over the phone. "You're with St. Ambrose?"

"Yes—"

"The auction house?"

"Yes, we have a manuscript that falls in line with your area of expertise—"

He cuts me off again. "You'll have to find somebody else."

"But—"

"I don't work with auction houses."

"Yes, but—"

"As a rule. I'm sorry—"

"You see, I have, or at least I think I have, what might be an original draft, a *handwritten* original draft, of *The Bell Jar*."

This gets his attention.

Nicolas Jacob arrives at St. Ambrose on a late-June morning. He is gingered haired with gold-framed glasses and a face that, by my estimation, is eighty percent beard. His shirt is buttoned to the top, though he wears no tie. His burgundy summer cardigan is missing a button. Standing over the three notebooks in the safe holdings room, Nicolas rubs his hands together, brushing away invisible particles.

Nicolas removes a small case from the pocket of his trousers. He places it on the table and unzips it to reveal a set of tools. Using padded tweezers, he pinches a corner and draws open the green-covered notebook.

My attempts to engage Nicolas result in only clipped answers, in yeses and nos. He does not smile, or maybe he does smile, but the beard disguises his smile, as it hides all of his facial cues beyond those suggesting conscientiousness and low tolerance. "It's extremely fragile," he says at one point. This, I already know. With poor temperature and humidity regulation, attics make for abysmal incubators of antiquity. I tell Nicolas about the Dyce brothers, and their probate purchase on Napoleon Street, and their discovery in its attic, and how it is my suspicion that the attic might have been Plath's at one point in time. "Not possible," Nicolas says. "If you'd said they found it in a house in Wellesley, Jamaica Plain, or even Winthrop, maybe. But Sylvia was not a Southie."

Nicolas scratches at his beard. He turns over his leather messenger bag and removes from it a document in a plastic sleeve. I ask him what he's brought, and for the first time in our short affiliation, Nicolas's tone changes from prim to a quality I can only describe as slightly more tender.

"It's a handwritten early poem of Sylvia's."

The title, I see, written across the top of the single page reads *MISS DRAKE PROCEEDS TO SUPPER*.

"I'm ready for that light rig now."

From the closet I wheel out a table-and-lamp apparatus. Nicolas carries the green-covered notebook and the sleeved document to the lamp and places both under the light with a magnifying glass top.

"If the handwriting in the notebooks is a different style than Sylvia's normal handwriting, or if the ink hasn't permeated into the notebook's paper, the content of the notebook is recent and likely a forgery," he says.

Administering his forensic handwriting evaluation, Nicolas compares an N, a T, and an R from one document to corresponding letters in the other. Another ten minutes pass without a word or signal. Nicolas pushes his fingers through his beard again, his fingertips searching for skin. If he believes it's authentic, or if he sees a detail that signals it's just not right, Nicolas is unwilling to say. Or perhaps he cannot say. Perhaps he does not know.

With his phone, he snaps color spectral photos of a page from the notebook. He opens his laptop, and, examining the photo on the screen, separates the words from the background colors.

Nicolas makes a small noise. He pushes his glasses up the bridge of his nose, then asks me if the Dyce brothers indicated who they bought the house from. The address was in foreclosure and purchased from a bank, I say. He thinks a minute. "All right, we can check with the housing records."

"It's authentic, then?"

Nicolas straightens his spine. Blinks. Nods.

"One of the great pleasures of my life in academia is having had the honor of seeing pieces of Sylvia's work before. Letters, notes, pages of poetry. But nothing this complete. Was there anything else the Dyce brothers found with the notebooks? Other items, like a letter that might explain how the manuscript got here?"

None, I say. I gather the green-covered notebook, take up the other two from the table, and place all of them back into the lockbox.

"A manuscript like this doesn't just fall into your lap," he says. "As far as we know, it's the only handwritten version of Sylvia's novel in existence. It deserves to be evaluated and studied." Nicolas rises from his stool and follows me to the cabinet drawer as I place the lockbox back inside. "Aren't you the least bit curious? How is it no one knows this version of the manuscript exists?"

Yes, I have questions, but there will be time for seeking answers. For now, there is much to do, and I am focused on relaying the good news to Quimby, focused on reaching the Dyce brothers before Elton and Jay Jay decide to bring the notebooks to another auction house, and focused on the one thing I do know, the one thing that matters. After fifty-five years, Sylvia Plath has returned.

5

Boston Rhodes, 1958

It wasn't that I felt threatened by Sylvia, or the prospect of inviting her to join our little group contest, yet every good contest requires some strategizing. I gathered my best poems and spent many an afternoon at the university library hunting for editorial contacts and reading the works of John Berryman and W. D. Snodgrass for inspiration.

No sooner had I set myself up before a spread of magazines one day when I sensed someone approaching.

"Of course I'd find you here." Sylvia was standing over me with that perpetually thin-lipped smirk, her skin olive, her hair short and dark, her eyes low-lidded. She was holding a copy of *The New Poets of England and America* to her breast. "I just want to say, I can't possibly tell you how much 'A Visit to Dr. No' moved me. As I read it, I said to myself, *Thank God someone, anyone, wrote that poem.*"

"You're too kind," I said.

If only that were true, I thought.

"I really do envy your passion. Ted says my work could use an infusion of it."

She noticed all the magazines I'd pulled from the racks. Each was sheathed in a cloudy plastic cover.

"Which ones are you thinking of submitting to?" she asked.

"Isn't it obvious? All of them."

"Which one will you be submitting to first, then?"

There was no first. Rather than picking and choosing my strongest, I'd decided to submit to the whole lot.

Not that anyone invited her, but Sylvia pulled up a chair and took the liberty of fanning out my sheath of poems. "Well, which piece will you be submitting?"

"Every one," I said.

Sylvia's good manners fell away, and here she became dubious. "All at once?"

I spoke slowly so there'd be no misunderstanding me. "I'm submitting every poem, to every magazine, all at the same time."

"I think you might be crazy. Either that, or fearless."

"In my experience they go hand in hand."

"Well, in my experience," she said, "the ego bruises far too easily to go through the process of submitting even one poem to a single magazine, if you want to know. Yet I do submit, like some horrible sadist."

"Rejection doesn't concern me, because I'll have fifty-nine other poems out for consideration at the same time. My father says the salesman's way is diversification."

Sylvia liked that. "What else does your father say?"

"Good product, like talent, is cheap. But as long as you've got the ambition to sell, it's just a numbers game. I'm not sure if that makes me a poet or a salesman."

"It makes you a professional."

I liked that.

Sylvia sat with me through the dreary process of identifying magazine submission editors. Afterward, she helped me fold copies of my poems and seal the envelopes. By the time we'd created a dozen small stacks, with every submission addressed and stamped, we'd burned through the afternoon.

Sylvia and I left the library and came upon Commonwealth Avenue, the air smelling like rain. Sylvia held the mailbox open for me. "Professor Lowell says you and I have a lot in common."

Let me ask you, Professor, what exactly yoked me and Sylvia to each other in your mind? Was it the way we both wrote about oppression of the self and of the body? Did the poetry she brought to your workshop hold a passing thematic, linguistic, or spiritual resemblance to mine? For such a perceptive man, you really were blind.

I dropped all my submissions inside the mailbox as though casting my bid for a title. Then, bashfully, fragile even, and lacking any hint of that smug self-assurance, she said, "I'd very much like to become friends."

Another question for you, dear Professor: How close would you allow yourself to get to the very thing you disliked the most, to protect the very thing you most loved?

I accepted Sylvia's offer.

I believe the workshop was feeling a bit protective of Sylvia. How else to explain why you and the others came to see Sylvia perform that night at the gathering of the New England Poetry Club in front of all those people? We came to listen, sure. We felt proud, too. But we also felt possessive of her, our own Sylvia Plath giving herself to a lusty audience in a Brookline apartment where Robert Frost once lit himself on fire and burned with jealousy.

I bet you can still picture her from that evening, Sylvia on the makeshift stage, the old girl dressed in a dark coat and boots, her lips at the microphone.

"A poem. 'Miss Drake Proceeds to Supper.'" And as she orated, her eyes closed, her hands behind her back, she did so with astonished intonation.

"'No novice
In those elaborate rituals
Which allay the malice
Of knotted table and crooked chair,
The new woman in the ward
Wears purple . . .'"

It was another strange little poem from our Sylvia, a study in madness and dread, revealed through the behaviors of a mind-crippled asylum patient confronting hindrances, hurdles, and hallucinations, all in an effort to reach the relative safety of the ward's dining room. It had some fine qualities, I admit. Yet there was little fair about the volume of the ovation Sylvia received as she lingered on the final word of the last verse. She waved, and she bowed to the room, and she devoured its esteem.

By now, you can sense the red rage building in me. Look how needy Sylvia was. Look how desperately she thirsted for approval. How I pitied you, Professor Lowell, leaning against the bust and applauding her, feeding her your love. How I pitied everyone else, too, fools placating Sylvia's desire for so much adulation. Did you not see you were feeding a machine whose only purpose was to consume for its own fulfillment? I might have lit the pages of my own poems on fire that night, but I'd already depleted my matchbook, slaughtering what was left of my cigarettes through Sylvia's performance.

Afterward, Sylvia had someone she wanted me to meet. Since becoming friends, at readings Sylvia was always introducing me to famous poets she knew and big-deal magazine critics and rich socialites who worked a room almost as well as she did, saying hello to so-and-so, preening, and hooting at some private joke.

"Boston Rhodes, this is my husband, Ted Hughes."

The way Sylvia said "my husband" was prideful and yet without a hint of gloat, surely a well-practiced performance. Admittedly, I was momentarily dazed, standing there in the presence of the great poet himself. Before me stood Ted, a tall, steeply shouldered man, striking, with a strong wide chin and hair the color of the pilsner in his glass. In person, as on the page, I found him to be without sentimentality. What I knew about Ted was that he came upon his notoriety riding a wave of seemingly effortless talent. One minute he was a simple rose gardener, and the next the so-called poet of a generation. In between, there was his opus collection *The Hawk in the Rain*, which you insisted was among the most tense and dangerous poetry you'd ever read.

In front of Ted, Sylvia heaped mounds of praise upon me. She went on and on about how my poetry was fearless and bloody and positively lit—as though her stroking my ego was a charity she was bestowing to the less fortunate.

"I enjoyed your reading tonight, Mrs. Rhodes." Ted spoke with a muddied Yorkshire enunciation. I assumed a shade of modesty, then told Ted how I'd paid close attention to his work, too, and quoted from "The Thought Fox," which impressed him considerably. I adored *The Hawk in the Rain*, I said, even if the collection did lack a bit of an interior life.

Ted was amused. "Well, then. Sylvia told me you were cheeky. And not just your poetry, which is delightfully guileless and leaves so little to the imagination."

Sylvia fawned. "Oh, Ted." She touched her hand to Ted's shoulder, as though to tame him. And then they were pulled away, off to say hello to others demanding their attention.

Sylvia turned around and flashed me a furtive thumbs-up. I'd passed a test. She then placed her hand against Ted's lower back again, resuming her place within their procession through people bathing the famous couple in adulation.

Have you ever known a shadow to mistake itself as human?

❋

Maxine immediately rushed over and begged to learn what Ted had said to me. They really were the perfect pair. Maxine fawned, admiring Ted and Sylvia hobnobbing from across the apartment. I'd witnessed Maxine going gaga over poets before. She'd practically dragged me to see John Ashbery's public reading at the Harvard Club even though I thought he was too avant-garde and probably on drugs. But Maxine's interest in Ted and Sylvia ran deeper than any other poets she followed. "They're one of those famous writing couplets, like Ginsberg and Orlovsky, or Hemingway and Gellhorn!" I couldn't help but picture Ted and Sylvia as a ruthless poetic force, spending their days together making love and writing in small rooms and bantering on Chaucer, Shakespeare, and Blake while sojourning with literary aristocracy.

My marriage was nothing like Sylvia and Ted's. With Kildare and me, there was no pageantry or style, and it carried no social authority by any stretch of the imagination. Its existence was predicated, in fact, on a loss of status, which began, innocently enough, with a letter I received years earlier at Frederick Hall, a prep school I found rigorous, prudish, and utterly pompous. The letter's author wrote that he'd noticed me from afar at the Longwood Cricket Club the previous summer and punctuated the note with a declaration of my beauty and my fashion sense, as I'd been wearing my crisp tennis whites and Brigitte Bardot headband the day he'd spied me. I reread his letter a dozen times before I had anything worthwhile to write back. I was flattered, I confessed, albeit surprised by his words, which were kind and thoughtful. In his next letter, which arrived five days later, he suggested we meet at the Longwood. As the date approached, all the bravado in me dissolved. I wondered if he was rich or handsome. What if he was rich *and ugly*? I secretly hoped he was depraved.

The first thing I noticed about him was not his medium build or thin lips or soft chin, but that he was wearing mismatched socks. Over lunch he said he was from Chestnut Hill and in his second year at Skidmore. His name was Charles White the Second, but because he'd wanted to be a doctor his whole life, everyone called him Kildare, as in Dr. Kildare, after the novels. "I hope I didn't scare you, writing out of the blue like that. I also had the hardest time tracking you down."

"I'm not an easy girl to find. I travel a lot. Some weekends I'm in New York. Some in Paris or Milan." I didn't know why I was lying.

"Time and circumstance. If I hadn't decided to go to the club that day, and you hadn't been at the club that day, I never would have seen you, and I wouldn't have written you, and you and I wouldn't be here now having lemonade."

I decided then and there that I was going to seduce him. After a splendid day together, I had him park his car outside my dorm, where I unbuttoned my blouse. He froze, completely helpless, not that I knew what I was doing any more than he did beyond what I'd read in *My Life and Loves*, which I'd poached from my father's study. I placed Kildare's one hand to my breast, the other to my hip. While he was occupied, I went to work unbuckling his pants. Soon, his breath was quick against my cheek. We made love, or a kind of love, brief, sweaty, clumsy, an endeavor we entered as novices and finished as budding connoisseurs. Afterward, he collapsed into me, blushing and marveling, his face sweaty against my chest. As inept as we were, I felt as though I'd activated some machinery within my body, its true purpose I'd never known. I knew its purpose now.

Was it even a month later that I was packing a canvas bag with brushes, a makeup kit, a nightie, a crushed blue spring dress, and a mink jacket from my roommate's closet? In the night, I slid my second-story window open and tossed my suitcase to Kildare where he was waiting. The roads at this hour were empty. I couldn't remember ever being out so late in my life. Kildare said we'd be in New Haven by morning, and by this time tomorrow, crossing into North Carolina, where we wouldn't need a premarital health certificate. By Kildare's estimate, we'd get to a church, get married, and get back to town by Tuesday, tops. No one was going to think to look for me at school until Monday at breakfast. As soon as Frederick Hall realized I was missing, they'd call my father. He'd be angry for sure, and angrier still after discovering I'd gotten married. But all of that would change, I figured, after he heard I'd married a boy from Skidmore, that he was a fine young man, responsible and kind, and that he came from very acceptable people.

"What do you want to do when you graduate?" Kildare asked as he drove the dark highway south.

"You first."

"Well, there's med school, obviously. And I've got a line on a residency program in Manhattan—"

"Manhattan?"

"You're okay with living in the city, aren't you?"

I laughed. "Oh yes!"

"Your turn."

I didn't have to even think about my answer. "I want to be the best. The best wife to you. The best homemaker. The best mother."

Kildare seemed pleased by this.

But fate's a funny thing. We play by the rules long ago established by a higher order—go to school, get married, make money, raise a family. Then Providence goes and reminds you that it's very much a competitor for the final say. Kildare and I were destined to never make it to Manhattan. We barely got farther than Pleasant Hill, North Carolina.

After I uttered two of the most misleading words known to womankind—"I do"—my disastrous tenure as a wife began.

Learning I was married, Frederick Hall handed me a notice of expulsion. My father refused to let my mother take us in. Obviously, I couldn't move into Kildare's fraternity, so he found a listing in the *Post-Standard* for a leaky, damp one-room flat with a sloping floor and windows painted shut that cost all of twelve dollars a month.

Straightaway I ran into my next problem. I think you'll agree, Professor, that in life it's a woman's prerogative to practice a certain amount of deceit, if for no other reason than to preserve the illusion of beauty. The truth was, my hands had never touched dishwater or cracked an egg. Now that there was an expectation I knew how to operate a homestead, I had to come clean to Kildare. I was a domestic neophyte. But becoming a great housewife was like acquiring any other skill, I told him, and I was determined to master it. Whenever my father eventually agreed to see the life Kildare and I were creating, he'd be satisfied. I was going to learn to be a good and proper woman.

So I drove to Mel's Five and Dime in Kings Station and bought copies of *Ladies' Home Journal, Family Circle,* and *Good Housekeeping.* Using heavy scissors, I cut out all the recipes. Despite my best efforts to follow the instructions, my tuna noodle casserole gave Kildare food poisoning. My honey ginger carrots were never quite sweet enough. Chilled melon was easy to master and difficult to screw up, but I always seemed to find the bitterest fruit. My crown roast of lamb was dry. My consommé Bellevue, bland.

The magazines said I should make my husband a lunch to bring with him for his day, but often I found them discarded and uneaten in the car. The magazines also told me to keep up with sewing repairs. I tried replacing Kildare's chipped and fallen shirt buttons, only to prick myself with the needle so often my fingertip turned blue. It seemed to me that I was not very good at "wife-ing." Moreover, with these endeavors I feared I was merely sublimating my loneliness, which had only gotten worse, not better, since leaving Frederick Hall. The apartment we shared was a desolate place. In the winters, there were days so quiet I wanted to scream. My malaise turned to apathy. I was certain I'd contracted rheumatic fever, but Kildare said I was just restless.

I knew what it really was, though. Something needed to change. I needed to change. I needed to *become* . . . whereas Sylvia would later show up in your workshop fully formed with her glamour, her worldliness, her education, and her esteemed husband, Ted. Sylvia was a success in all the ways I was not.

Looking at Sylvia here at the Brookline poetry reading with Ted Hughes, two titans mixing with their audience, how cruel it seemed that no one questioned her place or her position among the greats. I saw through Sylvia and her air of entitlement. I recognized better than most that *becoming* requires the act of commandeering the credulous nature of one's mind by simply acting the part. Where you saw Sylvia's confidence, I saw Sylvia's neediness consuming the love in every room she entered.

"I can just imagine being along for the ride on one of their many adventures," Maxine was saying. I mean, really! For someone as measured as Maxine, she really was making a fool of herself. She latched on to my arm and squeezed. "I just knew being friends with Sylvia was a good idea. You just wait and see, Rhodes. Now that you're in with Mr. and Mrs. Hughes, you'll be going places, too."

6

Ruth, 1953

NOVEMBER 12—

The line between insanity and art is a verse. So said the Mad Poet in the days before he left my charge. His words came back to me today as Nurse Edme scrutinized the vandalized pages of *Finnegans Wake* and the poem Miss Plath coded into its words one letter at a time. Nurse Edme chalked these exhibits up to the ramblings of an otherwise manic mind. That Miss Plath has chosen to write a poem about one of Codman Manor's porcelain bathtubs isn't nearly as important as the fact she chose to express her observations, I told Nurse Edme. "We are going to encourage *more* observations like this from Miss Plath, not less."

"But what's it supposed to mean?" she asked.

"It means we get Miss Plath more books!"

I have come to appreciate Nurse Edme's company. She has been with the hospital longer than most and even has a year of college education underneath her, where many of her peers were barely out of high school before the Nurses Corps came recruiting. When there is a question of conduct or procedure, timid and serious Nurse Edme is the resident rule book. Deviations from procedure bring her to contortions. "What about Mr. Butler? Won't he expect the books back in one piece?"

"We've only promised to use the books, not *how* we'd use them." I'm not opposed to feeding Miss Plath an entire library to deface if the intervention works. I have instructed Mr. Butler to order the full selection of James Joyce and Edna St. Vincent Millay. Still, Nurse Edme makes a strong point. Having a patient mutilate library books is only going to work for so long. I need a new plan.

NOVEMBER 14—

A fresh admission to the ward this week: a wilted, pale-faced creature named Penelope Drake. Wearing a long onion-colored dress with purple flowers underneath a squirrel-collared coat, and a carved shell cameo brooch clasping the points of her collar, Miss Drake arrived looking like a Kansas City schoolteacher. Her teeth are big and crooked, and her nostrils are wide. She hardly utters a word to anyone. Beholden to a kind of compulsiveness, she avoids stepping on certain patterns in the rugs, instead performing a kind of crab walk as she meanders from room to room. Nurse Edme says it looks like she is trying to avoid booby traps in the floor. And while Miss Drake has connected rather quickly with Miss Plath, whom she sits beside at group therapy and shadows through the manor, she mostly keeps to herself. She also ignores prepared meals and opts instead for pocketed saltines, croutons, sugar packets, and heels of bread. These behaviors point to a deeper psychosis that finds Miss Drake adhering to a strict and unusual code of cleanliness and routine from which she cannot break.

I have decided that the best course of action is to steer Miss Drake toward a healthy endeavor of some kind, something that interrupts the normal routines of Codman Manor, the daily structure of time, the implied safety of shelter, the warmth of predictability. So this morning, instead of gathering in our usual parlor for group therapy, I had Nurse Edme help gather all six women, each heralding from a wide cross section of healthy society—athletes, debutantes, academics. Together, we trudged across the fields away from the manor, passing the apple orchards in the direction of the water tower.

For her part, Miss Plath put up a bit of a fight. She grumbled and scowled as she high-knee walked through tall grass. "Can you even call this treatment? More like 'mistreatment.' Just wait until my mother hears about this!" We were a group, I told her, and not only in name, but in process. Miss Plath didn't much care for that answer, and sulked and threatened to go on a hunger strike. But as we approached the chicken coop, a confederacy of three milking heifers, a sounder of swine, and two dozen chickens, Miss Plath quieted, for on a side of the small wood structure stood one of the largest men surely either of us had ever seen.

The Norseman, as he is known, took off his straw boater, wiped a handkerchief across his forehead, and replaced the hat. "The women are here to work on the farm," I informed him.

The Norseman in his dungarees grunted and glowered at the huddle of women behind me. "Farm is no place for patients." His accent was dense, like his frame, which was all shoulders and thick bone of forehead and jaw and chin.

As though to make his point for him, Miss Drake bumped into a low bench and toppled it, spilling and cracking two buckets of orange and brown eggs. The Norseman took in the wasted, cracked shells.

"This is approved by the superintendent?"

Nurse Edme gave me a look, as the treatment plan has no precedent.

"I'm all the authority one needs," I said.

For all of his intimidating girth, the giant abandoned his fight with a shrug.

He led us past the farm and through a small ridge of fig trees. My pace slowed at the sound of a low, bright hum. As we entered a clearing, the hum deepened into a dissonant thwacking sound, like a convoy of twin-engine prop planes.

The group came upon a half-dozen white-on-tan hive boxes. Each was the size of a set of drawers and scattered haphazardly in the grass. Around us, thousands of bees whirred. The longer I stood still, the more pronounced the sound of the bees grew until the air was practically throbbing.

"Insects, better than chickens or cows. Hardier, too," said the Norseman. He ducked into a pitched-roof stone cottage overgrown with ivy. When he returned, he was pinching a mass of hessian and burlap, which he lit with a gas lighter and dropped into a smoker can he used to drown the insects in sleep.

After a demonstration of how one pulls the honey from the comb, the Norseman placed the smoker can in Miss Drake's fingers. Miss Drake took a single brave step forward and began swinging the smoker can wildly at the stragglers zipping past her face. Unable to escape the bees, she screamed, dropped the can, and ran away, obliging Nurse Edme, long-suffering, to dash after her over the hill.

Miss Plath sighed.

I, however, remain undeterred.

NOVEMBER 18—

I am pleased to report that, after some cajoling, the women of the group have taken to working with the Norseman's bees quite well. And each morning, an added surprise: Superintendent Frisch's two Dalmatians wind their way out of the Proctor House and, homing in on the activity in the bee yard, trot down the hillside to meet us at the hives. The Norseman shouts and waves his long arms after the dogs to shoo them away as the women of Codman Manor, hidden beneath dark veils tacked to hats, gloves, and cheesecloth smocks, pull beeswax sheets from the insides of the wood boxes. Lifting honeycomb undulating with brown insects, they touch the honey from the combs and then lick it from the fingers of their gloves.

Meanwhile, Miss Drake has thought less and less about the patterns in the rugs. Her feet no longer avoid the roses sewn into the fabric. Her handwashing has diminished to a manageable two times a day. And in a most apparent change, Miss Drake now joins the women of Codman Manor for meals in the dining room where she eats the food on her plate.

Having heard a rumor that patients are doing better cavorting with dispassionate insects than with doctors, Dr. Beuscher, like the Dalmatians, followed the clamor to the bee yard. Dr. Beuscher wanted to observe my technique, he said. "You're obviously doing something right. I'm just not sure what it is exactly."

I have come to appreciate Dr. Beuscher's sensibilities. I believe him to be genuine and sincere. He is tall and equable, uniformly kind to personnel and patients, and never goes anywhere without a little buoyancy in his step. There is no doubt that he is an intriguing man both in the spectrum of experience he has acquired at his age, midthirties, and his appeal for knowledge within a certain bracket of subjects, psychology and medicine among them, but also a rudimentary interest in my time at McLean. Am I finding my way? Am I doing well here? He addresses me with a delicateness that one might address a child having only just enrolled at a new school, and not a woman of thirty with all the proficiencies of a most gifted governess. His hair has gone white, a cruelty when leveled against any other young man, but not Dr. Beuscher. Its premature bloom of bright white, which is almost silver in the sun, offers a stark contrast against the smooth skin of his cheeks and fullness of his lips that, paired with his blue eyes, conveys a clarity of spirit, a fidelity to the field and his purpose. I hear the nurses always talk in whispers about his beauty. If there's a flutter of delight I feel in his presence, it is in deference to this fidelity. Dr. Beuscher believes in psychoanalysis, in structure, in tradition, but also in the value of observation and listening with an ear to receive.

In the bee fields, I asked him if he knew of the law of parsimony.

"I can't say that I do."

"The most straightforward answer to any problem tends to be the right one. Why stick with dated techniques when the patients tell us they need something else?"

Dr. Beuscher considered this. "The superintendent would disagree with you."

"He's allowed his opinions."

"Can I tell you about another law? The one about unintentional consequences?"

"Dr. Beuscher, do I look like I need protecting?"

His eyes were trained on mine. "No, I don't think you need anything, in fact."

He looked like he wanted to say something more. Instead, he turned his gaze toward the women working among the bees, mesh veils obscuring their faces as the wind picked up and bent the pines around us. When the breeze hit just right, it reeked of sawdust from the meatpacking plants ten miles east down Route 2.

Rain began to fall. The Norseman bellowed, "Equipment back to the *stugan*!"

The women of Codman Manor turned in, filing past the stone cottage, placing their smoker cans on a bench, dropping their hats and gloves in a pile until Miss Plath was the last patient left in the yard. I called out to her. She continued pressing long beeswax sheets home into her hive box.

The mesh of her screen grew less opaque as I approached. The hems of her pants and jacket sleeves, I saw, were caked in shimmering black mud.

"Come, Miss Plath, time to go indoors—"

I gasped and wheeled backward. My feet trampled on her protective gloves, which lay abandoned on the ground. The mud caked to her extremities was teeming with life. It wasn't mud at all.

Without thinking, I seized her bare wrists and shook them hard. The coating of bees held on to her, consumed her, refused to give her up. They moved up the small hairs on her arms and nuzzled the crooks and curves of her fingers.

The Norseman's wide hands appeared suddenly, and steadily, they grabbed and pulled swaths of bees away from her arms and neck.

Miss Plath, unflinching, wondered what all the fuss was about.

NOVEMBER 20—

Freud once said that of all human obsessions, the strongest is a desire to habitually rely on memory, when the truth is that memory is full of holes. We fill those holes with ghosts.

The infirmary has recently moved from its pre–Civil War–era site on Summary Road to a wing of Codman Manor. As I entered the large, airless room overrun with hard linoleum the color of spearmint gum, the ward with its dozens of beds struck me as familiar, suggestive of the scarlet fever ward, with its long hall of iron-framed cots, where I used to visit my daughter Tiffany.

Miss Plath's bed faced a window through which she could see the manicured lawns, the paths that cut northeast across the grounds, and several little cottages. When I first came upon her, she was slumped, her shoulders and brow sharing a delicate symmetry. Her hands in her lap were bandaged in honey-colored gauze. Mauve blemishes trekked across her neck and up along her cheeks, which were full and splotchy. The attending doctor said it was the insulin therapy we are using to treat her mania, and not the bee venom, that made Miss Plath inflate like this. "They all blow up like balloons," he said.

I told him to tuck in his shirt.

From a wicker chair opposite her bed, I sat close enough that my knees brushed the edge of her mattress. I resumed our daily reading together, choosing from *Look, Stranger!* Miss Plath says I have a lovely voice but a terrible oral presentation. I told her that I never claimed to be a poet.

"You don't have to be a poet to read poetry, but you're butchering it," she said.

I offered her the chance to read to me, but she refused. I closed the book of Auden and asked how she'd like to continue. "Why don't you write me another poem?"

She held up her bandaged hands like trial exhibits.

"I'd like to ask you about what happened yesterday, if that's all right. Why did you put your hands in the hives?"

"Dictation. I think I'd like to write a poem about Miss Drake."

"Were you trying to hurt yourself? It must have been painful."

"It makes me sad, thinking how lonely she must be. Her mother hasn't visited her even once. I bet she feels numb inside, closed in, shut down, and shuttered by people. I bet she's practically desperate to feel something." Miss Plath's grave expression broke into a broad smile. "She sure looks real funny out there, tripping all over herself with the bees, don't you think?" She laughed, and I could tell that laughing felt good to her. Then she grew pensive again as she took in the sight of her bandaged hands, the fingers all bound together. This seemed to bring her back into the moment, into this bright infirmary with the bedsheet pulled tight over her legs.

"Dictation it is." I returned to my clipboard, angling the pen against the page.

Sylvia shut her eyes. ". . . No novice in those elaborate rituals . . . which allay the malice of knotted table and crooked chair, the new woman in the ward wears purple . . ."

With this journal entry, I report that Miss Plath has challenged me to play a new game. A listening game. It is a game in which one must pay attention to the words underneath the words. It is a game I know how to play well. It tells me that I have finally begun to reach her.

NOVEMBER 30–

An unsettling incident today.

I have noticed that the visitors' list hanging outside of Miss Plath's room has gotten exceedingly long. Countless boys in letterman jackets come and go. There was a boy in a blue prep suit uniform one day, and another wearing the uniform of an officer cadet. The local Christian Scientist evangelist stopped by, and a Unitarian minister who knows the family comes to room nineteen on Thursdays. An English teacher Miss Plath had in high school brought her red licorice, and a college benefactor brought her sweet mints.

Of all her visitors, however, Miss Plath speaks most often to me about her mother. Aurelia attends to her daughter at Codman Manor almost daily. Mothers are a frequent topic in group therapy—mothers as delinquent caregivers, mothers as disappointed despots, mothers as sources of ire. If we might remove all mothers, then we'd get rid of half of all our problems, the Mad Poet once declared. His was ironfisted and manipulative, and when he thought of her, his soul, he'd said, burrowed underground.

"My mother's the worst," Miss Plath confessed. "I'm suffocated by her, always under her review. I feel lousy saying such things, but I'm being honest. Mother wants everyone to love her perfect daughter."

"Being everything to everyone, or even someone, can be a difficult way to live," I told her.

"I didn't ask for it. I've suffered through it."

"You're not obligated to anyone's approval, let alone your mother's."

"You'd make a good mother, Dr. Barnhouse," she replied. These words struck me. (Does Miss Plath detect that I *was* a mother, and then *not* a mother? Does she sense that at one time I cared for a life, now only the memory of a life?)

In response to our sessions together, I have ordered the head nurse to restrict Miss Plath's mother from visiting. These social calls are doing Miss Plath little good and ask far too much of her. I suspected this would not go over well with Aurelia, and when she arrived at the receiving desk this morning, I was not surprised that she raised a ruckus. "But I'm her mother!" Aurelia declared. She craned her neck over my shoulder to try and peer into the nearby parlor. "Sylvia! *Sylvia!*" she cried. "I demand to speak with a doctor immediately."

"I am Miss Plath's doctor," I said.

Her eyes narrowed.

"A *real* doctor."

"Any doctor here will tell you the same thing."

Aurelia bristled beneath her bowknot hat and sank with silent rage and injury. "How dare you. You have no right to keep her from me."

But of course I did, and I do. Powerlessness registered in her face. She called out for her daughter again, took a step forward, and would have broken past me to track down Miss Plath, I'm certain, had an orderly not arrived at that very moment and offered to escort her out of the manor.

"This is far from over," she spat and left, her shoulders so stiff that the end of her fur coat dragged along the rugs.

I do not for a second doubt her.

DECEMBER 1—

McLean Hospital is more than a hundred years old, and in that time it has had six superintendents. The institution now under Superintendent Frisch is procedural and tidy. He is a protégé of the great early American analysts. Among the first to translate Freud's writings from

Austrian to English, he made his name publishing books about Freud's thoughts on wit, the collective unconscious, and the topography of the mind. As I marched up the porch steps of the Proctor House, the prospect of defending myself against a man of such esteem brought me no pleasure.

Candidly, I do not blame Aurelia Plath for filing a complaint. During my daughter's convalescence, was my resolve to see Tiffany any less steady? Even after she was moved to a quarantined ward, I'd pressed for entry to see her. I'd waited with silent resolve in the lobby for whole days while the nurses brought me cups of tea. I did not leave, if for the small chance that Tiffany felt my presence. I understand Miss Plath's mother more than I let on; I understand that plea into the void.

Superintendent Frisch offered me a butter candy from a dish. I declined with a wave. He returned the dish to his large desk, with its photographs of the superintendent shoulder-to-shoulder with the Archbishop of Boston, and another of him huddling with the Emmanuel College bowling league.

The two Dalmatians trotted past my knees. They offered me a hasty sniff on their way to the superintendent, who bent forward in his chair like a vaulted conch shell and took their faces into his cupped palms. "Sigmund and Basil are inseparable. The animals have been that way since birth. I've raised seven generations from a single line, every one of them state champion show dogs." His demeanor was pleasant and a bit too well practiced.

He opened a desk drawer, removed a square of tinfoil, and unwrapped a sandwich. Pulling off two ends, he dropped them on the floor. The dogs snapped the corners up hungrily.

"Now about this business of restricting visitors."

Miss Plath's mother trades in the currency of nurturing while threatening to withdraw her love, I explained. Furthermore, I said I believe Miss Plath lacks self-reliance. "With her mother gone, there is no one for Miss Plath to depend on but herself."

As I spoke, one of the dogs moaned and passed gas at the superintendent's shoes.

"No one else but you, you mean." The superintendent's smile widened, imparting a sense of controlled authority. He drew in a breath between his teeth. Underneath his poise, I sensed disdain. "You do have an undomesticated approach. I understand that you've got my nurses traipsing patients to the apiary in the name of some inane treatment."

Inane or not, I thought, *the treatment is working.* Miss Drake's condition improved by the day. She remained shy and buttoned up, inclined to mope through the ward, and dubious of others, and yet no mood nor manner could subdue her reemergence of self. Miss Drake was good-natured and showed renewed interest in spending time around others in group. She possessed good and simple qualities, chief among them a gentleness and a blossoming curiosity.

"It's all highly unorthodox," the superintendent continued.

The dogs' ears twitched, sensing the shift in him.

"You'll reinstate Aurelia Plath's visitor privileges. And you will stick to psychoanalysis. No more deviations. I make my disapproval of you and your methods no secret. You won't succeed here, Dr. Barnhouse, if it means getting in the way of me running my hospital. Deviate again, and you will no longer be walking within it."

THIRD STANZA

The Agreements

History and one's past are like lovers. Both are liars.

—Boston Rhodes, "The Victor"

7

Estee, 2019

Early days, not yet a master curator though beginning to make a name for myself, I am chronicling the inventory of the Spanish National Library when I come upon a book in a decommissioned reading room. I am a young woman here, only twenty-two at the time, already inured to dusty rooms, a graduate student, my hair still brown and perpetually drawn into a ponytail down my back, dividing me like the seam between two pages of a book. Set among the library's shelves, I pull the unusual tome. It is heavy and bound in red leather, velvet, and gilt corner pieces. At once, I recognize it as liturgical, very likely a Rothschild, easily mid–seventeenth century. Even more remarkable than its age and craftsmanship, however, is the stamp I encounter inside the front cover. Bringing the book under a table lamp, I see the hallmark of the prayer book's original owner, a Roman Catholic church called St. Dominic's. A simple search and I find that not only does St. Dominic's remain operational after four centuries, but it stands not fifteen blocks from this very library. The book is not listed among the library's inventory. Its inclusion here among our stacks is a mistake. Patrons frequently return the wrong books. Librarians put these books aside, and without categorization, the books drift from one desk to another, from one pile to a second pile, and eventually join the misplaced, mishandled, and mislabeled. The migration of objects relies on such haphazard exploits.

So I set about returning the book to the Church of St. Dominic, walking the fifteen blocks one afternoon through the streets of Madrid, under the same deep blue sky that saw the book journey farther away, now observing its return to where it began. In his quarters, the pastor marvels at the item I've brought him. He postulates that it disappeared during the Spanish Civil War, when the parish was converted into a quartermaster's warehouse, and many of its books were moved to attics and cellars for safekeeping. His mounting disbelief that such an artifact from St. Dominic's past has found its way home gives over to wonder. The church will preserve the book in a place of honor, he says.

Several months later, my postgraduate work finds me curating for the Library of Catalonia when I read in the newspaper of a seventeenth-century Rothschild book of prayers having sold at Sotheby's Madrid for the American equivalent of thirteen million dollars. Perhaps St. Dominic's changed its mind about its ability to maintain the book, to offer it sanctuary. The more likely answer, however, is that the church discovered the book's financial worth.

Am I angry? Only to the degree that all agency of youth is predicated on hot-blooded crusades. Looking back now, though, what I feel is appreciation. The book, and the betrayal, turned out to be the first occasion in which I tracked down the record of an object. It set me on my way toward becoming a master curator. Over the decades, I have learned that the path an object takes throughout its life is out of our hands, while the role of a master curator is to see to it that the objects move safely from those hands to the next.

It is fitting, then, that my tenure as a master curator ends where it began, with me tracking the path of another misplaced manuscript. Nicolas is right, questions remain about the handwritten draft of *The Bell Jar,* questions that deserve answers. Like Nicolas, I want to know how the notebooks wound up in a lockbox in an attic, and not in a museum, in an archive, or with an estate. I wonder if someone purchased the notebooks, or if Sylvia Plath gifted them. The worst case I can imagine is that the notebooks are stolen objects, fully aware that if the notebooks are in fact stolen property, St. Ambrose cannot, will not, sell them.

To find the origin of the Plath notebooks, I return to my laptop and create a list of archives and libraries. My first stop is a phone call to the Mortimer Rare Book Collection at Smith College. A woman answers. I say, "I'm calling about Sylvia Plath." Oh yes, says the librarian, they have many valuable pieces of her work. I ask about *The Bell Jar*. *The Bell Jar*? Yes, yes, of course. Their rare book collection contains quite a few editions, in fact. The archivist has a soft voice. She lists items from memory. A rare edition of *The Bell Jar* from 1971. An edition of *The Bell Jar* with illustrations. An early print of *The Bell Jar* published under the name Victoria Lucas.

"What about notebooks?" I ask.

"Plath notebooks?"

"Yes. Spiral notebooks that contain early drafts of *The Bell Jar*. Have you ever had one of these in your archive?"

"Not that I'm aware of. But, like I say, we have many editions."

"Any editions that might have wandered off or gone missing?"

"Have we ever lost Sylvia Plath, you mean? I would hope not." I hear the click-click-clicking of a keyboard. The archivist finds no record of Plath manuscripts written in spiral notebooks, and no record of their collection ever having possessed such items. So I skip to the next collection on my list, dialing and moving the receiver to my other ear. Like the repetition of a line of poetry, my conversation with the librarian at Indiana State University mirrors the last. The man at this archive says his library has never held such a document. He directs me to the Stuart A. Rose Library at Emory University. I call Atlanta. The librarian who answers is more Southern burr than identifiably male or female. No, they have never possessed early copies of *The Bell Jar*. No, this archive only collects magazine articles written and published by Sylvia Plath. I place another call, this one to a small college in Worchester, and then to a college in Bedford, New Hampshire. Both have possessed original handwritten drafts of Sylvia Plath's poetry and her letters, but nothing so unique as three notebooks containing a draft of *The Bell Jar.*

I am spelunking a rabbit hole.

I dial a library at Brown University, then a library at Columbia University, and then a library at Harvard University. The closest the Massachusetts Historical Society came to possessing an original Sylvia Plath manuscript was a publisher's copy of *Ariel* with editorial marks in the margins that it traded to the Morgan Library & Museum several years earlier. So I dial New York. The librarian at the Morgan reads off a dozen texts that it keeps on-site. They include an edition of *The Bell Jar* with drawings by Sylvia Plath and a videocassette recording of the author reading excerpts from the novel. The librarian, a man who could not sound more disinterested in helping me, assures me that its archives have never contained a handwritten first draft of *The Bell Jar,* and furthermore, he is certain no such document exists. I'm wasting my time, he says.

At the end of my search, the only new information I have acquired is that the origin of the Plath manuscript is just as mysterious as its final destination, hidden and forgotten in a lockbox within an attic.

How relevant is Sylvia Plath? Just ask Scarlett. "Sylvia Plath is *super relevant*! There's, like, a massive interest in her brand!" We are gathered in the safe holdings room with the Dyce brothers and Quimby. Scarlett is dressed in a black formfitted sheath and the dark-framed glasses she wears even though her vision is twenty-twenty. Scarlett says she's performed a quick and dirty poll with St. Ambrose's online users. For eighteen- to thirty-year-olds, Sylvia Plath falls right between *elite* and *accessible*. The poll itself elicited five times more engagement than any other question St. Ambrose has ever posted.

"Is that good?" Elton Dyce asks.

Scarlett brightens. "Very good."

And when you look up the most-read books of all time, she adds, *The Bell Jar* comes up in the top five. I want to ask Scarlett if she's ever read *The Bell Jar*. She'd probably say yes. She'd probably be lying, because Scarlett does not read books, she reads trends and the temperature of rooms.

Scarlett presents mock-ups she's made of a logo that reads SYLVIA PLATH RETURNS. She passes out copies of a chart with overlapping circles, each circle labeled either GEN Z, GEN Y, GEN X, or BOOMERS. The Venn diagram looks like a cell dividing. Each intersects at SYLVIA PLATH.

"When you put all of this information through our audience appeal algorithm, Sylvia Plath is more popular among the thirty-to-forty-year-old demo than Kanye," she says.

Quimby seems pleased. The sale of a handwritten draft from Sylvia Plath will constitute a real success for St. Ambrose.

"That's not to say Sylvia's image can't use an overhaul," Scarlett continues. "With the right campaign, we can spruce up her persona for the twenty-first century and elevate our sales proposition at the same time." As Scarlett makes her plans, and talks us through the marketing and advertising campaign she envisions, it seems as though she's forgotten, or ignored, the fact that Sylvia Plath is already here in the twenty-first century. She is in front of us right now, split into three parts, separated on the table in the low cool light of the safe holdings room.

"So, how much are we talking, ballpark?" Jay Jay Dyce asks.

With a little glance in my direction, Quimby turns the floor over to me.

"The last item of Sylvia Plath's to appear on the public market was an unfinished poem. It sold for two hundred thousand dollars."

"Two hundred thousand dollars!" Elton pounds the table. "And that was just one little poem!"

"There are some collectors who do nothing but clamor for midcentury work of such fine caliber. We believe your item can fetch as much as three-quarters of a million," Quimby says.

"Someone's really gonna pay that much for a book they could just buy a used copy of on Amazon for a dollar?" Elton asks.

"We live in strange times. Vintage Converse sneakers sell for fifteen grand. Forty-year-old PEZ dispensers go for thirty," Quimby says.

Jay Jay pushes away the mock-ups and graphs. "Let's talk terms."

As far as compensation, St. Ambrose's commission is ten percent, Quimby says. Jay Jay scoffs. He counters with five percent, and here I learn that when it comes to negotiations, Jay Jay's languor disappears quickly. It's as though his jersey-wearing persona is nothing but a prop in a long con designed to get everyone else to let down their guards.

"Ours is a nonnegotiable set fee," Quimby explains.

Jay Jay is ready to walk when I wade into the arbitration. Master curators are equal parts psychotherapist, mediator, and diplomat. So I ask the Dyce brothers what it is that they'd really like.

Elton and Jay Jay glance at each other, and Jay Jay says, "I read somewhere that single-item auctions sell higher on average than regular auctions."

"That's true," I say.

Quimby demurs. "You'd like a single-item auction?"

"And a signing bonus."

"You mean a per diem," Quimby says.

"And St. Ambrose gets seven percent, not ten. That's our nonnegotiable set fee."

As the Dyce brothers and Quimby do their dance, an unplaceable feeling surfaces in me. Over the years, I have forged a kinship with many objects. Watching them leave the auction house is tantamount to a repetitive stress fracture of the heart, and yet I pride myself on my capacity to hold objects without forging feelings of ownership. The profession tasks me with containing, nurturing, and delivering these items. Someone, I forget whom, once called me a surrogate. I appreciate that description. And with the Plath notebooks, I want to be the custodian who receives them and the one who sees them off as I would any article of consequence. A simple transaction that will also see me through to my own exit from St. Ambrose. The sale of the Plath notebooks will be a good sale on which to close out my calling. The real difficulty is convincing all parties that they can each get what they want. The Dyce brothers want their money. Scarlett wants the sale. Quimby wants the reputation boost to St. Ambrose. A good master curator, competent and empathetic and tactical, will satisfy them all.

"I believe we can agree to these conditions," I say.

Quimby offers a strained laugh. "Well, let's not get ahead of ourselves—"

"Seven percent?" Jay Jay asks.

I nod. "And a single-item auction."

"What about the per diem?" Elton asks.

A per diem, too, along with the intangibles of St. Ambrose Auction House, our knowledge, reassurances, honesty, depth of expertise, fair assessment, reputation, and counsel. "When it comes to the Plath notebooks, there are no safer hands than ours."

Quimby forces a smile, and if he is hoping that it doesn't come off as insincere, he has failed. He is flummoxed and wondering how, exactly, he's found himself shaking hands with the Dyce brothers. But he is shaking hands with them, one after the other, because Quimby wants nothing more than for St. Ambrose to stay viable against Boston's larger, long-dominant auction houses, each expanding its digital tendrils and middle-market investments. Make no mistake, St. Ambrose is a lovely fruit dying on the vine. Sylvia Plath has come to us at the right time.

"Well, then," Jay Jay says, "it looks like we have ourselves an agreement."

8

Boston Rhodes, 1958

Despite volumes of evidence to the contrary, I do abide by a moral code. My aims always justify the means. To that end, I want to tell you the sordid details about my extramarital affair with George Starbuck.

No one will ever tell you art is a meritocracy. It's a business through and through. To be the best in any field, a person must angle, cajole, and coerce. Like my father always said, winning on the road, as in life, is about relationships, forging alliances, and creating allegiances.

I'd learned that, outside of the workshop, George was moonlighting as an editor at Houghton Mifflin publishers, which meant he was in a position to publish a collection of mine. Maxine could have her two *New Yorker* pieces. A book put out by a powerhouse publisher was enough to put me on top with the Ring. So I made sure that we became close, George and I. Our repartee both in and outside of the workshop was already an easy one. Caught up in a moment, I'd touch George's hand and watch for the color to rise in his face. I'd catch his eye or smile a little too long at his stupid jokes. As it turned out, the animal didn't take much effort to steer. One night, George took away my drink and drew me behind the unguarded coat-check desk. "I'm going to kiss you, and you're going to kiss me back." He pulled me close. Or maybe

I stepped forward. We tumbled into the hanging coats of muskrat, sheared beaver, stoat, and sable.

George sprang for rooms, usually at the Eliot Hotel, with views of the Back Bay Fens. We'd finish making love and soon after start again. We'd continue in this pattern until our bodies rebelled from exhaustion. George, with his sad brow, thinning temples, and small mouth, was not as handsome as Kildare. Still, the smell of his skin—maple and musk mallow—and his earnestness, which was straight and true, strengthened our affair into something honest. George never asked for any more of me than I was willing to give him. And what I gave him—my attention and my body—was enough to satisfy him. I'd come to understand that there was only so much one man was capable of accepting of a woman. After Kildare had had his fill of me, volumes more of me remained. That was the part I gave to George. There were the physical needs that he saw to, but it was always the business of poetry that brought us and kept us together, assuaging the guilt I felt over our affair, which wasn't much to begin with.

What I had only recently begun to learn was that I had a kind of power. I'm not talking about the power of seduction, but a power that comes from an acute understanding of human psychology. See, I outright told George I was using him to get published. George said he'd figured as much, that I was far too savvy and striking to start a random affair with a schlub like him. But George wasn't a schlub, and I did love him, and probably would have still had he not already promised he'd personally oversee the publication of my first poetry collection.

But therein lays the truth; let my more mercenary tendencies reveal themselves to you here, Professor. I was honest with George about using him to further my career, but it wasn't simply for the book. There was a second idea underneath the first, a manner in which to undermine Sylvia.

George's enthusiasm for Sylvia was boundless and by far the loudest among us in the workshop. George always had something complimentary to say about Sylvia, endearments ripe with flattery and obsequious praise springing from a place of fanaticism I doubt even he understood. But it was George's praise for Sylvia among the Ring that cinched it for me. I had more poems in circulation than almost everyone in the Ring's competition, and this put my standing among the implicit internal ranking close to, if not at, the very top. But recently, the Yale Younger Poets Prize singled out Sylvia as a finalist. This, in tandem with Sylvia's latest poem finding publication in the *Atlantic*, meant she was catching up to my lead, and fast. No one celebrated her one-two punch more than George. At the Ritz, he bought her martinis and toasted Sylvia all night. It was enough to make you sick.

But as our affair continued, George's enthusiasm for Sylvia's work waned. In workshop one day, you recited and analyzed Sylvia's newest poem. As usual, the workshop heaped acclaim upon it, yet George said he found that the poem, with its images of goose-stepping Nazis, rang emotionally false. "I don't know, it all seems a bit cheap."

Maxine pounced. "Are you daft, George? The poem's practically perfect, every word of it."

"It's just," continued George, "the poem reads like the writer's trying too hard."

That Sylvia was "trying too hard" was an observation I'd made to George not a day earlier. We were in bed, and I'd said that Sylvia was obviously talented and excruciatingly ambitious, but didn't he get the sense the old girl was trying a little too hard? And George had nodded, and George had sucked in the smoke from his cigarette, and George had made a small grunting sound that meant he agreed.

Sylvia's serene disposition at the Formica table hid any sting George's criticism might have inflicted upon her. Still, I'd cast the poison dye, and soon after, the workshop's fulsome commendations for Sylvia's poetry began to wither. The next poem of hers that you orated received lesser praise than the usual fare. When Sam said it wasn't nearly as strong as the other works Sylvia had written, I smiled behind my teeth.

Everyone in the workshop was finally catching on to the fact that Sylvia was a fraud.

Everyone except you—you, who extolled Sylvia's mastery of craft and tone and voice. I was shocked when you suggested that she apply for the Radcliffe literary prize. I asked George what you could possibly see in Sylvia that had earned her such an advocate. Maybe she was sleeping with you after all.

"Her poems are remarkably upsetting. Ominous, even." We were making love as he said this. I spooled my hair around my finger, spinning deeper into my thoughts as George pumped and thrusted into me from behind. Truly, there is nothing poetic, or remotely musical even, about the way men make love. Humor and arrogance, certainly. There's an element of negotiation, too, which I suppose you might call a kind of dance. I have always found my longing in that dance, there among sweaty backs, damp foreheads, wet thighs, and dry lips. "I don't think she's a well person. Have you noticed . . . sometimes her poetry . . . comes off frenetic? More confession . . . *than confessional*—!!"

George finished with a mighty heave. He rolled off of me and collapsed into his pillow.

After recovering some, he continued: "Do you think Sylvia's ever been hospitalized? I bet she has. I was thinking about that verse she brought to workshop once. Something about it being an accident the first time it happened, but with the next she meant to last it out and not come back."

I remembered that poem, and how Sylvia had recited it at the long table from memory. Not just from memory, but from someplace *deeper* than memory.

"What do you think she meant by that, to 'last it out'?" George asked.

We all have a little bit of madness in us, don't we, Professor Lowell? Is it an exaggeration to say that madness is the thing that joined my orbit and Sylvia's?

I'm thinking back to a time before I met you, before I'd ever heard of the workshop, before I'd written my first sonnet even. My infant daughter had croup. I spent my days picking up toys that never stayed on shelves, running laundry that never stayed clean, shuffling plates of half-finished meals from counter to sink, and emptying nests of crushed cigarettes in tin ashtrays in cycles that never ended. After an episode during which I remained bed-bound for a whole week, I overheard the visiting doctor tell Kildare that my slide into the depths of anguish was a combination of mania and postpartum depression. I continued to try my best to keep up with the house and the baby's needs, but it wasn't long before I felt that old boot pressing down on my chest, determined to crush me.

Then one afternoon in my half-aware state while undertaking the ironing, I heard a dryly melodic voice on the TV say, "How to write a sonnet . . ." The baby had just woken up from her nap and was crying for me in the next room, but all I heard was, "On this program in the series, the Divine Sonnets by John Donne will be read and discussed."

The TV's bars and static cleared. The camera panned left, holding on a bald and bespectacled host with a morose, small-lipped expression. His words entranced me to my core as he recited "Death Be Not Proud."

I'd never written a poem before, but I was bitten, and the inky venom merged with my blood. That night, when Kildare was asleep and the baby down, I heated water for tea. At the oak dining room table, I laid out a sheet of my father's stationery with EMPEROR FINE FABRICS stenciled across the top. For a long while, the tapping of my pencil against the page was the only sound in the whole house.

Two years later, my affair with the written word, as well as with George, continued unabated. The desired effect of the latter, to chip away at Sylvia's base of support, was working . . . until it wasn't anymore.

Sylvia was growing drunk at the Ritz, and there I was, not nearly drunk enough as she told me how much she appreciated the workshop's honesty about her poetry of late. "Especially George's. I need more criticism like that. Ted says I'll never find the limit of what I'm capable of if I remain satisfied with mediocrity."

I wondered how many times was she going to say Ted Hughes's name in one night.

"I haven't yet produced *great* poetry, with my own voice. I will someday, I'm confident. You and I, Boston, we're both geniuses of writing. We have it in us. Our identities are shaping! We shall, in the fullness of time, be among the poetesses!"

My back molar crushed an ice cube from my drink. Once skeptical of her seemingly interminable sanguinity, I was, as of this moment, unconvinced her ego was capable of incurring damage, even in the midst of the harshest criticism. Despite my best-laid plans, Sylvia remained unaffected by the piercing points of disparagement made by the slings and arrows of jealousy and spite flung by members of the workshop, the very people whose approval she craved most. And while I needed to understand what Sylvia was really after in this world, more than anything, I wanted to understand why she had crashed *my* world. I'd come from nothing to carve out a place for myself within it, and I wasn't going to share it.

"Tell me, why poetry?" My chin hovered over the rim of my drink. "Why not something more sensible?"

"Why not try something outside of Ted's domain you mean?" Sylvia grew pensive. "It's all I can do, if you want to know. I've been told my problem is that my heart is just too big. It lets in too much. I can't help but feel everything. It's overwhelming. So I put the feelings into poems. I like to think of each poem as a little room I drop into for short visits."

Given all your talk about our similarities, this was the first moment in my relationship with Sylvia that your assertion rang true. Have I ever told you, Professor, how I'd spent my whole life living in little rooms? Rooms the shape and size of every role I was supposed to play.

Rooms I'd either outgrown or I'd never fit in to begin with. I'd set out to be the best—the best student, the best wife, the best homemaker, the best mother. In the end, I'd failed at them all.

But I hadn't failed at *this*, at being a poet!

"I'd die to feel more than I do. It's the only way to be good at something," I said.

"Or *great* at something." Sylvia raised her drink. "Then we agree, we'll just have to push each other."

The cloudy cocktail sloshed over the lip of her glass.

"To building more little rooms."

To building more little rooms, I thought, *and to building bigger rooms.* To building a thousand-page novel, for all I cared, just as long as Sylvia left *this* room.

Just then, George sidled up to the table. "What are we toasting?"

"Pushing each other toward greatness," Sylvia said gaily.

"Hear, hear!" George clicked our glasses to his and swallowed some of his drink. The night continued with Maxine reciting the poetry of W. D. Snodgrass, and Sam and George flirting with Sylvia, and Sylvia reading from your collection, *For the Union Dead,* while mimicking your glacial voice. No one noticed how I was suffering through it all as I drank and I smiled and I laughed and I loved.

But the room in my heart was filling with a sulky, bitter spirit as my scheme to undo Sylvia disintegrated before me. Sylvia had firmly made a place for herself among us. She had also found a way to keep us spinning under her inescapable inertia, as though she were the sun in a universe I'd already conquered. I'd done so prostrating myself to you, and by proving myself to the workshop, and by fighting with the words that finally unlocked my place in your world.

No, Sylvia wasn't welcome in *this room. This room* was mine.

⁂

Four years before Sylvia came and conquered and set roots among us, Kildare and I wove through neighborhoods of grand homes along Oxbow Road. The Cougar pulled up to my childhood house. Using my pocket mirror, I adjusted my bangs, checked my color, and straightened my collar. My hair was washed and set, just the way my father liked it. He hadn't seen me since Kildare and I had gotten married, and I wanted to look my best for him and to show him how well we were doing, even though we weren't at all. We were broke, cut off from family, and approaching destitution.

We came before my father at supper. Harlan Rhodes had long ago taken over management of Emperor Fine Fabrics and was to this day both the ballast and the mast of the family. Here we were: a man of importance, his estranged daughter, and his son-in-law, all placed around a perfectly appointed table, while my mother, seated at the other end, held the silence. Gathering his courage, Kildare stood, his head low. He said he'd made a terrible mistake not asking him for his blessing to marry me, but that we were happy together, and we were expecting our first child.

Portly and grim, my father didn't stop tearing into his Cornish hen. Kildare glanced at me for support. I shot him an angry look: *Get on with it!* And so he did, stammering so as he asked my father for a loan to purchase a house.

My mother prepared my father's bourbon in a short glass, then he and Kildare retired to the study. Left alone with her in the den, I found myself wanting to tell my mother how much I'd missed my family, how I'd tried to make my father proud, and how I was sorry that I'd failed and disappointed them. I fidgeted with the hem of my skirt as my mother watched the clock on the hearth. At the same time, it was slowly dawning on me that by coming to my father we might actually have just walked into a trap.

The doors to the study parted. Kildare and my father came out into the vestibule and shook hands. When Kildare and I were back in the car and heading home, I cried that my mother and father were such horrible, horrible people!

"Your father offered me a job," Kildare said.

A pit forming in my stomach, I realize Kildare wasn't joking. I begged him to refuse it.

"You said it yourself, something has to change. We can do better than this," Kildare said.

I wasn't crying anymore. I wiped the old tears from my cheek with my knuckle. It was 1954. Scientists had discovered the double helix, a vaccine for polio, the cause of the common cold, and here Kildare was talking about dropping his dream of going to med school, to do what? *Make coats!*

"To sell them, actually." Sensing the dismay rising in me, he said, "Agatha, it's an olive branch."

"It's another way to keep us under his thumb." And yet, how I hoped Kildare was right. I missed my father so.

"Agatha, there's something more . . ."

My head was spinning, and my heart was sinking at the terms of this bargain.

"He's grooming me to take over the company," he said. "Someday, Agatha, we inherit everything."

The night I returned home from the Ritz Ring with Sylvia's recitation of *From the Union Dead* selections still in my head, Kildare met me in the living room, a man submerged in shadow, a drink in his hand, and burdened with news.

Harlan Rhodes was dead.

My father had been driving back from a business meeting in Philadelphia, and he never arrived home. Instead, a caravan of college coeds on the way back to Penn State after a night of partying had noticed his Cadillac on the shoulder of a road in a little municipality called

Norristown. Assuming the car was abandoned, they'd stopped at a roadside diner and placed a call to a local sheriff. A patrol unit rolled up thirty minutes later and radioed central.

When they found my father's body, he was clutching his wallet. The way I figured it, he'd wanted to make sure that whoever discovered him didn't rob him, so at some point between those first pangs of discomfort riding up his left arm and his last thought, he'd pulled off Route 8 and tried to stash his billfold in the glove compartment.

The funeral was open casket. The stationary scowl, the depressed eyelids, the pinched brows, the downturned chin—they presented me with that all-too-familiar disparaging mien of his. In death as in life.

Standing at the lectern to deliver my part of his eulogy, I read a poem, "Death Be Not Proud." Before me, the church pews were filled with faces that were mostly unfamiliar, except for yours, Sam's, Maxine's, and George's to your right. Kildare and George were separated from each other by a single oak pew, that and the secret of George's and my affair. But the affair mattered little here. For the moment, my father's passing nullified any interest I had in rising in rank or esteem in your world. My insides felt like shattered glass. My soul lay inert.

On your left side, buttoned in her dark wool jacket, sat Sylvia. Her hair was tied in a braid bun, and her hands were stacked on her lap like sheets of paper. Did I detect tears? Did I see a flicker of indisputable sorrow in her eyes?

"My father died when I was eight," Sylvia said to me a few nights later. The Ring was huddled together in the refuge of the Ritz's red-leather booth. We were sipping on crystalline glasses of cognac and liqueur with curls of lemon rind. "I didn't go to his funeral. My mother didn't allow it. I know this might sound peculiar, but I imagined your father's funeral as though it were *my* father's funeral, though I doubt his was quite as lovely. I particularly liked that poem you read, Boston." She recited several full verses by memory, then said, "John Donne. A classic. Imagine, a whole poem designed to make the reader feel sympathy for Death."

I disagreed; the poem was about the folly of pride. "Death is full of it."

"I think Donne's saying Death is doomed, forever locked to his purpose. It's kind of like the two of us, Boston. We're locked to our purpose. The only real difference between Death and poetry is free will. We can choose to write, and what to write, and when to write. But Death has no choice but to destroy."

This, spoken by a woman who had known nothing but unlimited choices! *How naïve,* I thought. *How young and asinine.* Sylvia had the audacity to lecture me on free will? What choices did I ever have? My father told me which schools to attend and what to wear. When I chose to rebel, my father took the money and his love away. Choice meant choosing what to sacrifice. What did Sylvia know about sacrifice, with her privilege, fortune, fame, education, and wellspring of unconditional love? She had a freedom that not even you had, Professor—you, who spoke about choice in terms of the words we picked and rejected to create a poem's greatest desired impact in meaning and tone and style.

Not long after my father's funeral, you paced through the workshop, circled the table and your twelve acolytes seated around it. In your hand you held Sylvia's latest poem. As you studied it, that little divot between your brows was throbbing. And then, when you read it aloud, this nascent draft of hers, this work in progress, this embryonic sketch, Sylvia's words and your voice mixed like a Molotov cocktail. Her words, the incendiary fluid; your voice, the flame.

That Tuesday afternoon was the first time I heard what true free will sounds like when Sylvia announced, "A poem about my father."

The piece she read conjured a man, a great man, as a statue, larger than life, so large that she might climb a ladder to rest on its brow, crouch in its left ear to brace against the wind, and hide under the roof of its immobile and silent tongue.

Dearest Professor, my teacher, my prophet: I don't mind telling you it stung to realize that *my* father's death had inspired Sylvia to write about *her* father's life. I can almost hear you asking me to justify such a bold claim. After all, we all have fathers. Who among us doesn't harbor a complex affiliation with the archetype of father in the form of God, giants, tyrants, kings, judges, devils, and holy men?

You will want proof, so proof you shall have!

Sam asked Sylvia what she was calling the poem.

"'The Colossus,'" Sylvia said.

"Brilliant!" George exclaimed. "I thought I detected allusions to the Colossus of Rhodes, what with the statue metaphor and all."

The Colossus of Rhodes? The Colossus of Rhodes! Sylvia had more free will than anyone, and with that free will she'd made a choice—to steal the Rhodes name from me!

Worse yet, with "The Colossus," a feat of poetic brilliance from a Major Voice, Sylvia had officially undone all the progress I'd made in undermining the Ring's fading perception of her. Despite my fucking George Starbuck for the past two months, George was more enamored with Sylvia than ever. Sam had discovered a newfound respect for her. And Maxine, who had never really lost all that much esteem for Sylvia despite my best efforts, cornered Sylvia as often as possible to have her look over her work, bounce ideas off of her, and further ingratiate herself.

And you . . . After that day, you might as well have handed Sylvia the keys to your kingdom.

While the emboldened muse within Sylvia persuaded admiring words of her father onto the page, my father's death provided me no such inspiration. In fact, as Sylvia's creative cup overflowed, mine had dried up. Ever since my father's death, I'd only written seven poems. Each was worse than the last. I reworked them until I loathed them, and then I threw them all away. It got so that I wasn't able to look at a pen, which really scared me. Writing bad poetry was better than producing no poetry at all. I felt the prize of the Ring wriggling free of my grip.

Poetry moves us, but nobody ever says *how* it moves us. For some, an absence of poetry leaves them buried alive and running out of oxygen. I worried I was never going to write again.

My daughter went to sleep without fuss that night. She asked me for a bedtime story, a glass of water, and an extra kiss on the forehead. Downstairs, I straightened the sofa pillows. I picked up toys from the floor. I wiped down the kitchen counter from the day, and when I was finished, I turned out the lights in the house my father had helped us purchase. All was quiet and still.

In the garage, the air prickled my skin. I opened the car door and placed myself in the driver's seat. For warmth, I blew one, two, three breaths into the cup of my hands. The old Cougar reminded me of Kildare. With the ownership of my father's company in transition, Kildare was on the road more than ever, in Chicago, St. Louis, Kansas City, Iowa, or Indiana. The objects he left behind—the clothes in his closet, his cigarettes on the reading table, the car in the garage—were no longer enough to keep me feeling close to him in his absences.

I fished his car keys out of my sweater pocket and put them in the ignition. The engine roared to life. I didn't want to fall out of the car when I lost consciousness, so I locked myself in and got comfortable.

Carbon monoxide filled every inch of the garage, editing the oxygen the same way I crossed out words on a page. I grew light-headed. A tingling moved from the tips of my fingers up through my hands, and soon my arms felt as though they defied gravity.

A few minutes more and the clouding air swallowed me whole. I closed my eyes. The world I struggled to contain on paper slipped away from me as though it was never mine to capture in the first place.

1

Ruth, 1953

DECEMBER 10—

During his few but vital moments of clarity under my watch, as he rose from his amphetamine delirium, the Mad Poet would mumble, "Poetry is a listening game. It's the only thing on earth born of grace."

Today, I can't help but feel as though I am losing at this game with Miss Plath.

We have started her regimen of electrotherapy. Four times a week, at seven thirty in the morning, she and I walk arm in arm to the basement level of Codman Manor. Superintendent Frisch has ordered me to stick to strict psychoanalysis and keep to these standard remedies. I believe him incapable of acknowledging that the shock treatment method is nothing more than a quick fix to a protracted problem.

Miss Plath has asked me to join her at each session. She finds comfort and trust in my presence. She climbs into a bed, and I remove her slippers for her. She receives a sedative while an attendant straps leather belts to her wrists. Two more bands of leather tighten across her lap and ankles. She accepts a tongue blade wrapped with gauze between her teeth. I wipe her temples with salt paste. The attendant places electrodes on her skin. Behind the bed is a number dial with a voltage symbol that lights. It is at this moment each session that Miss Plath appears most tormented, not with terror, but with shame. Her eyes close, and at the press of a red button, her back arches and her shoulders strain. The violence rages through her and mollifies into small, melodic spasms. Though she is out, her body continues to fight, to kick, to drum against the mattress. When the internal wave crests, her muscles ease. She remains still like this for another thirty minutes.

As promised, I sit by her side and wait for her to wake. The clicking of the clock's second hand mirrors her delicate pulse.

Do I believe the treatment is effective and affords Miss Plath a semblance of inner stillness? I do. And yet, it remains a shallow inner peace. Despite fleeting flashes of euphoria that follow each session, her depression deepens. She remains contemptuous, self-critical, and withdrawn.

Further hindering my ability to reach Miss Plath comes word that the superintendent has reinstated her mother's visiting privileges, freeing Aurelia to interfere with my care.

In no way do I feel more stymied in my therapeutic approach, however, than by the patient herself. If Miss Plath's stunt at the apiary is any indication of her willing escalation in her campaign of resistance, soon I will be left with few alternatives.

Upon her waking from shock therapy this morning, I asked Miss Plath how she was feeling. Hardly blinking, hardly moving her lips, she said in a voice that was hardly a voice at all, but a suggestion of a voice: "I was thinking about the poetry of Elizabeth Bishop. She's independently wealthy, if you want to know. Inherited a fortune from her dead father and traveled all over the world without a care, just writing and gathering inspiration. You and I should be so lucky, Dr. Barnhouse. Can you imagine the life? I'd just about give anything to have that kind of freedom."

Despite all of her wisdom and bluster, Miss Plath's worldly experiences remain scant at best. Her most significant to date was her summer internship with *Mademoiselle* in New York City. For six weeks she joined a crew of thin-calved, short-coiffed bobby-soxers. There were lunches at the Drake Hotel, eating duck bigarade and roast capon under a Belle Époque ceiling covered in stars. There were fashion shows at the Roosevelt Hotel. There were boys who took her to La Petite Maison, who bought her tickets to see *The Crucible*, who plied her with drinks at Delmonico's. No glamour nor gratuity lessened a feeling that she was not valuable or even good, she said once. "What I felt was mostly glum and disconnected, doing what everyone told me to do."

Listening to her wax impassively about a poet called Elizabeth Bishop and her wild freedom, it occurred to me that for a young woman who prides herself on having experienced life, Miss Plath has had very few experiences free from the authoritative direction of others: the guidance of her mother; the supervision of her editors; the expectations of handsome young men.

Perhaps I am back in the listening game after all, for an idea has grabbed me by the wrists! No force, save the Norseman himself, or a hundred and twenty volts of electricity, seizes with more strength.

DECEMBER 11—

Locating a table at the faculty dining room presents me with a daily challenge. The women sit together, but I am not a nurse. I could eat with the doctors, but I am not exactly welcome at those tables, either. Often choosing a table in the hinterlands between the two, today I purposely sought out a seat across from Dr. Beuscher.

"You're going to let me borrow your car."

"I am?" He placed a cherry tomato between his teeth. "For what?"

"To build my patient's sense of self and help her establish a foundation of independence and choice. I've decided Miss Plath and I will be going on an outing. Presently, I do not possess a car, though I have it on good authority that you drive a Woodie, with sufficient enough space to accommodate several passengers."

"An outing? To where?"

"It's none of your concern."

"It's my car."

"My patient, my treatment. We'll be gone for six, maybe seven hours."

He considered my proposition, and came back with one condition.

"As a rule, I don't accede to conditions," I said.

He brought his napkin to his mouth. "Let me take you to dinner."

"Absolutely not!"

Dr. Beuscher shrugged, rebuffed but unflappable.

"It's not that I don't appreciate your strict moral code. I'm sure there are any number of others at the hospital willing to lend you a car for some nefarious purpose."

"You'd be wise to watch yourself. I'm coming to you because I believe you, more than anyone, value what I'm trying to accomplish."

"My admiration for your methods only goes so far. I figure, if you're so hell-bent on breaking others' rules, maybe you'll see to it to break one of your own."

DECEMBER 19–

I conceded.

This morning I snuck into the dining room. While the kitchen staff was banging around pots and pans and dishes, preparing lunch for sixty women, I nicked two china cups and saucers, gold-trimmed and painted with wisps of blue-tipped forget-me-not flowers. One for me. One for Dr. Beuscher.

Balancing two cups of hot liquid without spilling a drop reminded me of Miss Drake's old walk, the way that she used to avoid stepping on the colored patterns in the rugs, the purple cabbages and the fist-size roses. Rather than carrying steaming coffee, I imagined they held an elixir, a kind of medicine filled with properties designed to change minds.

Dr. Beuscher was seated among a circle of patients and finishing his morning group. If someone pulled out a photo from the late nineteenth century showing the parlor's bookshelves and furniture, I suspect it would look exactly the same as the parlor did today. The elongated rectangles of sunlight that stretched and moved through the two windows slid across the floor and up the wainscot with the same long-established trajectory. It was the top of the hour, and after Dr. Beuscher's group dispersed, I held out one of the cups. He regarded it with wariness, the same surprised-yet-amused look he'd given me countless times.

"I suggest you take it. It's already getting cold, and we just have a few minutes before your next group."

"This doesn't count as a date."

"It's the only time I'm giving you." A coffee for a car. Certainly there were nurses and faculty members with vehicles, but I was unwilling to ask a subordinate to submit herself to any sort of trouble or retribution for aiding my cause. Dr. Beuscher already indicated his support of my methods, even if he didn't understand them. He had the means to supply the vehicle and the authority and autonomy to sanction its use.

He accepted the coffee. I sat, leaving a chair between us. "Where a person chooses to sit in group reveals her true state of mind," he said. "For instance, if you were to sit across from me, I'd understand you want my attention. Whereas sitting a seat or two beside me indicates distrust."

"I'm not about to be psychoanalyzed."

He apologized. "Force of habit. Sometimes I have to remind myself that not everything is analysis."

I jumped right in without dithering over small talk. "What do you want from me?"

"To know you a little bit better. You're an unusual woman."

"Unusual is beneficial. People come to this hospital because the *usual* options haven't worked."

"Is that why you do it? To break things that need breaking?"

"I fix things that are already broken."

He turned to his drink, his fingers interlaced around the cup. "That's the one thing people get wrong about this place. We don't fix them. If they're lucky, they get a little reprieve from their afflictions, and that's all."

"Is that why *you* do this? To facilitate reprieves?"

"Among other things, I'm also curious about people. I hope you don't mind me saying I'm curious about you, Dr. Barnhouse."

"Insight will gain you nothing. You'd be wise to leave well enough alone and let me do my job."

"Right, the keys to my car. For some mysterious treatment and details you won't discuss."

"Telling you would leave you without the benefit of plausible deniability when Superintendent Frisch asks."

"I think you believe I wouldn't understand, and that I'd try and shut you down."

"For every improvement I've enacted, the consequences have been swift and sharp," I said.

"Well, you can't have advancements in thought or science without some sort of corollary or pushback. It's the law of relativity. Every action has an equal and opposite reaction. Physics applies, even in an asylum."

It was a fair point. For each book of poetry I have ordered, there is a book of poetry Miss Plath has destroyed. For every exercise in countering obsessions and compulsions I have authorized, there is a woman determined to shove her hands into the beehives. For all brash restrictions I have enacted, I have received additional oversight. The listening game is always one of calculation of benefit versus harm.

"What if I were to tell you that I have no intention of talking you out of anything? I appreciate what you're trying to do. I want to help if you'll let me."

I turned up my palm. "The keys, then."

Dr. Beuscher retrieved a small leather tear-shaped key chain from his pants pocket. Latched to it was an enameled shield, red with a gold serpent climbing a staff. A perpendicular sword, also gold, divided it, creating a kind of cross.

"They're yours."

I reached for the ring, but he pulled it back with a slight tilt of the wrist.

Dr. Beuscher raised his eyebrows. "As long as you tell me why."

He didn't mean why did I want the car keys. He wanted to know why I was here in the first place, operating in the ward, dedicating myself to the asylum and to the women of Codman Manor. Dr. Beuscher smiled. It wasn't that bad a smile, a gentle downward slope of the lips in tandem with the quiet rise of cheeks against his eyes, which were steady and engendered in many nurses a certain loss of equanimity.

"It's just you and me for the next eight minutes. So talk."

Sidestepping the law of relativity, I once again came up against the law of parsimony. I knew I needed Dr. Beuscher's help. The simplest, most straightforward way to get it was to relent, to drop a toe back into the realm of memories, where I was eighteen and married to Francis Charles Edmonds Jr. and tending our very ill daughter. At the time, I'd picked up dozens of books on anatomy. Was it agency culled from the deepest well of grief, or was it happenstance that I found myself poring over them, *having discovered them* erroneously mis-shelved among our dead daughter's books? I set out to understand the body within their pages—layer upon layer of sinew, skin, hunks of muscle, lengths of bone, and the mind itself. Francis obliged the folly of my medical school pursuit fully understanding that I needed a vocation, a life away from the life I'd just buried. I kept my head down and my eyes drawn to the learning, to busying the mind, to deamplifying the noise of the ghosts, until these measures alone no longer held back the pain of Tiffany's death, and I grew taciturn. I fell into moods and rages. The fighting between Francis and me was relentless. By the time he left me, I'd long come to learn the chemistry of grief. To this day, my hunt continues for a cure to the elemental makeup of anguish, surely no match for a woman determined to smother the memories, to kill the ghosts.

But I did not tell Dr. Beuscher any of this here in our group circle of two. We drank our coffee. The sunlight followed its ageless course across the floor.

Dr. Beuscher's eyes flickered as he looked into mine. "I think you almost divulged something there. But it's all right. I understand. You don't like people asking questions about your life. And you're also not going to tell me why you need my car, are you?"

"I'm sorry, but I'm not," I said.

"It must be lonesome, always going it alone."

The heart and the head are separated by two feet for a reason. It's the only way to win at the listening game. To hear, we must surround ourselves with silence.

"I have to wonder if it's worth it, Ruth."

Just then, a patient with a snaggletoothed grin shuffled into the parlor. She was followed by two other women.

"Our time's up." I put out my hand again.

Dr. Beuscher gave me the ring. As I stood to leave, he asked: "What am I supposed to do when the superintendent comes looking for you while you're doing whatever it is you're doing with my car?"

Not wanting him to have to lie for me, I advised him to steer clear of the superintendent for a while. "Be mindful and alert."

"The same goes for you," he said. "I'll add be careful, too."

FOURTH STANZA

The Meal

Every heart is a cannibal, every beat a bite.

—Boston Rhodes, "A Death in Norristown"

10

Estee, 2019

How do you know a lost soul when you see one? He wanders into the lobby of St. Ambrose Auction House from the street, aloof, head low, hands hidden in his pockets. He wades deeper into the gathering, occasionally stopping to admire the art on the walls without really looking at it. This is all an act. He doesn't want to seem out of place. He *is* out of place. He dresses as though he does not want to be here, wears a sad trench coat, baggy pants, an untucked flannel shirt, and a buttoned sweater vest. He is a man who wears rumpled clothes among people who do not believe in rumpled clothes. Nicolas Jacob, the disgruntled manuscript assessor, is the last person I expect to see at the public unveiling of the Plath notebooks, yet here he is.

As Nicolas merges with the crowd, he passes a group of reporters that has gathered around the Dyce brothers. With the per diem I authorized, Elton and Jay Jay went on a spending spree and have shown up today in flamboyant purple and white suits, respectively, movie-star haircuts, and matching aviator glasses. At each cocktail party, at every photo shoot, at all media events that Scarlett orchestrates as part of the Sylvia Plath revitalization and publicity tour effort, the Dyce brothers arrive loudly, craving the attention, loving the spotlight, and never forgetting to shoehorn Dyce brothers Fix 'n Flip into the interview or conversation. Scarlett, meanwhile, has blown through the annual advertising budget, placing ads in papers and periodicals, on benches, and on the sides of MBTA buses. The Sylvia Plath Book Club she's organized with area bookstores has propelled *The Bell Jar* to the top of the local bestseller lists. For today's unveiling of the Plath notebooks, Scarlett has set all three of the manuscript notebooks on display near the center of the lobby in a glass pedestal showcase. Quimby stands beside it. He greets patrons of St. Ambrose with a convincing-enough smile, his teeth a vivid white, possibly even whitened, to a shade that makes me think of the Dorchester Heights Monument when the summer sun hits it just right. The crowd, far larger than the one that came to see the unveiling of Marie Antoinette's pearls—our most popular auction to date—drowns out the quartet Scarlett has paid for. The caterers she's hired struggle to maneuver through the throng. Between Quimby's grandstanding and Scarlett's machinations and the Dyce brothers' showboating, the auction, as a process and as an art, is morphing into a form I do not recognize.

This is not the auction that I promised the Plath notebooks. Having personally managed the cleaning and minor repair work of the handwritten draft of *The Bell Jar*, there have been times, alone with the manuscript in the safe holdings room, when I speak to it. Ordinarily, I do not make a habit of talking with inanimate objects. I attribute these recent one-sided conversations to the fact that the Plath notebooks will be the last objects I will auction. It is a unique connection that we share. I want our mutual departures from St. Ambrose to go well, with dignity, decorum, and grace. And yet here we are, with the voices of the Dyce brothers booming, and Scarlett orchestrating a photo opportunity with the mayor and the notebooks, and Quimby fraternizing and loosening the money in the room, all while a crowd gathers in density. So when Nicolas appears beside me at the catering table, in my view an ally has entered the scene, and I'm happy to see him.

Nicolas motions to a fig from a dish—motions but does not take.

"Thematic hors d'oeuvres. Interesting touch." Yes, *The Bell Jar* is particularly lousy with mentions of food experiences. When I suggested to the caterers we serve food mentioned in the novel, Scarlett thought it would be clever to put the trays of halved avocados stuffed with crab meat, platters of roast beef and cold chicken, and crystal bowls of black caviar all underneath glass bell jars. Then she laughed, all proud of herself. "Sylvia always liked a good party," Nicolas says. I doubt I would've been invited to a party that hosted Sylvia Plath. Neither would any of the people in this room, drawn by her celebrity and the allure of seeing for themselves a mystery object heretofore unknown and discovered in an attic.

Nicolas is here because, ever since he confirmed the authenticity of the manuscript, he hasn't been able to stop thinking about it. "I've been trying to track down where the notebooks came from through the housing records."

"Let me guess, the records are a mess, and you found nothing." I know this because I instructed the St. Ambrose Office of Restitution to devote considerable resources to investigating the provenance of the Plath notebooks, too. Attempting to find the previous owners of the house on Napoleon Street, we pulled up permit dates, permit numbers, scan dates, stamped dates, and status dates, only to discover that the paperwork is both vague and incomplete. The documents jump from nameless owners to bank foreclosure statements filed by the city.

"Correct," Nicolas says. "But then I cross-referenced Sylvia's last known address with local police records."

"You got a hit?"

Like me, Nicolas Jacob is a tracker. He knows that sometimes you have to look between the information to find the information you're looking for.

"Sylvia's last known address was in London," he says. "And eight days after she died, a crime squad responded to a break-in at her apartment. The incident is very likely the moment the manuscript disappeared."

But this new information is troublesome. "So it's looted art."

"Not exactly." Nicolas touches a fig, places it between his teeth, bites down, severing it in two. "The notebooks aren't listed among the dozen items reported missing from the flat. If they were among the items taken, then someone concealed them from the record."

Or it was an oversight, I suggest. The standard due diligence procedures of St. Ambrose include routine checks of databases of lost art and other historical records. The notebooks did not show up in any of them, nor did they appear in any will or personal journal of Plath's. "If Plath didn't formally catalog the items, it's likely nobody knew exactly what the thief took."

As one mystery is solved, half a dozen others present themselves. With fifty-five years of unknowns to fill in, I want to identify who took the notebooks and how the manuscript got from Plath's flat to the attic of the Dyce brothers. Was it the previous owner of the house on Napoleon Street who took them? Or was it the owner before that? Whoever put the notebooks in a lockbox must have known that they were valuable. And yet, if that is true, why then did the thief leave the notebooks behind in the attic?

"If the notebooks aren't listed in a police record, then technically the notebooks weren't stolen. No party has claim to them, not even the heirs of the Plath literary estate," I say.

"I'm sure St. Ambrose would love for that to be the case." Nicolas swallows the fig. His jaw works under the mass of his beard.

There's a surge of activity around the glass display, a swell of voices from people waiting to see the notebooks.

"I really do hate auction houses," Nicolas says. This offends me. "It's nothing personal. I dislike any institution that gives away antiquities."

"We don't give anything away."

"Worse. You sell to private buyers."

What Nicolas doesn't say, but what I hear loud and clear is that he believes people like me are thieves and crooks. "We offer objects a second chance," I say. "Without us, they'd fall into disrepair."

"You're saving them? To the people in this room, objects are trophies."

"If you want to save the manuscript so badly, you should bid on it."

"That's not the point. Some things aren't meant to belong to anybody."

"You'd have us throw them away?"

"They belong in a museum, or at least someplace accessible to the public."

I have forty years of experience curating objects that says otherwise. "You could have called and saved yourself the trauma of walking into enemy territory."

"It's easier to ask for a favor in person," he says. "I want clearance while I can still get it. In a couple of weeks, when somebody in this room buys the manuscript, another substantial scholarly find will be out of public reach. She's about to disappear again. When that happens, odds are we'll lose our opportunity to learn its secrets. There's not a lot of time left."

"You want time with her. What are you going to do with it?"

"Read the notebooks. Study them. See what they can tell us about where they've been for half a century," he says. "Please, Estee."

The way he says my name, drawing out the final Es, makes it sound like a little song. I want to help Nicolas. I feel bad for him. Besides, neither of us wants to see the Plath manuscript go until we've had our moments with it.

And then there's this: most nights, I try to decide which descends faster, the quiet or the loneliness. There was a girlfriend who, after several years together, left me and married a wealthy real estate broker. After her, there was my engagement to a writer who was never really going to get married, to me or to anyone, and then the woman I lived with after her, who died from cancer over the course of a year in my home.

Relationships are far less tangible than objects, yet they are more fragile. Many have misinterpreted my rigidness to mean that I am a solitary woman, but they are wrong. What all this has taught me is that people need people. Even people who are not good with people. Even people who are not comfortable among other people in this world. I see that Nicolas needs me. And if his needing me leads to answers about the Plath manuscript, then maybe I need him, too.

How do you know a lost soul when you see one? You recognize yourself in him. So I agree to talk to Quimby, to try and secure Nicolas a study pass. Nicolas's beard shifts as he smiles beneath it.

"Thank you."

11

Boston Rhodes, 1959

A knocking, light at first, registered through my thick unconscious state. I blinked once, twice. I was still in Kildare's car, still in the garage, and—somehow—still alive.

The knocking, I sluggishly realized, was coming from the window to my left. How long had my daughter been standing here in her pink nightgown and tapping her small fist at the glass to wake me? For a long moment I stared into her hazel eyes and noted the flecks of deep green in them.

My cheek was pressed against the steering wheel. The dead clam in my mouth was just my tongue. The air in the garage was clear of carbon monoxide. A red fuel light on the dashboard was blinking.

Never again was I to underestimate the value of running out of gas.

In that moment, I decided I was finished with poetry forever. I was through writing it, through studying it, and through competing over it. Poetry had done me in, and it had done me no good. Death may be forever locked to its purpose, while I on the other hand was free to walk away from my burden.

When he came back home from his latest work trip, I wasn't going to say anything to Kildare about the long night I spent in the garage. Instead, I was going to show my husband that his faith in my devotion to him was well-founded. I had crawled my way back from death for my Kildare. God knew I'd never been good for him, but I'd survived, I was certain, to make his happiness my whole life. It was high time that I grew up and became a mature woman and a fully realized wife. I was ready to make concessions, respect tradition, and let go of indulging in the excess of drinking and smoking and chasing tantrums.

Kildare was running Emperor Fine Fabrics, and he needed me more than ever. From that day onward, I'd greet him with a glass of bourbon at the door and take his briefcase and raglan overcoat from him. I'd usher him into the dining room, no longer buried under my notes, marked-up pages, and books of poetry, but set instead with place settings and two burning candles. I'd dress our daughter in smocks and shiny shoes and untwisted tights and brushed hair. Together, we'd eat a meal that I'd have spent hours preparing. Afterward, I'd scoot Kildare into the living room and have him take off his shoes. And when the house was quiet, I'd sit in the empty dining room and feel pleased with all I had done.

Didn't Kildare deserve a home like this every night? Didn't he deserve a wife who took care of him so well?

My mind made up, I got out of the car. "Let's go have breakfast."

Sylvia and Ted had lived for the past year in a small apartment in town that was six floors up a steep staircase. Two curved bay windows hovered above shadbush and chestnut trees. At dusk, the glass tendered a reflection of the Charles River to the west, and beyond that, the orange brick and white plaster façade of Cambridge.

In his oil slick–colored suit and dark tie, Kildare was dressed more for a sales meeting than a dinner at Sylvia and Ted's that night. For some reason, Sylvia was practically desperate to grow our relationship, and since I'd given up competing with her, I'd accepted her invitation. For his part, Kildare didn't like wasting a perfectly good Friday evening with people he had so little in common with. Or as he put it, why would anybody spend time with those who believe navel-gazing is the height of intellectual discourse? Once we were at the apartment, though, Kildare managed to turn on the charm. Like a gentleman magician, he presented Sylvia with the bouquet of assorted lavenders we'd stopped off at a T station flower shop to purchase. Sylvia babbled on a bit about how thoughtful it was of us as she untied her apron and led us inside.

The apartment had an oddly shaped living room with wood molding, a couple knee-high bookshelves, and a coffee table displaying *Sewanee* and the *Paris Review*. The flat was only three rooms, but they'd painted the walls cream to give it warmth. They'd also hung up a painting of nymphs with goat hooves, and another with an atlas of stars and constellations.

Their home, I observed, stood in stark contrast to ours, which was larger, but a den of bedlam by comparison. Despite my efforts to get out from under the laundry and the dishes, I was still struggling to keep a house. As part of my new and exquisite plan to take care of Kildare, I'd returned to those lovely housekeeping magazines and searched the feminine codex for instructions. I'd discovered just as many rules to being a perfect wife as there were to being a passable poet. There were the "dos": keep your husband happy, keep him fed, keep him satiated. There were the "don'ts": don't bother him, don't question him, don't leave a mess, don't forget to smile, don't pry into his business. The magazines ordered me to be glad when he came home from work and to show him sincerity in my desire to please him, but so far I couldn't tell if my efforts had made Kildare feel better, or even good, for that matter.

Later that night, Sylvia showed us a photograph of herself and Ted on vacation. In it, they were seated under an umbrella, and Truman Capote was getting them sozzled on screwdrivers, Sylvia said, mischievous and gleeful. There were more photos like this, one of John Steinbeck with his arm around Sylvia's waist as they were getting drunk on brandy, and one of Edna St. Vincent Millay, Sylvia, and Ted, the three reveling in a ballroom full of ceiling streamers and party hats and glasses of rum and sidecars in their hands. In another, Ted and Sylvia were lounging at a Copenhagen outdoor café with Marlon Brando and Audrey Hepburn.

Ted, dressed in a dark turtleneck sweater, slacks, and tailored charm tonight, peppered our evening together with dry jokes and observations, like American football was pure bourgeois and Boston was just like Yorkshire, only more British.

"Now tell me about this," Kildare said, pointing to a little shelf holding Ted's collection of smoking pipes.

"That one is Hemingway's," Sylvia said. "It's a billiard pipe, I think. The one next to it is Emerson's, though he's really a cigar man."

What was Sylvia trying to prove? She seemed to be getting a kind of thrill out of watching me suffer through this little parade of hers and Ted's. It was becoming clear to me why she'd summoned me for dinner. I'd gone to great lengths to erode the workshop's confidence in her, and Sylvia was returning the favor by playing the perfect host, all gay and perky and jovial in her pearls, petticoat, and heels while her husband served us from his expensive bottle of Gordon's. Sylvia made balancing fame and a home seem effortless. Maybe it was effortless for Sylvia. If so, she'd forged these abilities and assets from the mine of a charmed life.

She assigned us seats around the French painted dining table. As dinner began, I shook off these spiteful thoughts of mine. I felt sorry for Sylvia, actually. She was trying so hard to play the part of the gracious host, when in reality she was no more than a picture of naïveté and braggadocio.

Being served a traditional dinner of seafood, Kildare commented on Sylvia's cooking, not once but *three times*. Two trips back to the pot for more, and Kildare was fully satisfied in a way I wasn't able to satiate him. I'd never prepared such a beautiful meal or set such a beautiful table. *Housekeeping Monthly* said I needed to have dinner ready and on time for

Kildare, but he was always staying late at work. The food I made just cooled on the stove. There I sat, night after night, waiting for him like a fool with a red ribbon in my hair. When Kildare did eat my meals, he scarcely said a word about how good they tasted. He certainly did not emit the grunts and moans of delight I was hearing tonight, not even over my meat pie, something I actually cooked well.

The dinner conversation turned to Charles Van Doren's confession that *Twenty-One,* Ted's favorite American television show, was fixed. Kildare said he was as surprised as anyone by the scandal, even though I knew he never watched the show himself. From here, Ted steered the talk to the Algiers crisis and Charles De Gaulle's establishment of the Fifth Republic in France. Then it was all about education and Ted's yearlong appointment at Amherst. Sylvia, growing tipsy on wine, put an end to all this heavy talk and asked Kildare how he and I met. "We eloped," he said, and I kicked his ankle hard under the table.

Sylvia swooned. "Eloped and married to a salesman—how wonderfully American!" Rapt, she propped her chin on a canopy of her interlaced fingers. "Tell me about being on the road, Kildare. I so admire people who sell anything. Glass eyes, false teeth, rubber breasts, a rubber crotch! I have half a mind to write a poem about a traveling salesman."

Kildare was flattered. Poor thing—did he not see that Sylvia was making fun of him? "Oh, that's right, Mrs. Ted Hughes is a bit of a poet, too," he said.

Sylvia's cheeks colored, a trick that isn't all that hard to master, really. "I'm an apprentice, always in process of becoming a poet. I think that if I keep working, I'll be a serviceable Minor Voice one day."

I goaded her. "Why stop at Minor?"

Sylvia was overcome. "Oh, Boston! Really, I don't know what I'd do without your encouragement."

I said she'd have Ted's.

Sylvia glanced at Ted, who was rubbing the tines of his fork with his napkin. "Ted's a brilliant poet, even if he doesn't see my work as particularly interesting."

"About this confessional poetry Lowell has you both writing," Ted said, "it's so middlebrow."

I grew cross. "You don't approve?"

"Poetry on sexuality? Melancholy? Despair? Your audience doesn't want to know everything about the inner lives of their poets. It's all so exploitative."

Kildare piped up in agreement. "I said the same thing. Private thoughts should be kept private. We don't air our dirty laundry to strangers."

"I tell Ted all the time, he underestimates my readers," Sylvia said.

"Alienating your readers with descriptions of one's inner life will eventually cause them to abandon you, my love. Stir them, inspire them, but don't turn them into your analysts."

"And I say," rejoined Sylvia, filling my wineglass and holding both me and a shimmer in her eye, "readers see themselves in our poetry, don't they, Boston?"

Ted mocked her. "Why? Because it's honest?"

"Yes! Because it's honest."

"My cherished exquisite wife," said Ted, "truth isn't the same as honesty."

I nearly choked—Sylvia and Ted even argued like a dream, trading intellectual barbs as though making love.

I needed the night to end. When I saw my chance, I excused myself. I wandered down the hallway to the guest bathroom and sealed myself inside.

Reapplying lipstick and a splash of Chanel from my pocketbook, I regarded my reflection. Eyes of dark charcoal eyeliner, matte lips in deep red—tonight I was channeling Dorian Leigh. But the light washed me out and just made me feel more miserable.

Behind my reflection I noticed a pocket door. I put away my makeup and perfume, but instead of leaving the bathroom the way I came, I grew curious and opened the slider, unsealing a study.

Faint conversation carried in from the dining room as I approached two identical desks set side by side. One was neat and sparse. The second was a mess of loose pages, carbon copies of poetry, a typewriter, and an alarm clock. Beside a rhyming dictionary lay a sheet of paper on which Sylvia had written four stanzas.

Mildly interested, I glimpsed the work in progress. At the top of the page Sylvia had circled a title.

"The Rival," it read.

There is no better inspiration than conflict, jealousy, or hostility. Along with her seafood dinner, Sylvia had served each of these to me that night on a platter. For the first time since my father's death, and my own near demise from which I'd risen anodyne and passive into a flavorless world, I was once again hungry.

We were almost home from Sylvia and Ted's when Kildare said he'd had a good time. He could see what everyone liked about Ted. And that Sylvia, what a firecracker!

Yes—a fine cook, a fine wife, and a fine writer, Sylvia was the whole package. Even her minor writing was better than mine of late. Take "The Rival," I thought as I paced my dining room long after Kildare had paid the sitter and gone upstairs to bed. I ruminated over the charmed lives of our evening's hosts, and the poem Sylvia had clearly left on her desk for me to find.

If the moon smiled, she would resemble you.
You leave the same impression
Of something beautiful, but annihilating.
Both of you are great light borrowers.
Her O-mouth grieves at the world; yours is unaffected . . .

Who was this rival? Wasn't it obvious, Professor? Oh, I was on to her. Sylvia wanted me to figure her intentions. Was it not enough that she'd taken over my workshop, or captured your affection, or that she had the perfect life? I doubted she'd ever understood what it was like to have to fight for every word. I wanted to phone George right away to carp and moan, but it was late and I'd surely wake his wife. Not that I didn't already have an idea what George was going to say if I did call. How was Sylvia to know you'd go into her study and find that poem? And I'd reply, *Because Sylvia and I are similar, George. So similar, in fact, that she knew I'd go snooping. It's exactly what she would have done were the tables turned.* Then predictable old George would have said that I was being paranoid. And I'd have said, *But no friend knows you quite as well as your rival does.*

With one glimpse, that poem of Sylvia's had seared into my mind.

. . . she would resemble you . . .

. . . annihilating . . .

. . . unaffected . . .

Furiously, I pulled at a sheet of Kildare's stationery and, at the dining room table, I transcribed Sylvia's words. I hadn't written a decent word of my own since my father's exit.

Not since Sylvia's arrival, said the venom voice.

I was fully alive tonight, however, with new words spinning and moving in my mind. Under the point of my pencil, the words of Sylvia's poem *changed*.

I drew lines through them and replaced them with others.

"She would resemble you" became "She was a mirror."

"Annihilating" became "exterminating."

"Unaffected" became "untouched."

More of her poem came back to me. My pencil moved, my hand possessed by obsession.

Verses bled from me. In the morning, a new poem was waiting at the table like a place setting. In my fugue state I'd circled its title.

"The Competitor," it read.

Say what you will—that I copied Sylvia's inchoate poem, or that I engaged in the insider trading of creativity—but I didn't intend to formally submit "The Competitor" to any publication. I wrote the poem to break down my miserable brain block using the acid of spite.

And it worked.

After crafting "The Competitor," I found I'd entered a new period of unexpected productivity. An unstoppable surge of subjects, scenarios, and motifs came to me. Images appeared in my mind, fully formed and rich with detail. A direct channel had opened between my heart and my hand. Truly, if I'd ever known obsession or the fire of mania, all past experiences failed to match the fervor with which I tore through my rhyming dictionary, mapped rhyme patterns, typed pages upon pages, edited and worked the text. My father's death had smothered my inspirational flame. Vengeance reignited it and made it burn brighter than ever.

Maxine stopped by the house with a rhubarb pie, only to discover me half-starved but fully nourished in a state of half wakefulness and half sleep, my hair tied back, my clothes disheveled. Truly, I'd never felt more alive. All other needs, drives, and desires had vanished in me, replaced by the words, as well as the hunger to get them right.

Sylvia Plath was among my thoughts no more than a driver considers the gasoline in his tank. How could I focus on the old girl when I was using every spare moment to become the poet I was destined to be? I graduated from this frenzied state exhausted and spent. After sleeping for days, I rose and discovered a sequence of new poems I'd written: "The Victor," "The Gospel of Luke Rebuked," "The Hawk at Supper," and "A Death in Norristown."

Of all the carbon copies, submission forms, and magazine query packages I was busy preparing, "The Competitor" was not among them. So imagine my surprise when I sliced open a letter from the *New Yorker* one day only to read that the magazine was accepting "The Competitor" for publication.

It was a mistake, an error of envelope stuffing. *But of course it wasn't,* said the venom voice. *In a game of strategy, nothing is accidental.* Of course, I was euphoric as any writer who'd attempted to see her work laid out on those iconic pages would be when "The Competitor" appeared in the April issue. A few days later, an editor from the *Atlantic* phoned. He said he'd read and enjoyed "The Competitor" quite a bit, and he asked if I had anything else like it. I mailed him "A Death in Norristown" and several of the newer pieces I'd recently finished.

The magazine accepted them all.

The self-imposed moratorium on my writing life was over, and it had lasted far shorter than I'd expected it to. Sylvia had usurped my place in the workshop, so I'd undermined her standing within it. In return, she'd taken advantage of a moment of weakness to rattle my confidence in both my ability and my marriage by showing off her own. More than capable of pushing back, I was going to show Sylvia it wasn't all that hard to earn the prizes, the glamour, the notoriety. My voice had recuperated, and I had everything I needed to finally beat her at her game.

12

Ruth, 1953

DECEMBER 22—

A couple of weeks ago, a patient brought in a fashion magazine she'd lifted from the lobby to show to our therapy group. She opened it to a page and, in a stunned voice, declared that the young woman in the image was none other than our own Miss Plath. The model featured in *Mademoiselle* lay in repose on a short sofa. The collar of her blouse and the shade of its buttons, as well as the pearls in her ears, were all the color of bone. The model in the image was smiling, but it was a strangely posed smile. Her right arm, also posed, fell across her lap and held a single downturned long-stemmed rose. The article's heading, drawn in neat white calligraphy, read *WHAT A DISH!*

Miss Plath immediately denied that it was her in the magazine. "Dr. Barnhouse, will you *please* tell her she's wrong? It doesn't even look like me!" True, there were obvious differences between the model and the patient, what with the patient's short hair and the slow-healing gash over her left eye versus the model's long, flowing hair and flawless skin. The model also looked happy. Miss Plath was a blend of glum self-disapproval and resolute defeatism. Despite these surface differences, the model in the magazine was clearly Miss Plath. The image was taken the summer of her internship at this very publication. The longer I stared at the girl in the image and noted the noncommittal grip around that rose, the more I saw a sadness she shared with Miss Plath.

And yet, as I write this entry, it seems to me that Miss Plath was correct to deny that she and the model were one and the same. The real Miss Plath is neither the model in the magazine nor the young woman here in Codman Manor. There is another version of Miss Plath still to uncover. It is her true self, away from pressure and influence. The only way to get at it with any hope of permanence is by a demonstration of free will. And that is the point of the new exercise requiring Dr. Beuscher's car keys and some coordination.

In general, Miss Plath of late has been in an upbeat mood. I recognize that this temperament, artificially heightened by insulin and shock therapy, will soon diminish and leave her mired again in the muck of dull and deadly thoughts. At the same time, I continue to reflect upon Dr. Beuscher's observation: we do not fix patients, we merely offer them brief pardons from their afflictions, temporary exhalations from the chaos of madness and the loneliness and the grief. Experimentation in chemicals and in behavior modification are worthwhile if it means keeping that window of reprieve open longer, but I want something more for the women of Codman Manor than short respites of sanity; I want something more for Miss Plath.

I announced the intervention to the women of the group this morning. Autonomy. Self-determination. Unconventionality. Tomorrow morning, we will be leaving Codman Manor together for Boston Common, where they will have several hours to operate under their own volition, free of direction.

"I do love the Common at Christmas time," said Miss Plath. The others in the group seem excited by the prospect of engaging in this task, as well, even as Nurse Edme continues to undermine these atypical proceedings. Following group, Nurse Edme asked me if I was certain letting the patients go AWOL was a good idea. I reminded her that I am unable to officially ask her for her help, though we could use a wrangler that the women trust. I've watched Nurse Edme with the women of Codman Manor. She is good with them, what with the way she plays "The Chattanooga Choo Choo" on the grand piano, passes out chewing gum, and takes patients by the hand as they move through their days in the asylum. If Nurse Edme really wants to help the women of Codman Manor beyond the spinet and the sticks of chewing gum, she now has a chance to do so.

"I don't understand what this outing has to do with standard care."

Nothing. "Standard" has no business cavorting with "care." "Standard care" put my daughter in the ground.

"Nurse Edme, how many people have suffered under the conditions of conventional thinking? We do not, and will not, sit idly by."

Despite my early successes, I retain the sense of being an outsider at the hospital, a lone operator with few allies. Nurse Edme remains my sole reliable confederate. Her thoughts on the subject of nonconformity remain intact, but when it comes to working by my side, she is my indispensable enabler. Accordingly, I am pleased to report that she has agreed to assist me.

We leave first thing in the morning under the cover of darkness.

DECEMBER 23—

A jarring start to our journey. Having planned to rise in the predawn hours, instead I was roused by a face in the dark calling my name. I cried out to the intruder, "Identify yourself!"

The intruder whispered back, "It's me! Nurse Edme!" and switched on the desk lamp. I oriented. My vision was groggy, my mouth dry. Nurse Edme herself appeared a bit stunned in the light. I followed her stare. She was looking at the tiny amber bottle of extract. I had fallen asleep holding it as I was drawn in the long hours of the night to the dulcifying delirium of an opium drift.

Trying to seem as though she hadn't seen it, she whispered, "I've woken the women. What do we do next?"

I had Nurse Edme retrieve Dr. Beuscher's car while I struggled to shake the fog and dressed. At five thirty a.m., Miss Plath, the other women of the group, and I were gathered outside underneath Codman Manor's covered entrance. Exhilarated as they were by the maneuverings of our stealthy adventure, no one complained of the dreadful cold seeping into our clothes.

I kept my gaze fixed on the darkness just beyond the porte cochère for Nurse Edme's signal. Finally, in the predawn gloom, headlights flashed twice. Together, crouching, hunched and bracing against a whistling wind, our little federation slunk along the dark road in a short line, five women, followed by Miss Plath, and then me. Nurse Edme had pulled over a couple of yards away on the side of the Nine-Tenths Mile Loop. At the station wagon, I opened the driver's side. Behind the steering wheel, Nurse Edme looked stricken. Clearly, she was having second thoughts.

"Did anybody see you?"

No one had seen us, though we still had to remain very quiet. Having done her job well, I invited Nurse Edme to hop in the back and let me take the wheel from there. She agreed and joined the women piling into the seats and the carriage, with Miss Plath taking shotgun.

Driving somebody else's car is like wearing somebody else's shoes. Neither feels quite right, but in a pinch they both get the job done. I drove Dr. Beuscher's station wagon half a mile in the dark before turning on the headlights. Then we were on the other side of the hospital's stone archway and rolling along on Trapelo Road, the manors disappearing behind the trees.

By six a.m., the sky was brightening. From Route 2, we passed groves and fields of scattered haystacks and sagging barns. The women were quiet, the drive having lulled a few of them back to sleep. For some time, the only sound was the occasional whimper coming from Nurse Edme.

We were passing over the steel rib cage of Longfellow Bridge when, at its central towers, Miss Plath glanced wistfully beyond the span, not quite at the view of the city skyline but at the river below. I remembered then how Miss Plath had spoken about jumping from this bridge, and all of the things in her life that made her want to end it.

"What are we doing when we get there, Dr. Barnhouse?"

"That's up to you."

"This really does seem like a foolish exercise. It's not like I've never been to the city before."

True, but add methodology to any simple enterprise and you will find that all roads lead to Rome. Or in this case, to *living.*

"What do you want to do?"

She thought about it. "I really don't know."

"So I guess we'll just improvise."

"Is that part of the therapy, too, Dr. Barnhouse?"

I said that it was.

"Have you noticed psychiatrists don't ever say what they mean? And they absolutely never talk about themselves, either. For instance, all the ladies think you're secretly married. I told them of course you're not married. Greatness takes sacrifice. I for one will not allow myself to be toyed with by any man."

"You'll never get married?"

"My mother would certainly like me to get married and have a pack of kids someday. I worry it would sap my creativity and positively annihilate my desire for written expression. Marriage is the abandonment of the intellectual and the thinking self."

"I bet she didn't like hearing you say that."

"My mother looks at me like there's something wrong. She's bound to have a heart attack someday, trust me. I can't stand her unbearable air of self-importance. It masks her lack of intelligence. She's voting for Eisenhower, you can bet your life on it. She's bought into our noble war hero's absurd plan to fly to Korea like a white dove. Can you believe that, Dr. Barnhouse? Some people are just so ignorant. I bet you're an Adlai Stevenson enthusiast. Mother calls him a communist. But everyone's a communist nowadays if you've signed a peace appeal." Growing reflective then, she pulled a lock of hair down over her forehead, as though measuring it with the slide of her thumb. "When I get home, mother will act like none of this ever happened. Do you think she'll ever forgive me for causing her so much trouble?"

"There's nothing to forgive. You've broken no laws."

I believe in rules, in order, in cause and effect. You cannot have one without enduring the other. I do not risk my livelihood or the safety of others without grave reservations. Yet, when weighing actions of consequence against consequence of inaction, the need for her outburst, like our sojourn from the ward to Boston Common, becomes obvious.

I parked the station wagon across the street from the State House. In the snow, the Common was a patchwork of untouched white padding. Pine and sidewalk salt and chimney smoke filled the air.

Outside R. H. Stearns Co., where women with thick coats and Salvation Army buckets swung brass bells, the women of Codman Manor fanned out and stormed the park. Nurse Edme was overcome, and I was forced to endure her listing of the abundancy of ways the patients might lose us. Couldn't she see, though, that this was the point?! The women were to detach from their patterns of behavior. They were to lose us entirely.

Miss Plath headed off in the direction of the mangers with their wax shepherds, sheep, oxen, and angels. She carved her way toward Flagstaff Hill, where children in winter coats and mittens and scarves were sledding, and where some of the women of Codman Manor shared a toboggan down the slope. Later, Nurse Edme and I spied Miss Drake, stocky, standing statue still, and sticking out her tongue to catch the snow. Miss Plath hurled a snowball at her, striking her dead center in the face. Miss Drake attempted to return the favor, but was too uncoordinated to pack the snow tight. The two walked off together to the duck pond benches as the clock on the Old Boston Church struck noon.

Later, Nurse Edme and I paused at Frog Pond, only to see all the women of Codman Manor having negotiated the acquisition of skates and traipsing on the ice. What a sight it was! A gaggle straight from the asylum, spilling and tumbling and intermingling with people of high fashion and good taste. If only these people knew where the women slept at night.

As evening advanced, the weather turned. The sky opened with sleet. Nurse Edme said we should rush back to the car (and back to the manor, no doubt), but Dr. Beuscher's station wagon was all the way on the other side of the park. Instead, we took refuge at the S.S. Pierce department store, and that's when I saw Miss Plath struck with wonderment.

We had entered an enchanted village of lavish holiday displays, full of sparkly jewelry, wooden toys, expensive coats, and a child-size Lionel electric train set.

But it was the centerpiece that drew Miss Plath: an expansive exhibition of manger dioramas, each one housed underneath tiny bell jars. There must have been a hundred of them, each diorama set like prizes beneath these small inverted glass domes.

Miss Plath and the other women of Codman Manor walked out among them as though wading into a glimmering lake. The glow of the lights above and the flashes of gleaming tinsel cast the bell jars and the women in a special light that imbued them all with uncommon grace and elegance. Or perhaps the luminosity came from within the women themselves, grinning, ambling, and existing in the open, listening to the subsonic thrum of the moment.

I believe even the most afflicted patients are capable of exhibiting blips of normalcy, seconds when the fog clears and their true selves emerge. I have witnessed these windows of reprieve in their laughter, their stillness, and in the banality of their most ordinary endeavors. Within S.S. Pierce, I was witnessing Miss Plath for the first time rising above the taciturn constitution that has confined her these many months.

She moved freely among the display of bell jars glinting under the star field of lights. If one was so inclined, one might believe Miss Plath herself was a piece of the display, that she belonged here just as those old wax statues with their expressions of passive serenity belonged in Boston Common.

"The thing is, Dr. Barnhouse, I'm constantly at war with others, but also with my own worse demons," she once told me. When I'd asked what she meant by that, she'd replied that the pursuit of one's passions has a corrosive effect. Indeed, Miss Plath's had landed her in my ward. But in the department store, it seemed to me that Miss Plath was no longer at war. And those worse demons? They were enclosed under all that domed glass.

She was free.

DECEMBER 26—

The patients of McLean Hospital are not prisoners. We derive the word "asylum" from the Latin "*sylum*," meaning the right of seizure. But with the addition of a simple letter A, the word *changes*. *Right of seizure* becomes *no right of seizure*. We protect our charges. We listen to them. The moment we stop listening to them is the moment we've lost the listening game. In fact, the only way the women of Codman Manor are prisoners is as captives of their own daily routines. While our little group was off visiting Boston Common, not once did anyone at the ward notice the absence of six patients. Ordinarily, this might leave me with serious concerns. Given the circumstances, however, I am grateful for the predictability of human nature.

Yet after our return, I received bewildering news. At breakfast in the dining room, where patients sat among tables arranged with white cloths, porcelain teapots, and polished silverware–settings befitting the dining car of the luxury Super Chiefs—a nurse said to me, "Oh, it's so tragic, isn't it?" She was busy preparing pills in paper cups on a rolling tray. "Those poor, poor dogs." When I replied with only puzzlement, the nurse dropped her voice low. "You didn't hear? Oh, it's awful! The superintendent's Dalmatians *died*!"

Truly, for I thought I must have misheard her, I asked the nurse to repeat herself.

"Someone killed them. Well, not *someone*. They were stung to death," said the nurse. "If the Norseman hadn't spotted the dogs when he did, no one would have found the bodies until spring thaw . . ."

How often had the routine of the hospital's prized Dalmatians found them traipsing down the hill from the Proctor House, drawn to the bustle of our activity among the beehives? Only we were at Boston Common, and hadn't been at the apiary to shoo them away.

With the burden of culpability weighing heavy on me, today I sought out Dr. Beuscher. "This isn't your fault," he said, but in the same breath he urged me to choose my next moves carefully, as the superintendent isn't soon to forget about this. Dr. Beuscher is a kind man, and I believe his intentions are good. He gave me his car keys not because he trusted me, but because he wanted me to trust him. I must mind myself and my surroundings. I am no longer on safe ground.

DECEMBER 27—

Having on prior occasions come before Superintendent Frisch and addressed him on matters of alternative treatments, I recognize the futility of trying to sway him from his new threat of decommissioning the apiary.

Conceding my part in this tragedy left me with little leverage to plead my case this morning. If I was going to talk to the superintendent, my approach could not be a forceful one. I had to choose my words carefully, remain measured, and not show any desire or weakness. I'd get nowhere if I didn't sound calm and rational with him.

At the Proctor House, I told Superintendent Frisch that I do not feel it is fair to take away the beehives, an object of affection that my patients find therapeutic. Would he remove a scalpel from a surgeon's hand in the middle of surgery? Why then was he endeavoring to take away an instrument of such obvious service?

"Basil died quickly, we think." The superintendent's fingers massaged his temples. "When we found him, Sigmund was alive, still breathing, but blind. They stung him in his eyes."

"I'm sorry."

"That line of thoroughbreds reached back a century. It's all gone." He cast his gaze at the spot on the floor beside his desk where the dogs had often curled together to keep warm. He said he wasn't sure why we even have those damn bees. The livestock and poultry, they produce milk and eggs and service patients and faculty, but who among us requires honey? The cooks do not cook with it. No one demands it with toast or tea. Bees have nothing to do with therapeutic treatment, navigating the unconscious mind, or whittling down defense mechanisms.

The superintendent said he doubted my intervention met the criteria for sublimation of harmful urges. After all, hadn't one of my patients—who was it? Ah yes, Miss Plath—stuck her bare hands into the hives?

"But the apiary, it's terribly important to the patients," I said. He's a fool if he can't see that Miss Drake and the women have benefited from this treatment.

I might have continued to argue my point, but instead I chose to heed Dr. Beuscher's advice. I left Superintendent Frisch and the Proctor House, having concluded that, unlike our previous confrontations, I'd sensed no arrogance in him today, only grief, an emotion impervious to negotiation.

DECEMBER 28—

A new thought: perhaps loss itself is a kind of intervention, a way to confront the fact we hold no power over much in life except over how we respond to powerlessness.

Wrapped in a coat, scarf, and wool hat, alone I trundled across the snow-covered grounds this evening. From a distance, the stone shack on the path beyond the small farm looked like nothing more than a pile of rocks, or a small mountain rising from the bluish ice.

The Norseman stooped through the hut's doorway and came out into the cold hauling two tin cans of gasoline.

"You're sure you want to see this, Doc?" he asked.

I did, I said, bracing against the wind. I needed to stand witness for the women of Codman Manor.

For a long moment the Norseman faced the dozen pine stacks. There was no sign of activity from the bees, all tucked away, hidden from the winter. The evidence of their bristling capability, their full killing might, was as masked as any pain the Norseman might have felt by the task at hand.

He unscrewed the cap of the first tin. Approaching the stack closest to him, he splashed gasoline across the top.

I put a glove to my nose, the smell of fuel instant.

The Norseman moved on to the next stack, delivering the gasoline as though watering rosebushes.

Within the boxes, the insects were alerted to danger. Scouts lifted off and began to hover around the drawers. Against the relief of the snowfall, the bees looked like confused snowflakes refusing the draw of gravity.

The Norseman emptied the first tin and moved on to the second, swinging gasoline across the last of the stacks. When he was finished, he pressed the canister into the snowbank and reached into his coat for lengths of burlap. With a flick of his butane lighter, he ignited the fibers. The flame cast his jaw, nose, and forehead in a brass-colored glow.

One by one, he tossed the igniters. Stacks went up in flames. There rose a furious tap, tap, tapping from within the boxes like rain hitting a log roof. Mud-colored smoke mixed with the night. Instead of insects and snowfall, embers spun in the air. I backed away from the heat of twelve pyres.

Behind me at the mansion, the women of Codman Manor, pulled from their once-immutable evening routines, watched from the windows as flames rose and twisted in the purpling sky.

FIFTH STANZA

The Law of Unintended Consequences

What kind of worship is this? Are we demigods or are we artists? Or are we two arcs of one circle?

—Boston Rhodes, "The Gospel of Luke Rebuked"

13

Estee, 2019

In 2001, I assist in preparing for an auction of Charles Lindbergh memorabilia. I am cataloging typed letters, medals of honor, flight logs, and items of clothing when I come across a matchbook emblazoned with Lindbergh's image, his brow furrowed, his eyes staring into the near distance. This particular matchbook is rare, so rare I never thought I'd see one in person. Upon opening it, on the underside of the cover, I discover what might be, though it's difficult to tell, the indentations of a signature, in pen, the ink long faded. I place a sheet of tracing paper over the surface of the matchbook and with a charcoal pencil create a rubbing. The question then becomes, why does the world's most rare matchbook contain what appears to be the signature of the poet Robert Frost?

A master curator will go an entire lifetime without coming across such a double find. When we do, we must engage in our abilities as polymaths, as historians unraveling myth, as the investigators of partial fingerprints. In my inquiry, I zero in on a night in 1927, when this matchbook first debuted. It is one of two hundred special matchbooks made for attendees of a ceremonial dinner at the Astor Hotel in honor of Charles Lindbergh. After that night, many of the matchbooks disappear, yet one makes an appearance again, nine years later, in Middlebury,

Vermont, where Robert Frost is lecturing at the Bread Loaf Writers' Conference. In attendance is the poet Anne Spencer Morrow, who also happens to be the wife of Charles Lindbergh. Maybe Morrow offers a match to light Frost's cigarette in exchange for an autograph. Maybe Morrow asks for an autograph and has no surface except for a book of matches she carries in her handbag. Regardless, matchbook meets the man.

And like so much ephemera, eventually the matchbook is left in a hotel room, or at a bar, or on a subway seat, is picked up, reclaimed, moved from pocket to ash tray to drawer. The signature rubs away, as ink will do. One by one, the matches are plucked until only five remain folded within the square of its body. Then, in 1994, a weekend collector spots the matchbook at a garage sale in Long Branch, New Jersey. It is lying in a cigar box among buttons and pins and other matchbooks. He has the wisdom to buy it for fifty cents, and years later, to sell it at St. Ambrose Auction House for four thousand dollars.

These days, when I see Nicolas Jacob come to St. Ambrose to study the Plath notebooks, I consider how some people possess the ability to look at objects and see things others do not. A date hidden on a lithograph. A serial number imprinted within the gear of a watch. A hue of paint that points to a pendant's origin. An improbable signature in a matchbook.

Nicolas visits the notebooks at St. Ambrose throughout the autumn and early winter, always with the strap of a tan leather messenger bag across his torso. From the security feed on my laptop monitor, I'll see Nicolas hand over his satchel to the front desk and, in exchange, receive a security badge that he pins to his sweater. Each evening, I will see him exit through the lobby elevator, return the badge, retrieve his handbag, and head out into the gathering night. Every so often, through the camera feed, I will drop into the safe holdings room and see Nicolas sitting perched over one notebook, or all three of the notebooks, his head low, his shoulders hunched, a hand at his forehead. He will remain like this, stone still, for hours. Occasionally, he moves a pencil across his notes, or pushes his fingers through his beard.

I wonder what he sees in the notebooks that I have missed. Has he learned anything more about them? Has time revealed their details? Has patience unlocked their secrets?

So one morning in early December, as snow quietly falls over the city and a shiver has taken its hold of me, I join Nicolas in the safe holdings room. What has he discovered? Very little, he says, except that the years the notebooks have spent shut away in an attic have made them exceptionally fragile. Every turn of a page is a calculated risk, and so he works carefully using small movements and soft instruments, felt-tip tweezers and rubber gloves and magnified lenses. It is a marvel, really, watching him in his element, his half-moon-shaped glasses set at the end of his nose and Nicolas occasionally jotting notes into his own notebook. I find myself thinking about what might have brought him to Sylvia Plath to begin with.

I ask him, "Why Sylvia Plath?" Was it scholarship alone, or was it something more personal? Is it the crystal lens through which Sylvia saw anguish, isolation, betrayal, and death? Or the candid and uncompromising words she used to describe them, a thump-thump-thumping heart on the page, each poem operating under its own parasympathetic nervous system? Or the desperation in her poetry, how she strived to be understood? Is it her struggle with madness, her fixation on achieving control? Or the way Sylvia's poetry broke life down to simple moments as one dismantles a weapon?

"You'll laugh," Nicolas says. I won't laugh. "You will. But it's all right if you do. I had a dream once, when I was younger. I fell in love with a faceless girl. A couple of years later, when I discovered Sylvia Plath, I knew I'd dreamed of her. It's always been her." Her? Her face? Her body? "Her voice, actually. Of course, by then she'd been dead for something like thirty years." With a finger, he motions at the notebooks on the table. "But it's here."

Objects have voices, yet the notebooks are not saying who deposited them in a stranger's attic, though Nicolas still believes that if he keeps reading and looking, they will bare him an answer. I have my theories, some more plausible than others. Maybe the previous owner of the house on Napoleon Street was an obscure relation of Plath's, a distant niece or a relative through marriage. Or maybe the manuscript belonged to a secret lover Plath wrote to, a man who hid in his attic all evidence of their affair. I'd be a fool not to also consider that this whole endeavor is a con put on by two brothers. Nicolas says it's possible the manuscript wound up in the house as a fluke, a culmination of random, mathematically dubious connections, in which case we may never know how the notebooks got from Plath to the attic. Nicolas understands just as well as I do that the unintended consequence of discovering an item is so often a heartbreaking lack of closure.

"Can I show you something?"

Nicolas takes adjacent corners of the green-covered notebook and tilts it toward me.

"*The Bell Jar* . . . this version of *The Bell Jar* . . . is something special. That's because these notebooks aren't just telling one story, they're telling several . . . and all in perfect agreement with one another."

I draw up a chair and join Nicolas at the table. I smell him, his sweat mixed with wool.

"The first narrative is the story of the novel itself. It's Sylvia's tale of Esther Greenwood, the one we've all read. Most people will be tendering their bids entirely based on this fact," he says. "But here's the thing: this version has a *second* narrative coded into the first."

Nicolas points the end of his tweezers at a page to where Plath has crossed out the word "din" and replaced it with the word "tumult." Plath has also crossed out "tumult" and landed, finally, on the word "hullabaloo."

"We walk with Sylvia through trial and error and see her thought process. *This* is the second narrative. It's the story of Sylvia Plath creating this document. In her handwriting, one experiences the literal moment of her life when her pen touches the paper. The more discerning bidders will be bidding on this narrative."

Into this mix we add a third narrative, he says, only this one isn't written on paper.

"The legacy of the document. It's this narrative in which we currently find ourselves."

Nicolas might as well be reminding me that the manuscript's legacy is entirely in my hands.

"You know you can't sell the notebooks," he says.

"You act like I'm feeding them to a shredder."

"There's still so much we don't know about them."

I can tell Nicolas that the Plath notebooks are going to a good place after the auction, to a safe shelter where they will be admired and cared for, but I know such arguments have the impact of small stones bouncing off of his chest. No—Nicolas believes the notebooks will be going to the highest bidder, the kind of person who doesn't know the value of money, the kind of person who doesn't know the value of objects, the kind of person who collects objects and puts them in vaults and into the dark. The exquisiteness of Sylvia's work isn't in the words but in the servile trust she's placed in her public. Nicolas believes this with every fiber of his being. Would he prefer I counsel the Dyce brothers to donate the handwritten draft of *The Bell Bar* to the public library? The notebooks wouldn't survive the day.

"They'd be better off rotting in that attic than in a private vault," Nicolas says, and I can't tell if what I hear in his voice is grief or anger, only that it's directed at me. Would a private vault really be worse than a hot attic? Of course it wouldn't be, but Nicolas refuses to see this, or perhaps he simply can't allow himself to

Suddenly, I feel a need to defend my livelihood. "I was five years old when I found my mother asleep in her car in the garage. Only she wasn't asleep. She'd tried to gas herself. She was a poet, too." I stare at him hard, but in the reflection of his glasses I don't see his eyes, just my own. "I know what it's like caring for something beautiful and fragile. I've been doing it my whole life. So please stop looking at me like I'm the enemy."

Nicolas is quiet. He appears somehow smaller than he was just moments ago. I realize that I have gone too far, that my accusation has hurt his feelings. Conflict breaks fragile things, and Nicolas is unquestionably a bit fragile. I see now that it is best to let Nicolas have at the notebooks in silence, just as he prefers. His time with them is running short. I do not want to make this farewell any harder for him than it already is, or will be.

I consider leaving the safe holdings room, but reconsider at the undesirable thought of going back up to my office, currently in disarray. If an office is an expression of one's self, then mine is a thousand experiences packed into photographs and files and artifacts, much of which, as of this week, are in bubble wrap and moving boxes. I try not to think about my retirement as an ending, deciding instead to focus on how wonderful it is that my life and the life of the Plath notebooks are intricately intertwined. Nicolas and I are both in the safe holdings room today to hide from an inevitable future.

As I watch him work, I discover that, when it comes to experiencing awe, Nicolas has a tell. A pointer finger and middle finger maneuver through the thick brush of his ruddy-colored beard. As Nicolas moves through the last notebook, minutes pass in silence. I find myself feeling even worse for having picked a fight earlier with him, when Nicolas suddenly raises his head.

He's found something, something new, a clue to unlock the code, the signature under the top of the matchbook.

"My God . . ." he murmurs so quietly that he must be talking to himself. "I know who took it."

14

Boston Rhodes, 1959

Rejoice! Your poetry revolution was upon us!

The summer after "The Competitor" appeared in the *New Yorker*, I continued to spin the senselessness of my world into defined poems. I didn't like any poem I wrote nearly as much as I liked "The Competitor." Maybe that was because it had been so woefully difficult to come to that poem. "The Competitor" was a stick of dynamite that detonated a dam of my own unchallengeable construction. The barrier blown to bits, I wrote and wrote and wrote in a voice, whiskey-smooth and hot.

But was it my own voice?

For inspiration, I'd lifted a sketch of a poem from Sylvia's work desk. Whenever Sylvia got around to reading "The Competitor," if she bothered reading it at all, I doubted she'd recognize her words underneath mine. "The Competitor" was not nearly as derivative of "The Rival" as my dead father was to Sylvia's now-iconic poem, "The Colossus." "The Rival" as I'd stumbled upon it in her study was full of difficult and far-flung images. I'd go so far as to say "The Rival" was hardly a poem at all at that stage, while "The Competitor" went straight to the point, its intent and its target clear, even without its explicit mention of Sylvia by name.

If there was a voice I channeled, it was not Sylvia's, it was yours,

Professor Lowell. One's influences are intractable. I knew that to move forward, I had to shake off my parents and peers. Still, try as I might, I was unable to shake you as your fingerprints pitter-pattered up and down my body of work, leaving impressions in my poems as they might in wet clay. Oh, dear Professor, how I got you all mixed in my mind with my dead father, with my lover, with my husband, with my divinity. We have always been two pyres burning within the same plot, you and I. So few poets sparked me with enthusiasm. Beyond you, there were no new gods to find.

So instead of fighting you, I took it upon myself to accept your orders as though spoken directly to me by my general. I was going to lead your poet uprising and usher into the twentieth century your great movement, the revolution of confessional poetry. Suddenly, it was all that mattered, this perfect thing you forged. I was armed with a goal to be a leader of this literary transformation. Waving the movement's banner, I was going to make you proud—you, who taught me discipline, substance, and technique.

Let's be honest, teaching me was as easy as filling an empty bottle, for that's what I was when we met in that Brookline pen of self-absorption. Back then, I didn't know a damn thing about any poetry, really. But you chose me. You took me from "Polaris," and you guided my galloping spirit. You taught me to hook into my mood and siphon it onto the page. I was influenced by your critical sense, your teaching, your insistence that I keep my ears clean and open. In certain manic moments, I said to myself, *Heck, I'm better than you, Professor Lowell!* How's that for misplaced pride? All this to say, I was beginning to feel and speak like a living woman, my own woman, independent and loud and heard.

Once the *Yale Review* took a poem of mine for the summer issue, it became official: I had almost no unsold poems. Young poets were writing to me! Their letters fattened my mail stacks. Honestly, I found this more threatening than flattering. I am a distrustful creature! But it wasn't only the poetry they admired. They claimed to believe I, Boston

Rhodes, was someone to emulate. How was I to tell them that poets are such phonies? Sure, here or there we might have some valuable insights, but we hardly live by them. When you read us, you might think we knew something about life, but usually we are all just messes.

Yet, that didn't stop the *Saturday Review* from calling to ask about sending a reporter to my home. I was so excited, I practically pounced upon Kildare when he came in from work. Figuring he'd be in a foul mood as he so often was these days, I prepared him a drink, and as I handed the glass of bourbon off to him, I told him the news. The magazine was sending none other than M. L. Rosenthal! M. L. Rosenthal was the type of critic who carried a poem in his cheek as one savors a piece of hard candy. To think, he'd interviewed and written about my favorite poets, and here he was, coming to interview and write about me. "He wants to see how we live," I said. Kildare grunted. He was half paying attention to me, but mostly he was fixed on the mess in the dining room and den and kitchen, which he got onto me about. I begged Kildare to come to the interview. "He's going to talk to all of us." Kildare grumbled a little and made his way to the bedroom. At the top of the staircase, he nodded. It was not a full-throated yes, but an inconvenienced yes, a yes that was more a question than a statement of affirmation: *What are you pulling me into?*

The next week, in my kitchen stood Mr. M. L. Rosenthal, a balding man with white sideburns, dark-framed glasses, and a mole on his chin. Kildare and my daughter, who was dressed in her new yellow jumper I had purchased special for this occasion, joined me in the bright kitchen. Rosenthal set a recorder on the table, pressed a button to start the tape, and posed the most sober questions you'd ever heard.

The first went to Kildare.

"Sir, how does it feel knowing your beautiful wife is the voice of the new poetry movement?"

Kildare adjusted in his seat. Caught without an answer ready, he took a minute.

"Well, I don't know about that, but she is beautiful."

"With all of the attention she's been getting, is there still time to keep a house and raise a family?"

I waved across the table at my daughter, sitting quietly. "As you can see, we're doing fine here," I said, answering the question for Kildare.

Rosenthal addressed his next question to me. "Have you ever felt at a disadvantage in your profession as a woman?"

I laughed!

"What do you tell people who say women don't strive to make anything real out of poetry?"

"Maybe they're right," I offered in my driest, most droll demeanor.

"Let's talk again about this movement you and your contemporaries have started, this school of extremist poetry. I use that term, by the way, only as a matter of critical convenience and mean no offense by it."

"People don't expect confessions in their poetry, especially poetry about masturbation, adultery, or any unsultry and deeply personal moments," I said.

Kildare choked and coughed into his fist. How striking these words must have sounded to poor Kildare, coming from his lovely wife. If only he understood, these words had been in my head my whole life, and only now was I brave enough to verbalize them, in an interview, no less, for all the world to read.

"Until recently," I continued, "people only knew what poetry was, not what it could be. And yet one might look at confessional poetry as one degraded branch of Romanticism. What we're doing is placing the sensitivity of the poet at the center of concern. And no offense taken, Mr. Rosenthal, you sweet, small, Semitic man."

"I admit, I'm not clear what audience is eager to read these solipsistic self-advertisements."

"You're certainly not the first man to call me an egoist. You won't be the last, either, especially after this article appears. Let me preemptively set your readers right. Our revolution is nothing less than courageous self-exploration in the face of grave psychic risk. Humanity will no longer silence us."

"I hesitate to state the obvious, that the Romantics embraced silence," said Rosenthal. "And by 'humanity,' I take it you mean the male culture?"

"Not explicitly. But it's almost 1960, Mr. Rosenthal. What's fair and right to talk about in polite society is no longer relative. Back to your question of audience, though. I'd say that my readers are those who embrace this new paradigm of frank individuality and don't want to risk slipping into a profound sense of alienation by refusing to acknowledge our voices."

"It's your right to tell us what's on your mind."

"Every confession requires a listener."

"Are you asking your listeners to absolve you?"

"Hardly. The Sacrament of Reconciliation is to God. God's the only listener that can absolve us from the secret sins of the heart."

When the *Saturday Review* ran its interview, I was as staggered as the next person to learn that it put yours truly on the cover. In the photo, I was seated with my legs angled against a bookshelf. In my right hand I held a pen. The main cover line read, *THE AGE OF CONFESSIONAL POETRY HAS ARRIVED.*

But when I landed at the second line on the cover, my world stilled.

"Meet Boston Rhodes: save for the likes of Sylvia Plath, debatably the movement's most prominent champion."

I stood stunned, leaning against the kitchen counter with the magazine in both hands, and felt the joy draining from me. In its place was anguish, soon replaced by silent rage.

Save for the likes of Sylvia Plath?! What was Sylvia Plath doing anywhere on my cover?

And what was that odd, awkward phrasing supposed to mean

exactly? That Sylvia Plath was arguably the movement's most prominent champion? Or that I, Boston Rhodes, held that designation, except when compared to the famous Sylvia Plath? And as for the term *debatably* . . . Who, exactly, was doing the debating?

Any way you sliced it, this declaration gutted me. That middling, minor poet who'd crashed your workshop had seized the mantle of the revolution right out from under me! I'd won the cover, but Sylvia—strange, beautiful, intense, with her perceptive, celebrated, handsome husband Ted—once again took center stage.

On a walk through Cambridge en route to give a talk at the ladies' auxiliary, the magazine cover followed me through the city, this Jerusalem for bookstores. Showcase windows staged copies of the *Saturday Review* featuring Boston Rhodes, sly and seductive and strong. But the magazine might as well have placed an asterisk by my chin more prominent than M. L. Rosenthal's meaty black mole.

**Save for the likes of Sylvia Plath!*

I was seeing my face, with Sylvia's name, in the newsstand settlements at the T station, the convenience-store counters, the news bodegas, and the awning racks in front of the half-dozen drugstores along Massachusetts Avenue, when I spied none other than Ted Hughes coming up the opposite side of Appian Way.

I called out to him, but quickly abandoned this effort when I realized he wasn't alone. His arm was around the shoulders of a young woman in a green summer dress. A thick twist of ponytail swung between her shoulder blades.

They were walking hip bone to hip bone, attentions intertwined. Ted was talking to her, but I couldn't hear what he was saying. Whatever it was must have been hysterical, because the Mystery Woman laughed into Ted's chest.

❋

Later that afternoon as I prepared dinner, and into the night while I cleared the table and washed pans and plates, I struggled to shake what I'd seen in Cambridge—what I thought I'd seen, anyway. I landed on several reasonable explanations for such familiarity between Ted and this Mystery Woman. She might have been an old friend of his, or an admirer. Ted was currently giving a weeklong guest seminar at Harvard's department of comparative literature, and this Mystery Woman was just as likely to be a student, though an overly playful and affectionate one. Ted had smiled and gone along with her, but had he acted improperly? No more so than when he'd charmed his way through our dinner, before growing drunk and notably unfriendlier.

Yet I'd seen the way that this woman touched Ted's chest as they'd walked along the boulevard. There was knowledge in that touch, and reciprocated intimacy, too.

Finding parking in Cambridge the next day found me circling for a while. I told myself I was headed back to Harvard Square to run more errands, to stop by the shop for typewriter ribbon, to visit Felix Shoe Repair and pick up my heels. And since I was going to be here anyway, why not stop off and see my friend Ted? You'd agree it was a perfectly reasonable endeavor.

I saw a spot on Massachusetts Avenue near Prescott Street, jammed the gas, and crossed two lanes to a chorus of bleating horns.

On foot, in big dark sunglasses, a trench coat, and floppy hat, I bounded across the campus and set myself up behind a large locust tree between the faculty club and the English department.

Every few minutes, I checked my watch and fingered the camera strapped around my neck. It was Kildare's camera. We hadn't used the Leica since our rash and secretive wedding years earlier.

And here, as the afternoon grew breezy, I waited.

From its high-up vantage point, a hawk carving loops in a perfect blue sky will see everything below without making suppositions. What it sees, it accepts as fact. If I'm honest with myself now, I had no such aptitude. My mind continued to swim with scenarios and questions. Time and circumstance had brought me to this moment. Poets are mirrors. We are detectives. You said so yourself. We are those who operate within an asylum from reason.

A quarter after four o'clock, I saw Ted in a tan sport coat coming out of the building with a large group of people. I fumbled with the lens cap. The camera's flash went off in my face.

The group thinned, and soon Ted was talking to just a few who'd stayed behind after the lecture. Then, there was just Ted and the Mystery Woman in a short daisy dress.

She and Ted stood close. He smiled at her. They walked off together, Ted's hand momentarily touching her back.

I raised the camera and twisted the focus, but missed the shot as they rounded the building corner and headed south toward Massachusetts Avenue.

For a while I walked behind them as they crossed Harvard Yard to the square, where they took the steps down to the T station.

Probing my coat pocket for a token, I found one and proceeded to follow them through the rotary. The station was teeming with people. Coming to divergent stairways, I looked to my right and to my left. Ted and the Mystery Woman were gone.

Among the dull tiles and ramps, the crowd moved around me as though I were a boulder settled in the middle of the Charles. The hiss and squeal of the Braintree line announced a train's impending arrival. Betting that they were headed into the city and not away from it, I ran to make the train and slipped inside just as it was set to close.

I observed them seated together at the other end of the train car. To stay hidden, I pushed the brim of my hat low. In the reflection of the glass I watched them. Ted must have looked directly at me a dozen times as we rode, but he didn't see me.

At the third stop they stood and left the train. I followed Ted and the Mystery Woman onto the platform and, perched behind a tiled pillar, snapped a photo of the two ascending the stairs. At street level, I found them again and kept with them as they entered the Athenæum.

The foyer of the library was large. Ornate gilt wall lamps with petals of pink and white glass, and furniture that was all scrolls and filigree, engulfed me. Tall elegant book stacks carved garden-like pathways through the tawny-lit collections.

That afternoon, I was making a collection of my own.

Ahead, I watched Ted pointing out the paintings, prints, and wall drawings he admired. The Mystery Woman opened a book and tested Ted's knowledge of the American Civil War. Eavesdropping, I heard Ted sharing his thoughts on Audubon's *Birds of America* with her.

Between the fourth- and fifth-floor reading rooms I lost track of them again, only to wander eventually into a secluded area where the stacks grew narrow. I heard movement and whispers.

In the next aisle over, through a slim space between the tops of books and the bottoms of shelves, I saw a hand hiking up a dress. Ted leaned forward and kissed the young woman, and the young woman took his ear—not just the soft lobe, but the whole ear—into her mouth. Ted took a step and pressed her into the shelf, a motion that sent books toppling from my row and me hopping out of their way to avoid falling objects.

I ducked, but then I did not duck, because I felt unseen behind my camera, the shutter's click masked by the sound of falling books and the blood rushing in their ears. Ted and the woman operated in the protected void and grew feverish and bolder in their perceived concealment. Her hands took the sides of his face; his hand moved up her inner thigh. His other hand tugged at the shoulder of her blouse, revealing a black wire bra and the edge of a small breast that Ted immediately consumed with his mouth, his thick hair falling over his face. In a swift, singular move, Ted turned her around, revealing a fierceness once concealed behind the composure of a man who above all else understood control.

My camera captured hunger, lust, and caprices that changed by the millisecond. What my lens could not see, I heard in the changing cadence of hushed breathing between two people.

They looked up at my camera, but they did not see past the single bookshelf that separated us, or the shadows beyond that. I felt removed from the moment, even as they seemingly wanted to draw me closer to them. *Look at us, capture us, envy us.*

Fingers interlaced fingers. A body folded over another body. I wondered if Ted had ever fucked Sylvia like this. I bet there was a time when he did, when the stakes were not quite so high, when Sylvia needed his body for its beauty and not for the notoriety it might bring her. There was a time in Sylvia's life when Ted needed her body as much as she needed his, but that time was over. Then I tried imagining what it might be like to feel so devoured by Kildare, by George, or by something other than bitterness.

Ted retucked his shirt. The woman untwisted her dress. I put the cap back on the camera.

After they left the stacks together, I waited behind. When enough time had passed to guarantee a safe escape, I gathered my things and headed downstairs.

I started for the exit when Ted and the Mystery Woman rounded the corner.

"Boston!" Ted seemed both amused and baffled to see me. A wire in my chest grew hot and rattled like the filament of a light bulb.

To play it off like everything was fine, I leaned in and kissed Ted's cheek, which was flushed, and I smelled the woman's mouth on him.

"Just call me the most impulsive woman on earth! I had a sudden desire to see the busts of Raphael and Rubens." I talked fast, praising the reproductions of William Marshall Craig. All the while, I was aware of the Mystery Woman beside Ted. She was studying me.

Ted noticed, then turned to his side and introduced the Mystery

Woman as a friend from Cambridge. "And this," he said to his companion, "is the incomparable Boston Rhodes."

The Mystery Woman went pale. Suddenly she was fumbling with the clasp of her shoulder bag. She took out a copy of the *Saturday Review* with my face on the cover.

"It is you! Oh, wow! What an honor!"

She was young—younger than me, younger than Sylvia even: a college girl. Her zealousness counterbalanced a clear lack of sophistication. She asked me for an autograph.

As I signed the magazine cover, I noticed Ted eyeing the camera strapped around my neck.

I handed back the magazine. Ted said, "It was good to run into you." He kissed my cheek this time, and then he and the Mystery Woman headed off in the direction of the hall of rare books.

I was outside again and struggling to slow my heart rate. *That was close,* I thought, grateful that Ted hadn't asked too many questions about why I was there or what I was doing with my camera.

When I reached the sidewalk, though, Ted came out of the building and called out after me. Leaving the Mystery Woman behind on the steps, Ted jogged over. His hair was loose and falling down over his brow.

"Ted—" I started, but he cut me off.

"You're a good friend to Sylvia. The best kind of friend. Close as sisters."

"Yes."

"So you understand just how fragile she is."

I smiled, but my smile came off as the phoniest work I'd ever produced.

"That's why I'd prefer it if you didn't mention this encounter to our Sivvy. No need to upset her or give her the wrong idea."

"Of course." My stomach was turning like a staircase.

"Good." The warmth was returning to his voice. He brushed his hair back into place. "I can always count on you to do right by the old girl."

15

Ruth, 1953–1954

DECEMBER 31—

The mind, by its nature, renders us unreliable participants in the listening game. This happens for one reason only. Memory is flawed. I consider the memories of my daughter, Tiffany, who is now an idea that no longer exists for me. Her memory endures on a tapestry strewn with holes. Each of us is subject to the acidity of grief. It eats away at the truth.

I write this entry with the knowledge that soon I will be asked to mine my memory for details of what happened here at McLean Hospital. Each word I put down on the page will come under scrutiny. Let this be my official record.

Reports of the impending New Year's Eve nor'easter sent nurses closing and latching the mansion's shutters and the orderlies hauling in dry wood and auxiliary heaters from the storage sheds. The storm arrived as the last fingers of daylight vanished in a blur of bluish white. I spent the night seeing to the women of Codman Manor as the wind howled and stirred the patients.

I later learned that during the storm a truck carrying the arboretum crew spun out on the main drive, swerved, and crashed into a ditch. One of the orderlies who got caught outside without gloves was rushed to the infirmary and lost his pinkies to the cold. Also, the pipes in Men's Belknap and Wyman Manor burst. A great red oak froze its old roots, toppled over, and smashed into one of the greenhouses by Mill Gate.

But the worst of the damage came from within. Doesn't it always?

Come morning after the storm, the chief night nurse, a perpetually disgruntled woman with a penchant for strong perfume, presented me with the room-check register. "We have a problem."

Moments later, our footsteps were quickening along the corridor rugs. Upon entering Miss Drake's room, I saw a bureau, a flowered chintz armchair, and a bed, each empty. Her closet was bare, as well. Miss Drake's suitcase was gone.

The patient, said the chief night nurse, was last accounted for at four a.m. Assuming that no one miscounted during rotations, this meant that Miss Drake had left her room within the past three hours. The chief night nurse said Miss Drake couldn't have left the manor. The doors were locked, of course, and then there was the blizzard that would have kept Miss Drake from leaving, too. I was inclined to agree with her assessment, and therefore organized the nurses into search parties, one for every floor of the mansion. I ordered each to move carefully and unhurriedly. "Miss Drake is not dangerous," I said, though really, her state of mind was as much a mystery as her location at the moment. So I added, "If she's feeling threatened, she might act defensively. Be calm."

Teams scoured the parlors, the music rooms, the library, the dorms, and the laundry facility. When patients wander off from a room or scheduled activity, either by deliberate infraction or distractibility, we often find them within minutes, but at eight a.m., the teams regrouped and reported no sign of Miss Drake.

Nurse Edme was struck by a shrewd thought. "What about the baths?"

I gathered a group of nurses and started down the service stairs.

Bitter-scented soap hung in the air. As I moved through a room with its white-tiled walls and claw-foot porcelain tubs, I sensed that Miss Drake was down here, or at least she had been. That's when I noticed the high row of pebbled glass, milky white and snow-covered from the outside. The windowpane nearest the end was open but a sliver, as it always is for ventilation.

Nurse Edme followed my gaze. "You don't suppose she somehow wriggled out through that tiny crack, do you?"

But by then, something else had become clear. It didn't matter why or how Miss Drake had gotten out. What did matter was that Miss Drake was not in Codman Manor any longer.

The blizzard had severed all the lines in and out of the hospital, and so I directed the chief nurse to radio the orderlies and tell them that we'd had a patient leave Codman Manor unauthorized and unaccompanied. At the front desk of the receiving hall, the chief nurse switched on the control panel and tapped the mic. "We need some assistance with a search and rescue."

"A patient went out in that storm?" It was the Norseman on the radio, his accent stark, his meaning bleak. There was wind and cold exposure to worry about, also twenty-two miles of inhospitable woods if our patient had erred and wandered north.

I shut down those thoughts immediately. The most logical possibility was that Miss Drake had taken refuge in one of the workmens' sheds. In the chance that she'd gotten herself to Trapelo Road or, less likely, all the way to Route 2, we'd need to radio the local deputy for assistance. Complicating matters was the fact that all of central Massachusetts was digging itself out from the storm. The roadways were completely cut off in or out of the hospital, with the plows a good twenty-four hours away. This was assuming the weather continued to hold.

Inside the estate, five feet of snow buried McLean such that it took some time for the search party to gather at the flying cherub fountain, frozen over like cake frosting. There was the head of the orderlies and his crew, who worked the manors, the gymnasium, and the rehabilitation center. The Norseman had gathered a couple of men from the stable and the service building. Bundled in matching wool coats and fur-lined hats, these were maintenance men, not trackers.

The head of the orderlies unfolded a map and fought the wind to keep it open. With a gloved finger, he deputized us into companies—one to cover the north stretches in the direction of Proctor Yard, one to head west toward the Mill Street greenhouses.

Nurse Edme and I joined the patrol heading south toward Higginson Manor. We trudged the interior of the Nine-Tenths Mile Loop, passing a parking lot of snow-buried cars.

"Why would she do such a foolish thing?" Nurse Edme asked me, as though I had an answer. "I don't understand what she was thinking."

I didn't know, nor do I now. Still, I admit here that I have often considered the way Miss Drake's outward silence has reflected a deep and mystifying internal quiet. In other words, Miss Drake played the listening game well. I wondered what voice Miss Drake was listening to in the storm, what it might have said to her, what it might have called upon her to do.

Cutting perpendicular to the walking path was a semi-decipherable path of shoe prints. It led away from the hospital and into a copse of hickory and pine trees. In a small clearing, a purple blouse blew across the white expanse. My pace quickened.

Several yards ahead, Nurse Edme came upon a pair of shoes and a pearl-handled hair brush. A trail of clothing pulled us through a quarter mile of denser pine and created a path that ended at the corner edge of a marbled sea-green suitcase jutting out of the snow like a shiny rock.

The sky was darkening, with word coming through on the orderly chief's radio that a second storm system was on its way. The temperatures were going to be dropping again by early afternoon, and the cold was already biting my toes like rattlesnakes.

A high-pitched whistle rose urgently from beyond thickets. Blackbirds beat their wings and scattered. I broke into a sprint, fighting for every step against the snowbanks.

A silvery sun glinted off stretches of bluish gray ice and feathered through the branches until the water appeared before me. The sound of my breathing fused with the rush of Beaver Brook.

By the time she caught up, Nurse Edme was lumbering, wheezing, and falling out of her scarf. We'd emerged at a steep embankment of limestone boulders along the water's edge.

Members of another search party were wading into the creek, while another blew into his whistle, his cheeks large and pink. Casting my gaze along a gasoline-colored slick of water, rocks, and chunks of ice, my heart boomed in my ears, and my breath stopped short in my lungs.

Behind me, Nurse Edme screamed.

The dam, one of many that chokes the waterway, was a thick tangle of branches, torn clothes, and the lifeless moon-colored face of Miss Drake.

JANUARY 5—

Meaning making is the coping mechanism of the hopeless. I struggle to keep myself from conjuring the significance of the nor'easter, but I believe it to be a manifestation of my failure to protect Miss Drake. Why did she leave Codman Manor during the storm? Where was she running?

The listening game offers only one answer: I alone set the pieces into motion.

I continue to try for sleep, but I close my eyes and I see Miss Drake, her face turned up toward the sky. Memories and ghosts have led me into fixations and compulsions. I rely on the opium these days and nights as a body relies on air. The linctus fuels a kind of rest. It keeps the beast in my head from bursting through my skull.

"I've always been surrounded by death," Miss Plath said during the day's session. "Dickie Norton, before he came down with TB? Well, he worked at a hospital, and this one time I made him take me to see the cadavers. Gruesome things, really. But I was very mature about it, if you want to know. I'm afraid of death, but death's very natural."

Here I state for the record, as clear as I possibly can, that I am worried about Miss Plath more than ever. Since the death of Miss Drake, any and all progress we have made has stalled and unraveled. Miss Plath has sunken into a dreadful state. She is neither eating when summoned to the dining room, nor conversing with the women of Codman Manor. Group sessions have become a circular vortex of despair, during which Miss Plath no longer possesses acuity or exuberance. Her drive toward self-actualization and independence has ground to a halt. Books of poetry lay untouched on her nightstand.

The death of Miss Drake rests heavy on the minds of the women of Codman Manor. Coming and going is the way of this place. Patients either move to the more restrictive wards for long-term treatment, or they leave the hospital and reenter the world. Yet Miss Drake's exit has struck a mortal blow to morale. Even the dissociative patients express causal loss.

But Miss Plath is not depressed. In fact, she possesses what I might call *a scarcity of grief*. Perhaps this is some form of denial. They were close, Miss Plath and Miss Drake. Miss Plath is not after comfort or reassurance from me. Rather, she has assumed a kind of mission to collect details about Miss Drake's demise.

How did I find her? Where did I find her? How did she look when I came upon her? Miss Plath approaches her friend's death with curiosity and, I fear, a kind of admiration.

"I imagine Penelope looked beautiful." As she said this, it struck me then why grief has not made its appearance.

Miss Plath is no longer chasing literary prizes, top marks, or perfection. I fear she is chasing death itself.

JANUARY 9—

How I have struggled to find the intervention that will pull Miss Plath from her spiral of death obsession! There will be no more extracurriculars, no more excursions from the ward. Electroconvulsive therapy will only realign the neurons in her brain so much before the human machine suffers its greatest toll. I am at a loss in terms of her treatment. And so, this day's measure will be Miss Plath's final intervention at Codman Manor before her mother comes to collect her.

At nine thirty this morning, the Mad Poet once again entered my ward.

No longer a patient, he wore civilian clothes, a brown jacket and sagging khaki pants. His dark hair was trim. He sported rounded tortoiseshell glasses, as well as an air of stillness he has mastered in our months apart. "You have a guest," I told Miss Plath, poking my head into her room, and she looked at me, confused.

"I don't want guests today."

"He'd really like to meet you."

The Mad Poet entered the room as I said this. Miss Plath's stare lingered on him. "I don't know you," she said.

He drew a chair across the room to the side of her bed, where she was sitting, cross-legged. "I teach poetry at a local college. Dr. Barnhouse is a friend. My name's Robert Lowell."

"I asked Mr. Lowell to visit," I added.

Miss Plath studied his face. I half expected her to shout at him to leave. Instead, she said, "I *do* know you. That is, I know *of* you. I've read

The Mills of the Kavanaughs and like the shorter poems in it. But I enjoyed your *Lord Weary's Castle* compendium more."

He appreciated her saying so.

My guest had brought with him a small book of poems. "I thought we might read together," he said.

Miss Plath cautiously agreed to it, and after an entire hour of hearing him gently recite poetry at her bedside, he put his coat on to leave.

"Would it be all right if I come back sometime, maybe later this week, to read some more?"

"Knock yourself out, Professor," Miss Plath said.

JANUARY 20—

For his visit today, the Mad Poet brought with him a box of Turkish delights wrapped in a gold-colored bow from Exotic Confections on Newbury Street, another book of poetry, and a deck of playing cards. With his successive social calls, I have begun to see in Miss Plath a flicker of warmth and the rebirth of acute curiosity.

"I've been wondering . . ." he said to Miss Plath this afternoon. "Why haven't you been able to write or read? Dr. Barnhouse says you're upset."

Miss Plath looked over at me, as though I might feed her the answer, but I said nothing.

"I used to be able to," she replied, "but the words on the pages just sort of merged together. I found myself counting the letters instead. After counting to a hundred or maybe two hundred, I no longer recognized the English language."

"Do you mind if I show Mr. Lowell some of your recent work?" I asked her. She nodded, and I opened my file.

He read "Tale of a Tub" to himself, and then her second poem, "Miss Drake Proceeds to Supper."

"Why did you choose to write about these subjects?" he asked her afterward.

"Dr. Barnhouse instructed me to be observant and write about what I see," she told him. "I 'spose I could have written about any one of the patients in their pajamas or the yammering orderlies."

"I like your work. It's skilled, intense, perceptive . . ." he said.

Miss Plath blushed, her cheeks gaining a color I'd yet to see in them here in Codman Manor, or even on Boston Common.

"I believe," he continued, "that these poems are more than just studies of your environment. It seems to me that they are tools designed to expunge the morass in your mind as though it were a kind of poison. It's a beautiful poison that becomes no less toxic when it touches the page." He smiled. "Except the more you write, the less it will hurt you."

Then he pondered aloud what it might be like if Miss Plath tried writing more of these poems, only not through dictation or by crossing out letters in a book with a soft-lead pencil, but by putting the poison on the page herself.

Miss Plath shook her head. "I won't. I can't."

"You have to start again someplace," he said.

"There's no place to start and no place to go. I'm my own worst rival."

"This rival," he said, "tell me about her."

The rival in her head, Miss Plath explained, tells her that she is good and praises her all the time. The rival sounds like a friend, but Miss Plath isn't so sure. Every time Miss Plath holds a pen, her hand shakes. It makes her worry that maybe she'll never be a real writer. And if she never becomes a real writer, then she will never be great or fulfill the potential that her rival promises her she'll eventually achieve. Miss Plath has a sense that she wants to undermine her rival, with pills, with falls, with rope.

"Then this rival of yours," he said, "is where you will start."

SIXTH STANZA

The Last Intervention of Robert Lowell

Passion! We display our hearts' capacities for love by caring for those who are left behind and those who know no love at all. We are bestowed with the responsibility to protect them from the outside, and at times protect them from themselves. We are sanctuary, like any great church, and a place of sanctity. Poetry, like theology, is the shrewdest path to tame the burdened soul.

—BOSTON RHODES, ESSAY, "THE ASYLUM FROM REASON"

16

Estee, 2019

A well-known novelist whose name I will not dignify here, and whose popularity is strong, quite strong albeit faded some over the years, celebrates the fortieth anniversary of his most notable book. The novel is equally famous for its cultural impact as it is for its ambiguous and indeterminate ending that has confounded and frustrated a generation of readers. The novelist asks for a meeting with St. Ambrose Auction House. He presents me with a folio, four pages, handwritten, never transcribed to typewriter or computer. This is, he says, the *real* final chapter of his novel, an ending that promises to answer every question and flip all that came before it on its head. "You think you know this story? You don't."

The novelist has come with an offer to sell this final chapter, at auction, to the highest bidder. Of course, the winning bidder has to promise not to tell anyone else what lies within these four pages, ensuring that the secret ending remains just that: a secret.

I decline to host the auction, for let us be clear, this is nothing but a publicity stunt, and a cruel one at that. How pitiless it is to hold over readers a heartbreaking lack of closure. It's the pinprick of a deep, unreachable itch, the tingle of a phantom limb, the name of a song one can't place. It is Sylvia Plath, searching for, and failing to find, her *hullabaloo.*

This afternoon, in search of some closure of our own, Nicolas Jacob and I take the T to the Kenmore stop and disembark onto Commonwealth Avenue. In the time it's taken us to get from St. Ambrose to the campus of Boston University, it seems autumn has ended and winter has arrived. Leaves skate across the sidewalks, and invisible brooms thrust them through the streets. As we cross Marsh Plaza, the bike racks and flagpoles cast long, lanky shadows. Nicolas hands me a set of keys to his office and tells me to let myself in. "Go to my desk. In the front drawer, you'll find a second set of keys."

"Keys to what?"

"Various buildings and other rooms on campus. We'll need them," he says. I ask where he's going to be, and he says Mugar Memorial Library, but when I inquire about what he's looking for there, he doesn't answer, or maybe he just can't answer because he's not sure, not yet. But if he finds it, and if his working theory is correct, then we will meet up again in an hour in front of the College of Arts & Sciences, where he promises he'll explain.

Nicolas's office is a ten-minute walk east across campus to a beige building with gothic aspirations, and a journey down a flight of stairs to the only part of the English department the college hasn't bothered updating. Nicolas's name is on a plastic plate beside his door. Using his keys, I let myself inside. The door swings open and comes into contact with the edge of a file cabinet. The walls evince a grouping of diplomas and a poster that reads BERNIE 2016 in white letters, and underneath that, FREE COLLEGE, CANCEL DEBT!

In the front drawer of Nicolas's desk, I find a ring fat with bronze and shiny silver keys, then cut back across campus to wait for him.

As I sit at a bench, a cold afternoon becomes a much colder late afternoon, the kind that makes the sky look like the chalkboard of a manic math teacher. Nicolas arrives almost an hour later than we agreed, and by now, my cheeks burn in the wind, but he glances at me, his dark eyes gleaming. He's found something. The cold is no longer a bother.

I follow Nicolas into the College of Arts & Sciences building. We climb a staircase and come to a numbered door: ROOM 222.

Nicolas asks for the key ring and I hand it over. He unlocks the room and flips a light switch. There's a long table with a dozen or so empty chairs around it. The windows look out on the Charles River and a couple of other campus buildings draped in ivy. The classroom is only a fraction of a normal-size classroom, its hardwood floors well-trodden, its area rug dulled by years of direct sunlight, its walls unadorned.

"I don't suppose you've ever been in here before. Room two-twenty-two, otherwise known as the Robert Lowell Seminar Room. A long time ago, Robert Lowell led his famous poetry writing workshop in this space."

"Of course," I say, now picturing this table inhabited by poets, and Robert Lowell, the professor and virtuoso of complex-patterned poems, famously pacing this space, circling the table, critical and watchful of his pupils.

Nicolas and I sit down on two chairs at the end of the table. "Lowell is the key to this whole mystery," he says.

"Did the notebooks tell you that?"

"No, you did, actually."

Nicolas unclasps his messenger bag. He removes a folder wrapped and drawn closed with twine.

"It was something you said in the safe holdings room today. A bell went off. Your mother. She was a poet?"

"A poet, yes."

"A poet, woken by her young daughter the morning after she tried to gas herself in her garage. I need two hands to count the number of writers who've attempted to die by carbon monoxide poisoning. John Kennedy Toole, Émile Zola, and of course, Sylvia Plath. But it was the detail, the one about you finding your mother the morning after her attempt. It just sounded . . . familiar. Turns out, it's familiar because it's a story I've already heard before. Even stranger, it's a story very few people *have* heard before. And those very few people who've heard it, they only know it because they've read this."

He pushes the folder toward me.

"A couple of years ago, I was producing an academic survey on confessional poetry and its relation to truth. My research required a deep dive into dozens of original and obscure documents, including a letter written to Robert Lowell."

He unwinds the twine and reveals within it a stack of typed pages.

"I went back to the archives this afternoon, and there it was, just like I remembered. It'll take you some time to read through it, but I think you need to read it to understand."

I need him to clarify.

"Your mother's name, it was Agatha White."

"Yes . . ."

"She went by another name. A pen name."

"Boston Rhodes."

"I imagine it's impossible to escape the legacy of one of the most controversial poets of the twentieth century."

I've never tried to escape it. I've kept it no secret from the world, though I have moved my life beyond my mother, so adept at infiltrating and infecting every aspect of the lives she touched. I can so easily become the child observer again. Here is my mother, ranting and shouting after my father through the house. Here is my mother laughing that highbrow laugh she reserves for others, and she is always laughing, except when she is screaming or doubled over in tears, which sometimes happens behind closed doors but often takes place in the middle of the house in a kind of show. Here are my mother's papers strewn across every flat surface in the dining room, her world literally sketched out, scratched out, revised, rewritten, and pieced together just the way she needs it to be. Here I am, a child up in my mother's study above the garage, sitting under the table between her legs, picking at her gray stockings as she click-click-clicks away on the typewriter, the toe of her black patent Pilgrim shoe tap-tap-tapping the floorboards. In my memory, as in the most famous photos of her, my mother is a high-cheekboned beauty with black hair and black eyebrows and lips that somehow move from seductive to scornful without the benefit of her activating a single muscle.

Nicolas opens the document before him to its final page and taps at the signature. My mother's signature.

"In this letter to Professor Lowell, Boston Rhodes chronicles a rivalry between her and another student of his—"

"Sylvia Plath . . ."

"Surely you knew, Estee. On some level, when you first saw the notebooks and asked yourself the question *how?*, you must have made that connection."

If curating has taught me anything besides persistence, it's that history is rarely kind to those searching for tidy resolutions. People profess they know my mother through her work. They claim that my mother knew them as though she had a line channeled directly into their innermost lives as evidenced by her poetry. And they also assume that a daughter must know sides and depths of a mother that no scholar or devotee will ever know, the parts that even my mother was blind to. No memory, poem, or recovered letter will ever bring one closer to truly knowing Boston Rhodes—poet, louse, lover, liar.

"My mother was a lot of things, Nicolas, but I can promise you, she didn't steal Plath's notebooks."

"That might be true. But our search isn't just about the Plath notebooks any longer. This letter proves it. There's more."

Nicolas looks at me reproachfully, patiently waiting for me to meet him on the other side of some monolithic revelation that he's discovered, but one I cannot yet fathom. "And it all leads back to Robert Lowell."

17

Boston Rhodes, 1959

My dear Professor Lowell, prophet of meter, keeper of rhyme, teacher of observation. Let me teach you about the math of the universe's scale of fairness. Since Sylvia's arrival in your workshop, I'd waited and I'd watched and I'd listened. Quickly, pieces of a grand design were falling into place.

At Central Square Pharmacy, I had the film developed. Uncertain what to do next, I brought the photos to Maxine. We were seated on a stiff white sofa in her suburban dream of a home, our shoes sinking into plush carpeting. With matching teacups in our hands, Maxine surveyed the spread of glossy images of Ted Hughes and the Mystery Woman. The photographs of the two were obscured by trees, by crowds, by bookshelves. The people were either too far away to make out, or out of focus.

"They could be anybody," Maxine said.

"Look again."

From the low coffee table I picked out a photo of Ted and the Mystery Woman between the stacks at the Athenæum, their lips no farther apart from each other's than the width of a dime. Maxine wanted to convince me there was no way to tell for sure if these photos meant Ted was having an affair behind Sylvia's back.

"You just don't want it to be true," I said.

"And you do," she replied sharply.

I considered denying the charge, but at this point I didn't see any reason to lie.

Maxine, nonplussed, stared into the mouth of her teacup. She picked up another photograph, studied it, and then shook her head. "Were you following Ted?"

"Oh, I shouldn't have," I cried. "I'm a horrible person. I don't know why I did it." But obviously I knew why. I just couldn't bring myself to say it out loud.

So Maxine said it for me. "You wanted to hurt Sylvia."

My mind flashed back to my dinner with Ted and Sylvia, and how, when Ted criticized her work, Sylvia placated him with a playful touch to his shoulder. In that gentle exchange, I'd seen fear in Sylvia, as though she knew Ted was capable of withdrawing every ounce of his devotion to her. I'd always detected a distinct hunger in Sylvia for Ted's adulation, not that I was unfamiliar with such desires. I understood desperation for the love of a man who was larger than life. I'd buried my father, yet I'd continued to live in his shadow, and would until I made him proud.

Maxine looked at me in a way that led me to feel trivial. "I didn't ask to see what I saw," I said.

She sighed. "Well, you saw, and now I saw. The question is, do we intervene? Do we show Sylvia the pictures or not?"

My encounter with Ted outside at the Athenæum had gotten me thinking. "So you understand just how fragile she is," he'd said. It made me wonder just how fragile Sylvia actually was.

"This will crush her," I said now.

"We don't know what it will do," reasoned Maxine.

But I knew, because I knew Sylvia. You said it yourself, Professor, that she and I were so alike. Sylvia's poetry and my own were sisters in theme, language, and soul. Yet as I saw it, these similarities hid one vast and critical personal difference between us, and therein lay the problem. In a contest between perceived equals, the person with the slightest advantage was going to win every time. Because Sylvia's advantage was the famous Ted Hughes, she'd perpetually draw top billing, the biggest applause, and the magazine headlines.

And without him, Sylvia's only advantage disappeared.

"We have to show her," Maxine said.

"Yes," I said. "It is, after all, the honest thing to do."

Maybe I was all wrong, and maybe I didn't know what I was doing, but I was of two minds about Sylvia. One told me to place the photographs of Ted and the Mystery Woman in an envelope and address it to her.

The second said to be careful.

The reasons for this dread had nothing to do with potential backlash or damage to my own reputation. Rather, I knew the power of the weapon I brandished. Forget all the vitriol I've spouted in this letter; I'm no monster. My mission of dominance was clear, yet the emotion I felt about delivering the photos was not warm and not happy, but complicated. I had thought about the problem of Sylvia Plath for a long time as seriously and as wisely as I could. Yes, we were two of a kind. An abundance of love and hate ran wild in us both. I can tell you, quite honestly, that I was frightened to do what I needed to do.

Still, I moved ahead, placing the envelope with the photos in my pocketbook, ready to deliver the payload, the final blow, the knockout punch, the . . . whatever you call the end . . . when Sylvia dodged it!

With no forewarning, she announced to the Ritz Ring that she and Ted were leaving town for good. Ted was completing his appointment at Amherst, and at the end of the summer they were moving to Northern England. "Yorkshire's very, very rural and has nothing but sheep and rabbit catchers," Sylvia lamented. Still, the change was for the best, she said, as Ted found he was less productive in America and had grown terribly bored with it, too.

Just like that, Sylvia called off the rivalry.

There would be no more workshop sessions for her, no more Tuesday evenings at the Ritz bar, and no more Ring. Having conquered each and accomplishing everything she'd set out to do, Sylvia was enacting a truce. She was leaving us having been crowned the de facto leader of a literary movement and a Major Voice in American letters, as though these prizes were hers to abscond with! Time was running out for me to get my due.

My dear, dear Professor—you who have made a pastime of memorizing the military histories of the Napoleonic wars—I ask you, have you ever known such a cowardly strategic battle-time move?

Notwithstanding the unfairness of it all, I was relieved to see Sylvia leaving us. With her out of the country and out of the picture, I was free to reclaim the workshop and the Ring and the eminence she'd taken from me. We entered Sylvia's last day at the workshop, which might have otherwise been a celebratory moment for me, but instead it became cause for concern.

You were running late for the class. (And you never ran late.) For a half hour, we, your devoted disciples, sat waiting for you. Eventually, a woman walked all the way over from the university administration office and announced that the workshop was canceled for the afternoon.

Sylvia cried, "We simply must find the professor. I can't imagine leaving town without saying goodbye."

I never understood the power that you and Sylvia had over each other. From her first day in the workshop, your connection was extraordinarily familiar. At first, I thought that you were merely lusting after the young and pretty little thing. After I learned who her husband was, there was a part of me that wondered if you were using her to get close to Ted Hughes. Then I wondered if you had accidentally fallen in love with Sylvia, and she in love with you.

I came to understand how wrong I was. Sylvia's resolve to impart a farewell was not a lover's resolve, I saw then, but a daughterly resolve. Your affection for her was never a lover's affection, but that of a father's, the kind that I have never known. With that realization, I saw a familiar longing and fear of loss in Sylvia. She was leaving, and you were nowhere to be found. It was possible that you had forsaken her. Maybe she'd failed to live up to your expectations, or had outgrown them and left you envious. The cruelest thing a colossus like you could do to Sylvia was rebuff her wish to say goodbye.

I wanted to believe this was true, and so I agreed to follow Sylvia as she went to find you. Hell, I even volunteered to drive.

The most logical first stop was your home in Beacon Hill. Sylvia pressed the buzzer to your unit. Eventually, a woman in a bathrobe came to the door. When Sylvia asked if you were here, the look on the woman's face was a difficult one to interpret—unless you're as well versed as I am in rendering such pity and anguish in others. How often had I procured it in Kildare, curating in him a kind of uncertainty familiar only to those who had endured a spouse whose madness turned in the wind like a weather vane?

The woman was disgusted. "Who're you? Two more of his little projects?"

Neither of us knew how to respond. We just stood there like doormats.

"We're his students, over at the college," Sylvia said. "The professor didn't show up for workshop, and, see, we were worried."

"You should be worried." The woman then shut us out, locking the dead bolt behind her. I don't mind telling you, Professor, your wife was a cold and cruel woman to us that evening. I still felt bad for her. What kind of torment must a man put a wife through to turn her into such a block of ice?

Back in my car, Sylvia said, "The professor was supposed to read at the Elks Lodge last night," and so that's where we went next.

Waitstaff were setting chairs in a grid in an open, gym-like space. A banner beyond a podium read LODGE #0010. A secretary confirmed for us that you had, in fact, shown up for your reading Monday evening.

You'd arrived drunk and left drunker, but not before hurling a glass of beer at the wall and proposing to a waitress.

Was I surprised? Not even a little. You collect, with an obsessive fervor, first-edition books, odd pens, and reams of notes in notepads, but what you collect most of all are followers. The secretary of the Elks Lodge had seen you leaving with several new ones that night.

Sylvia asked if there was a phone she could use.

An American flag dangled in the night outside the municipal police station. The waiting area looked and felt a lot like your workshop, with the same harsh lights and the same flimsy chairs with backs that give a little too easily when you lean into them. I smelled old shoe rubber and cigarettes.

The police officer in the front booth had a fat lip and remained unmoved when we ask to see his prisoner.

"You're here for the professor?" He said "professor" as though it were parenthetical.

I asked what the charges were.

Public intoxication and disturbing the peace, he said. There'd been a scene at a restaurant. They'd picked you up crying out against devils and homosexuals.

"You can't just shout obscenities at people," said the officer. It took four policemen to overpower and handcuff you! Given the officer's busted lip coupled with his disdain for you, I had to assume he was one of your victims.

Sylvia asked how much bail was. The officer said three hundred dollars, and without a word, she snapped open her checkbook, but the jail only accepted cashier's checks. The bail bondsman was open twenty-four seven, the officer said.

We returned to the station just before midnight. I slid a bondsman's check under the window. Forty minutes later, I nudged Sylvia awake as you appeared through a side door. You dragged your rumpled jacket along the floor. The knot of your tie was loose and low. You looked like a wall with some of its bricks punched out of it. Your hair was a fleet of sails.

You stopped at the little window and collected your wallet, glasses, and keys from the clerk, then redistributed them to your face and pockets.

Approaching the two of us, never abandoning your stride, you whispered, "I've discovered the secret of the universe."

Sylvia looked at me. "We can't drop the professor back at his home."

I agreed.

We considered taking you to a hotel and even talked about bringing you back to my house until we could figure out our next steps.

Sylvia said she had a better idea.

Exposed to the night, you were a man possessed.

As I drove, you harangued us and soliloquized a one-man reenactment of Napoleon's battles, with occasional side lectures on the dangers of unchecked power. Your words clanged and crashed together. Your body reached for the doors and the roof.

You sniffed the air, grabbed the two front seats, and wrenched yourself forward between us. "Do you smell that? Brimstone. The devil's hiding."

"Okay, Professor," I said. "You just sit back there and take it easy."

"I'm indestructible. A messenger from heaven. I've walked upon the waters . . ."

After a while on the Concord Turnpike, Sylvia had me exit the narrow, two-lane highway onto a rural road. The passage was dark and winding. She told me to slow down, as the turn was coming up.

Soon, I was veering through a stone arched gate.

Rain tapped against the windshield, making the central thoroughfare difficult to maneuver. Coming over a small ridge, I saw light from the windows of what looked like a half-dozen scattered mansions and hospital buildings. Just ahead, a large brick manor appeared.

I came to a stop under the covered entrance and put the car in park. For the first time on that whole drive, you were quiet.

Sylvia looked over at me, and I turned around to face you. Each of us was waiting for something to happen.

Then you grabbed up your coat and touched the handle, but you hesitated before getting out of the car. Marbled light moved across your face as lines of rain slithered down your window. You grew sincere and sober.

"I thank the universe every day that it brought you two together."

I couldn't find the voice to correct you, Professor. The universe hadn't brought Sylvia and me together. You had.

You stepped from the car and into the possession of an orderly who had appeared holding a large umbrella. "Mr. Lowell, welcome back to McLean Hospital."

"It's good to be back."

"We have a nice room waiting for you."

"In Men's Belknap?"

"Why, yes, I believe so."

"Good," you said and followed the orderly inside.

Sylvia and I returned to the city and said very little along the way. The farm roads clung to brambles, scrubs, and old trees that held the darkness. Route 2 grew busy with delivery trucks. The sky betrayed the touch of dawn, wrapping arms of haze over tall glass buildings.

Soldiers Field Road curved along the Charles River, and Harvard University ascended on the left when I asked Sylvia how she knew about that place.

"It's never hard to find your way back home. My mother used to say that."

"You were a patient?"

"I'm always a patient," she said.

"Why were you there?"

"Tried to hurt myself."

"So you understand just how fragile she is," Ted had said that night at the Athenæum, but until delivering you to the asylum, I had not understood the depth of Sylvia's past despair.

"You mean kill yourself?"

"Does that surprise you?"

Had you met Sylvia before the workshop, Professor? Did you recognize each other from your time at the madhouse? Had you heard each other's voices crying from different ends of a locked wing? I wasn't able to bring myself to ask Sylvia about it because, despite having just witnessed you in your decompensating state, I still couldn't really imagine you locked up in a mental asylum, all mad and shattered. That you were capable of experiencing such pain broke my heart. And if I'm honest now, I was also a little jealous, thinking that you may have experienced these intimate moments with Sylvia at one time, long before she arrived at your workshop. Unlike the university classroom, or the cozy rooms of the New England Poetry Club, the rooms of McLean Hospital were those I had not been able to share with you. If true, your bond with Sylvia was forged in conditions nothing in heaven or on earth could challenge. Once again, I felt at a disadvantage, only instead of fueling my anger, it just left me feeling sad and left out.

"Maybe it should surprise me, but it doesn't, not really," I said.

"There's a terrific tradition of mad artists. Roethke, Berryman, Eliot." Sylvia said this brightly.

That night, we added you to that list—you, the only person I know, besides Sylvia, who seeks, with a compulsive desire, that perfect, slow, complex stanza, that equilibrium of rhythm and rhyme, and who lives as though poetry is of the greatest importance and everything else is disposable. No wonder you and Sylvia were so familiar with each other. You were both haunted by familiar dybbuks.

"Anyway," Sylvia continued, "then came the psychic regeneration, and I went back to college and reconquered old broncos that had thrown me for a loop." She smiled. "I'm here now."

Yes, she was here now, but *who was she?* Sylvia presented herself as a strong and confident woman, an independent woman, but beneath all that sheen and polish and talent was a person with an ineffable desperation for—

For what exactly?

For greatness? For Ted Hughes?

It came to me then, like the most perfect verse. Sylvia was desperate for love.

I pulled up to her building. As Sylvia gathered her coat and bag to leave the car, I once again became aware of the photos of Ted I was still carrying in my pocketbook. I reached for my purse and touched the edge of the envelope, only to decide I could not bring myself to show her. The thing of it was, I no longer needed the photos, not after tonight. You were tucked away in a mental asylum, ending the workshop for the foreseeable future, and Sylvia was leaving.

I closed my pocketbook.

"You're going to visit me in Yorkshire, aren't you?" asked Sylvia. "Ted has all of his friends in England, but where I'm headed, I don't have a soul to call my own. Oh, you must come and visit! You already promised me."

I'd promised a lot of things lately. To George, that I'd keep our secret rendezvous. To Kildare, that I was his and always would be. To my dead father, that I was going to make him proud. To myself, that I'd keep Ted's infidelity, and the flaw in his heart, from Sylvia.

You must believe me, that in that moment I had every intention of keeping those promises, even if in the end I broke every one.

18

Ruth, 1954

JANUARY 30—

Pain, sorrow, grief, memory. These are languages. A true listener understands each. And empathy is the Rosetta stone.

But empathy was absent in the wood-paneled den of the Proctor House today. Embalmed in the smells of floor wax and oil finish, I sat at the oak desk, which might have made for a defendant's bench in a courtroom. Finding no such benevolence among my peers-turned-judges, I waited for an adjudication.

At the front of the chamber, parallel to the stone hearth, was a long table where the members of the ethics and disciplinary committee sat in wooden armchairs. To me they looked like a gallery of tin soldiers that I might knock over one by one with the flick of a finger. Each was robed in a thin cotton white coat and dark necktie cinched in a small knot, all except for Superintendent Frisch, who wore his customary bow tie. A carnation was twisted through the lapel of his seersucker blazer, too. He presided over the hearing with the sturdy posture of a man who'd waited a long time to impose judgment.

The superintendent addressed the committee. "With regard to Dr. Barnhouse's conduct in the case of Penelope Drake, at the very least we're talking incompetence. At the worst, it's nonfeasance. Dr. Barnhouse's negligence was thorough. Her unwillingness to abide by even the most standard rules and ethics that govern this hospital led directly to Miss Drake's death."

Every time he uttered her name, my body winced.

Dr. Beuscher spoke next, a familiar kindness emanating from him. "Miss Drake's death was a tragedy. And yet, to any reasonable observer, this was the result of a confluence of unforeseeable circumstances. I remind the committee, this institution has never called Dr. Barnhouse's integrity or character into question."

The superintendent replied, "The question is, did Dr. Barnhouse act honorably? Let's put aside for a minute that she's fighting for her future at this hospital. She places our institution in jeopardy."

For the benefit of the committee, the superintendent asked me to describe Miss Drake's condition upon intake.

"She was exhibiting common manic-depressive behavior patterns, combined with anhedonia and obsessive-compulsive tendencies."

"And there's a standard protocol for these conditions," added the superintendent. "What is that protocol, Dr. Barnhouse?"

"Observation and analysis. And when these don't work, insulin shock or electroconvulsive therapy."

Superintendent Frisch addressed the panel again. "But in Miss Drake's case, Dr. Barnhouse failed to administer anything resembling standard protocol. Instead, she chose to engage in a pattern of operating with little discernible strategy."

Dr. Beuscher said, "So it's your position, Superintendent Frisch, that if Dr. Barnhouse had followed your orders and recommendations, Miss Drake would still be alive?"

"Dr. Barnhouse is reckless, obstinate, impudent, and combative, not to mention opinionated. In my estimation, this and nothing else led to the patient's demise."

"And yet, according to her progress reports, Penelope Drake saw rapid recovery under the care of Dr. Barnhouse."

I defended myself. "Miss Drake's death is a tragedy. I did everything within my power to treat her, even when this hospital failed to."

Superintendent Frisch pulled on the lapels of his jacket. "And that included making a practice of coercing her into physical labor."

"It wasn't a practice," I objected, "it was a treatment. After a week, Miss Drake was eating again and experienced fewer symptoms of obsessive-compulsive tendencies. During these moments, Miss Drake was no longer the sum total of her illness."

"You say she was recovering, and yet no sane person would run out into the worst blizzard in half a century. Isn't it true you failed to see the patient was relapsing?"

Now Dr. Beuscher was the person who objected. "One of the benefits of effective treatment is a patient's ability to fully come back into the knowledge of her own comprehension. Isn't it possible the patient chose to leave on her own and saw the storm as a perfect cover?"

"If Miss Drake chose to leave the manor during the storm, she did so because Dr. Barnhouse put the idea of liberation in her head," the superintendent said.

"And I say Miss Drake choosing to leave was the ultimate act of self-determination," Dr. Beuscher said.

Superintendent Frisch turned his attention back to me. "Let's talk about self-determination. You were married, Dr. Barnhouse?"

I paused.

Exhaled slowly.

Closed my eyes.

"The marriage produced a child?"

I pressed my hands onto my lap. "Yes."

"And she died."

I wanted to crawl out of my skin.

"She did."

The members of the panel stirred. Dr. Beuscher said, "What does any of this have to do with the day's hearing?"

The superintendent folded his hands in front of him. His expression softened. "I wish upon no one the pain of losing a child. Still, we must take into consideration Dr. Barnhouse's mindset. What does the death of a child do, I wonder, to a woman who has so much to prove? She's the youngest doctor on staff. She's its first female psychiatrist. I submit that, in her desperation to prove her worth, she neglected to see she was damaging her patients. Miss Drake was a victim of Dr. Barnhouse's aspirations, grief, and self-doubt."

"You're wrong," I said, though I did not believe the words coming from my own mouth. They rang false, flat, dead. I had to admit to myself that I had not helped anybody. I was unable to protect Miss Drake. I defied the protocols of this hospital and the superintendent. The panel had every reason to trust that my techniques and all of my professed interventions have done nothing to cure a single patient, that they in fact led directly to the death of one of them.

As the superintendent concluded his deconstruction of my experience, expertise, and acumen, from the back of the chamber the double doors unexpectedly slid apart. I turned, and there in the entryway stood Miss Plath, the warm light of the chamber behind her spilling into ours.

The superintendent balked. "This is a closed hearing."

A nurse was standing at Miss Plath's side. "I'm sorry for the interruption. I'm here with a resident of Codman Manor. She would like to speak on behalf of Dr. Barnhouse."

I demanded the nurse promptly escort Miss Plath back to the ward, but my command fell on deaf ears. Instead, Miss Plath quietly, carefully, and without expression approached my table.

"I'm a patient of Dr. Barnhouse's. I was also Penelope Drake's friend."

Miss Plath brought an object out from behind her back.

"If it pleases the committee, I've written a letter I'd like to read aloud."

Despite the science and methodology of psychoanalysis, the controlled inroads we make into the cradle of thoughts and behaviors, the measures that allow us to lift the mad from the wet fog of their psychosis, there is and will always be, due to the unknowable makeup of the mind, a glorious mystery to human nature. For the first time since the spirit of impenetrable self-doubt lodged in this slim, sad-faced young woman, Miss Plath, I saw, had picked up a pencil and written lines of script!

She began to read aloud, shaky at first, but growing in confidence.

"It was a queer, sultry summer, and I didn't know what I was doing in New York. I knew something was wrong with me because all I could think about was how all the little successes I'd tatted up so happily fizzled to nothing. At my internship as a guest editor, I was supposed to be having the time of my life. I was supposed to be the envy of thousands. Look what can happen in this country, they'd say. A girl lives in some out-of-the-way town for nineteen years, so poor she can't afford a magazine, and then she gets a scholarship to college and wins a prize here and a prize there. Only I wasn't driving myself. I couldn't even get myself to react. I felt very still and very empty, the way the eye of a tornado must feel, moving dully along the middle of the surrounding hullabaloo."

As she read, the pages in her hands shook. Over the course of several sheets, the words plotted a story. It was about Miss Plath's life before coming to my ward, a life of obsessions and contradictions. She tracked the spark of her disillusionment and a private loneliness that made her feel empty and gloomy, yet the world still expected her to showcase a jaunty wit and sophistication, and to earn scholarships, and to win awards, and to eventually become an attentive wife. But there was the pull of her own ambitions, too. A man might care for her, but not grasp her fervor for poetry. A man might usurp her desire to write and to create. Yet she wanted both, even while she wanted neither. Obsessions and contradictions at every turn.

Miss Plath read on. The future she imagined, one in which she was destined for greatness, cracked under the weight of her indecision about which path to follow. The thought of killing herself appeared in the fissures. It formed in her mind coolly as a tree or a flower. Death was an exercise in control, like holding a pencil and moving it across a page. Soon, even the suburban landscape of her childhood home became a simulacrum, a shadow realm in which she calmly considered the method, the moment, and the milieu to properly end her life. A bottle of sleeping pills. A crawl space under the home. None of this brought her death, she said. Instead, it brought her to me.

She read on. At McLean Hospital, she met her new psychiatrist. A female psychiatrist, as queer a sight as any she'd seen in a mental asylum, even one as fancy as this one. She said that I dressed her and told her that I wanted to see her looking fine for me. Here, with this letter, Miss Plath was dressing me! "When the loveliest mirror cracks, it is not right to rest, to step aside, and hope that it mends without intervention. Dr. Barnhouse is beholden to an inescapable spirit of dignity and integrity so profound that it must be capped."

She read on. I had visited Miss Plath in her room, she said, and I was calm and I was careful, with a reservoir of understanding. Often, she had wanted to burst out in tears and say, *Comfort me! Hear me! Take me to your heart! Be warm and let me cry and cry and cry. Help me be strong.* She was tired and discouraged by all that despair. There were many times she'd given into that fury and desire for death. She fought and fought to free herself from it. "But Dr. Barnhouse saw which treatment wasn't working. I didn't think anyone could help me. The proper methods only made it worse. Dr. Barnhouse had new methods. She told me how to report on the world around me. This is what I see: Penelope Drake was alive. Today she is gone. To suggest that Dr. Barnhouse brought harm to her is a delusion worthy of the doctor's own care. She treated Penelope, just as she's treated me, and many others. Her only crime is that she helped Penelope discover free will."

She lowered the page, and recited the rest from memory.

"I've come to understand that we can address the madness within, but we cannot contain it. Look at a swarm long enough and you'll see what appears to be cohesive movement. It's all an illusion. We can't tame the bees. They are only in the brood boxes because they choose to be, because they allow us to be their keepers."

FEBRUARY 2–

The journey from McLean Hospital to town this morning was a somber parade. Dr. Beuscher drove me. I know I should have felt appreciative, but instead I just felt thin. I was fading like an afterimage in one's eye following the flash of a camera.

As we rode, the competency hearing from three days earlier was front and center in my memory. The members of the tribunal panel had listened to Miss Plath's prepared statement, but she was nothing more to them than a committed patient whose perspective was suspect and whose observations were unworthy of validation. She was mad, after all.

Then Superintendent Frisch had called a surprise character witness of his own.

Nurse Edme came forward. She edged into the seat next to mine, and, taking up the armrests in her fingers, she refused to look at me. I was jolted by her presence, and staggered, too, when she placed two small brown jars with glass dropper tops on the table before us.

The superintendent told the tribunal that he had a signed deposition from Nurse Edme, in which she spoke to certain observations. Nurse Edme then testified that on more than one occasion, she had observed me self-administering the contents of these jars.

The superintendent asked what was in them. I answered for her: "Tinctures of amphetamines and opium."

It was Nurse Edme's observation that I suffer from malady of a chronic, relapsing nature. Superintendent Frisch asked me directly if I currently was under the influence of either of these substances? I grew cross. Does one ask a one-legged man what it takes for him to walk? Or cast doubt on a person's vision simply because she wears glasses? I mustered every ounce of strength within me simply to stand in the morning from my bed, to walk a straight line, to focus on the work without Miss Drake's death overtaking me like some sick spirit. I am a fine and competent doctor! I felt no sadness or shame, yet my eyes filled with tears as the impact of Nurse Edme's disclosures became clear.

Do I feel any anger toward Nurse Edme? I've pushed her too hard and shattered a delicate threshold within her. No, I've failed her as much as I've failed Miss Drake. She broke my trust, but not before I broke hers.

With that, the superintendent announced that my services at the hospital were no longer required. Dr. Beuscher started to speak in my defense, but I raised a hand, and he remained silent; it was finished. Instead, I asked Dr. Beuscher for one last favor.

A ride.

At the city's West End now, Dr. Beuscher turned onto Fruit Street, whereupon we approached a white granite building with a columned portico, chimneys, and a domed top.

Inside, the ward at Massachusetts General Hospital is a mirror image of Codman Manor, literally its precise opposite, with linoleum floors instead of warm rugs, overhead fluorescents instead of lamps, hard plastic chairs instead of sofas.

A nurse bearing a striking resemblance to a broomstick showed me to my new room. It is on the third floor of this pale monolith clinic. The view through the metal screen is of a grassy courtyard surrounded by a brick wall and, beyond that, lots of city streets.

To find myself here, from giver to patient, it is as though the earth has suffered a blow so forceful that magnetic north and magnetic south have switched polarities. My heart aches over the cascade of recent events. I am driven to seek release, only here I am left with only my own insufficient apparatuses to get by.

A team of doctors visited me. I laid on my bed, and they entered one after the other, introducing themselves throughout the day. Then a nurse came in, and she did not introduce herself. She merely handed me a paper cup. "Please take these." I asked what they were. "To help the withdrawal," she said. I regarded her as though she were mad. They mean to rid me of the pain for good with these two little pathetic pills? To say I am skeptical is an understatement. Do I want to take these pills? What am I without my pain? Carl Jung writes that life consists of a complex of inexorable opposites. Day and night. Birth and death. Happiness and misery. Good and evil. Pain and relief. One is not meant to prevail against the other. Life is a battleground for eternal rivals.

But what does Jung know? He might be a renowned psychoanalyst, but he's also a diagnosed psychotic after all, and as far as I can tell, he is not in this ward with me.

FEBRUARY 10—

How wrong that wretched nurse was! These pills help not one little bit. I move through a gauntlet of amplified sensations. Bottomless hunger tears at me. My skin is aflame. A damp chill refuses to release me. Though I cannot lift my head from the pillow, I do not sleep. Trembling and wired and sick, I'm going mad.

But worst of all is the listening. I cannot shut it off! I listen to memories and to ghosts.

I hear my daughter crying with fever. I hear the rattle in her chest when she draws breath. In the waking state of my delusion-filled detoxification, Tiffany's small body rests beside mine.

Logic fights me. I have instead come upon an approach of pure surrender. This requires a sorting of my losses. For so long, where there has been sorrow I have replaced it with purpose, a will to drive the current of my own great meandering river toward some far-off and lofty fantasy.

A horrible, violent, poisonous dream last night. My daughter was sharing the room with me. Only we were not in my room, but in Miss Plath's room, room nineteen at Codman Manor. Tiffany sat on Miss Plath's bed with a blemish under her left eye. I heard a tiny sound. It was weak but steady. I came to see that the mark below her eye was actually a perfectly circular hole. The sound I heard coming from within it was the murmur of bees, thousands of them, that might as well have been the sound of an electrical current charging within the electrotherapy machine. I watched, frozen in terror, as a set of antenna emerged from the hole, followed by fiber-thin legs, thorax, and abdomen.

As my body lets go of this drug, I feel a tremendous void. I lie languid and lost. Tonight, all I hear is the sound of breathing. My own.

FEBRUARY 17—

Treatment continues. A treatment of nothing. A treatment of abstaining and of swallowing pills for the pain.

The nurse came into my room yesterday and handed me my paper cup of pills. I swallowed the capsules with a sip of water. "Those were your last." She delivered her cruelty with cool indifference. In the night following this sudden cessation, suffering without a wink of sleep, I banged on the door and shouted and spat and cried for the orderlies to bring me a sedative. No one came. Finally, a boundless emptiness overcame me.

An object of great importance has been stolen from me, nothing less than my potency, my power to exist.

MARCH 10—

The nurse came by today and told me I had a guest.

I figured it was Dr. Beuscher coming to check on me. Given the state of my wan appearance, I had half a mind to tell her to send him away. Though some of my energy has returned, I remain a drawn and ashen sight, as well as twenty pounds lighter than when I arrived here six weeks ago.

Instead of seeing Dr. Beuscher when I entered the lobby, Miss Plath rose from the sofa.

She was elegant in a box suit of worsted flannel and a pair of French shoes. Her hair was dark and groomed slick and neat.

Since her own discharge from McLean Hospital, she has returned to Smith College, just in time for the start of spring quarter. She is taking a couple of classes, nothing too strenuous, except for nineteenth-century American literature, which is turning out to be her favorite this year, she says. She has picked up her life again, a renewed, reborn self, surrounded by peers only dimly aware of how far off the rails their lives are capable of going. The underclassmen have received her as a kind of a hero, she says. What with her notoriety from the previous summer as the so-called most infamous girl in New England, and everything that followed her disappearance, she's become a person of intrigue among her peers. There is a history major at Yale she is in love with who claims to be related to a famous French poet. She is also fond these days of quoting Nietzsche, Rimbaud, and Baudelaire.

She brought forth our copy of *Finnegans Wake*. "We didn't have the chance to finish reading this together back at McLean."

I told her that the hospital library was going to be sore she hadn't returned it.

"If they want to charge me, they know where they can find me," she said.

I believe I will always remember Miss Plath this way, with a beam of sunlight from the common room window of Boston Hospital holding her face, *Finnegans Wake* in her lap, her voice a gentle balm as I smoked my cigarettes.

"I imagine it's not easy for you to see me like this."

"You don't make me uncomfortable, if that's what you mean. You're my psychiatrist, but my friend, too."

Such a response revealed the true intention of her visit, to satisfy some insatiable, bothersome curiosity about me. The great psychologist Alfred Binet wrote that if we were to look into the head of a chess player, we'd see a world of feelings, images, ideas, emotions, and passions. Miss Plath continues to work to pry me open and find mine.

"I bet you don't have very many friends," she said. "Everyone needs somebody. Until recently, I thought I needed everybody. I felt an arcane loneliness."

"But not anymore?"

"Neediness is a dangerous proposition for people like us. Lowell said my problem is that my heart is just too big. It lets in too much. I tried to shut it off and pretend that I felt nothing. It was the only way to survive. Either that or jump off a bridge."

"I'm glad you didn't. And I'm glad you're alive."

"Well, if you want to know, I think you and I have the same problem, Dr. Barnhouse. With it all bouncing around inside, we can't help but feel everything. The thing is, at some point I just realized the trick wasn't to close off my heart, but to instead allow myself to feel the world in its entirety."

A beautiful sentiment, I thought, though not an easy challenge to accept, and a terrific burden for those who do. No one has ever said empathy is painless. Not even Alfred Binet. Miss Plath's heart can hold the world in its entirety, but I worry the body that holds that heart is not nearly as strong.

It was good to visit with Miss Plath. I don't expect that I will be seeing much more of her. Before she left, she said she hoped I was going to be all right. I didn't have the resolve to tell her that I hoped the same for her, as well.

SEVENTH STANZA

The Letters

Freud said, "Everywhere I go I find a poet has been there before me." I endeavor to meet that poet, and to always be one step ahead of her.

—BOSTON RHODES, INTERVIEW, *The Saturday Review*

19

Estee, 2019

Life is poetry. It's symmetry and rhythm. We return to the places where we begin.

In the safe holdings room, I observe the three notebooks of *The Bell Jar* laid out before me on the table. It is early, half past six in the morning. St. Ambrose is quiet. The chamber I share with these objects possesses a somber air, but also one of wonder over the strange clockwork of the universe, the mathematics of coincidence, the propulsive instinct of objects, inanimate and otherwise, to wind their way back to places and people. I do not believe in fate. Objects find a home the way a river deposits sand. Sometimes, however, time and circumstance align again and again. Such is the case, it appears, with the notebooks, my mother, and me.

At seven thirty, two junior curators join me in the safe holdings room. With soft brushes, together we perform the final surface cleaning of the notebook covers. I rub a grated vinyl eraser along the initials, *V. L.* The junior curators make occasional comments about the format of the auction and the size of the audience St. Ambrose anticipates. One by one, we install notebooks into the glass pedestal showcase on a length of yellow satin. I am quite pleased with the arrangement. The junior curators level a blue blanket over the top of the glass pedestal. "Ready, one, two, and lift!" They carry the stand with the notebooks out of the room and into the hallway, toward the elevator.

In the upstairs lobby, the crowds arrive as though from a party that's already raging and spilling in from the street. The Dyce brothers do a parade wave as they enter the sales floor. They are wearing slick tuxedos, Jay Jay's of custom black and gold velvet embroidering with a mandarin collar, and Elton's of red velvet with gold bars on its sleeves. Plainly, in their minds, Elton and Jay Jay are the guests of honor. Connoisseurs, aficionados, spectators, advisors, dealers, poets, groupies, and arbiters of literature gather in praise of the Dyce brothers for rescuing the manuscript from obscurity and certain demise, bestowing upon them a toady's deference often reserved for the hero who plunges into a burning car to save a baby.

One of the Dyce brothers grabs my hand. "Scarlett says this thing's gonna last only twenty minutes," Jay Jay bewails. "How's that enough time to get the bidding up to three-quarters of a million?"

The Dyce brothers are nervous. They've flipped and staged enough flimsy houses to know that all the flash and finish in the world can't guarantee a high sales mark. The notebooks will sell fast and sell well, I say, and it is in everybody's interest that they do. The Dyce brothers will claim their money, Scarlett will claim a triumphant event, St. Ambrose will claim its seven percent fee, and the Plath notebooks will claim a new home. Then the time of the Dyce brothers and of St. Ambrose will be over. The draft of *The Bell Jar* will move beyond our reach, as it should.

Quimby finds me. "I admit, I had no idea how this was going to play out. I've never questioned Plath's relevance—you know that—but just look at this outpouring! There's at least three hundred people here."

Around us, there is conversation and socializing. Our regulars are here, men in suits and women in dark dresses, some in gowns. There are also the younger executives and the newly monied. The mood is charged and volatile.

A puzzled look comes over Quimby. "You all right? You look . . . I don't know. Distressed?"

If I look distressed, it's because I'm having trouble comprehending this auction is my last. It's just as well. Auctions at St. Ambrose used to be intimate affairs, formal social gatherings during which the house assumed the qualities of a small country, bordered with customs, driven by currency, its people in allegiance to the value of objects. But Scarlett has turned the showroom of St. Ambrose into a backwards world awash in heavy gray wall drapes and flat-screen televisions. An EDM artist with lip piercings and the side of his head shaved to the skin works behind a bank of audio equipment. Scarlett has also trucked in shell-back chairs with blue upholstering.

I'm present, but I'm no longer occupying the space beside Quimby. Rather, I'm looking through the crowd at Nicolas Jacob, who has just entered the sales floor in his winter coat and fur-trapper hat, his messenger bag suspended at his hip. Once again, I'm surprised he's here. Then I think, *Of course he's here*. With the Plath notebooks leaving us, he can't imagine being anywhere else. He wants to know where they will go. He wants to intervene in the proceedings, to tell me again why selling the Plath notebooks is a huge mistake.

"I'm bidding on the manuscript," Nicolas says.

"You can't afford it."

"I can't afford not to try."

"*You can't afford it*," I repeat.

"You could stop the auction. You could call it off," he says.

Even if that were in my power, why would I?

"The letter," he says. "What your mother did to Sylvia in the end—"

"What my mother *thinks* she did."

"You've read her letter," Nicolas says. "You know what she set out to do."

I have read the letter, a diatribe by an unraveling poet, a confused confession for a crime that, if true, is far, far worse than stealing three notebooks. But if Nicolas believes that by showing me the letter, he'd change my mind about auctioning the manuscript, he's mistaken. Historians and critics have picked apart each facet of my mother's personality left on the bone. And while my mother saw Sylvia Plath as an impediment to her own success and may have turned every act of poetry and passion into a weapon against her, to know my mother the way I did, none of this comes as a revelation. No, the only revelation here is the potency of inspiration. Robert Lowell was the catalyst; there was no telling what he was capable of inspiring in my mother. But does any word of this letter change a thing about the legacy of the notebooks? Not a syllable. In the end, an object still moves from hand to hand. The object doesn't care where it's been or who's owned it or why it exists. An object's purpose is to spark inspiration and nothing more.

The lights on the sales floor go down. Beatless ambient music transforms into a thumping sound, fat with drums and bass. Nicolas finds a seat in the middle of a row just as blue lasers stride overhead. They swing into a unified beam at a front riser where Scarlett emerges from backlit smoke in her swing skirt and a petticoat with flowers and cactuses.

Striding across the stage, a headset mic bent before her lips, Scarlett delivers a speech to provoke the emotional center of the room, to stir the room, to lift the room, to sell the room on the singularity of a most unique lot, a significant find, a one-of-a-kind, heretofore-unknown, handwritten first draft of Sylvia Plath's tour de force, *The Bell Jar,* in multiple pieces.

The music plunges to a final gripping note. The flat-screens—five are attached to the walls throughout the sales floor—slide through images: Sylvia Plath in a button-down plaid shirt, trousers, and ski boots; Sylvia Plath, posing with a group of male poets by a fireplace; Sylvia Plath, midtwenties, sunbathing on a rocky beach; Sylvia Plath in a long sweater, a white beaded bracelet attached to a fragile wrist; Sylvia Plath, lounging on a sofa, a long-stemmed rose dangling from her hand.

I wonder if my mother is in any of these moments with Sylvia, just out of frame, or perhaps occupying a place in Sylvia's mind in these very moments. In each photograph, Sylvia Plath appears brash and amazed. She displays a faintly upturned smile that is, in reality, just a suggestion of a smile that betrays either indifference, sadness, or possibly humiliation. For what can a photograph tell us about a person really? Very little, I think. We see what we want to see. And what do I see today? I see a woman who, through her words, was a custodian of a world she no longer fit in, and never really did.

I see a master curator.

The montage closes on a final image, a slow-motion zoom onto a slate-colored headstone. It is set among long blades of grass. The epitaph reads, IN MEMORY, SYLVIA PLATH HUGHES, 1932 TO 1963.

Like life, death is also poetry. An ending marks the beginning of a legacy. Every person in this room wants to own a piece of Sylvia's.

The auction has begun.

20

Boston Rhodes, 1963

You might ask me, Professor Lowell, about how I felt when I later learned Sylvia had taken her own life. I would tell you that the world as I knew it came to an end. But you, my faithful editor and collaborator, who worked over my poems with skill and ruthlessness, would never allow me to get away with such banality. So allow me to throw off the guardrails. No more benign words.

Sylvia had left for England with Ted. I was happy to be free of her. All the dramas of worry and competition were gone, and I was able to get back to my work. Life returned to how it was before Sylvia showed up in your workshop, when I did the fraught, solitary, and heartbreaking labor of writing.

Occasionally, Sylvia did dip her toe back into my orbit, if indirectly. Sylvia was gone, but one night Maxine, laughing and tipsy, rose from the Ritz barroom booth and read aloud from a small literary journal.

"'I'm a riddle in nine syllables,
An elephant, a ponderous house,
A melon strolling on two tendrils. . . .'"

So opened a clever new poem from our girl Sylvia. When she finished reading the little offering, Maxine lowered the magazine and frowned. "Well, if it's a riddle, I don't understand it."

"You're dippy," I said. The clues were all over the piece. A riddle, in nine syllables? Nine syllables per line? Nine months? Feeling as large as an elephant? "Sylvia's telling us she's pregnant."

George's face dropped, and Sam's face lit up. I sipped from my glass of sherry. No doubt, Sylvia believed she'd be a better mother than I am, she raising her offspring to know nothing but the benefits of belonging to parents of literary royalty, traveling and fine living and the ease of a life without limits. There were times when Sylvia had asked me about my daughter. We would talk in your workshop and here at the bar, and she would say things like, "I can't imagine being a mother," and, "Tell me more about your girl." Can you hear Sylvia's passive aggression?

My failings as a mother are vast. No, no, don't try to convince me otherwise. I am neglectful, unsteady, and inconsistent, and struggle to tap my reserves of compassion. But there is infinite love for my daughter, who looks like Kildare and who has my eyes, my smile, and my shrewdness. God willing, she does not have my fickle and angry heart. I ask you—as though you might know such things—what woman has the ability to be both a good mother, or even a halfway decent mother, and be the most renowned poet of her generation? No one, that's who. And yet, here was Sylvia, who apparently had decided motherhood suited her, and that it was compatible with writing and fame.

Maxine's chest heaved. "Oh, how clever! Oh, how wonderful!"

For some reason I thought about the photos again. After Sylvia had left for England, Maxine had asked me about what I'd done with them in the end.

"You never showed them to her, did you?" It didn't sound like an accusation so much as a hope. When I told Maxine that I hadn't, that I couldn't, she'd said, "Well, it's for the best." Despite her once-adamant stance on doing what she'd felt was the right thing by having me tell

Sylvia the truth about Ted, Maxine at the moment seemed relieved the issue was put to rest without casualties.

Now that Sylvia was expecting, I was certain Maxine would be doubly relieved to know the photographic evidence was no longer in play. Like the others in the Ring, I, too, rejoiced at the news—not for the life Sylvia was bringing into this world, but for the weight the world was about to drop on hers. I knew there was no more surefire a way to wick away the writer's vitality than feeding mouths, changing soiled clothes, and rotating laundry. I felt a thrill just imagining Sylvia losing footing in our now-quiet, though hardly dormant competition as she managed the distractions of child raising and the heft of everyday motherhood.

"Giving her those awful pictures would have been tragic. Can you imagine?" Maxine said. "And now, you can't ever show them to her. Not with a baby in the mix. It's like I always say, relationships defy rubric. If you still have them, Boston, you'd do well to burn them to a crisp and never think of them again."

I agreed with Maxine, for I no longer needed the photos to derail Sylvia, what with Sylvia both living in some far-flung country and soon to find her time conquered by a disruptive task of her own making.

New poems came to me slowly at first, though they were good and strong poems, "Night's Journey" and "Lost Captain" among them. George said I finally had enough work for a collection. He was confident the book was going to be well received, adding, "I have a sense for these sorts of things."

And George, with his critical and soulful eye, was right. The early reviews of *To the Lip,* which he mailed to me from the offices of Houghton Mifflin with their marvelous thick-bond envelopes, were among the most positive of my time as a poet.

As I took the bronze letter opener to George's latest delivery one afternoon, I glanced from the dining room table to the backyard where my daughter, framed by the window, was playing on the rope swing tied to the great oak.

Unfolding the newspaper clippings George had sent, I came to a review penned by none other than Robert Frost.

I put on my reading glasses. *To the Lip* was good in spots, Frost wrote, but between a kind of simplicity in technique and egocentricity, the work was intensely uninteresting and painfully unapproachable.

I guess I should have been flattered that Robert Frost, the man who despised, heckled, and engaged you, Professor, in rivalry, also seemed to despise me. But I'd be insincere if I didn't articulate to you here that I had, in fact, detected indignation stirring in my belly as I read these words.

The kitchen door flung open, and my daughter appeared with a black cut on her knee, which I acknowledged with a glance in her direction before returning to the review—this cruel, mean-spirited reproof.

My collection, reported Frost, sounded as though I'd written every poem in it all at once. It would be near impossible to dig up a writer who dwells more incessantly and pathetically on the dark and morose aspects of a woman's emotional and physical experience.

My daughter was going on and on about her leg, and I kept shouting at her to *give me a goddamn minute to breathe.*

What to do with such a review but go sour and stop reading? But I did not stop reading.

"Boston Rhodes's motives, artistically speaking, are all wrong," wrote Frost. Wrong? Had the man forgotten our encounter at the New England Poetry Club? Did he not remember I was the woman who'd put out his fire?

No, said the venom voice. *A man like that never forgets the person who extinguishes his flame. He is battling for relevance like salmon fighting the upstream current to spawn.*

My eye was then drawn to an article on the same page. Just above my review was the review of another new poetry collection called *The Colossus*—

It was by Sylvia Plath.

Kildare was in the kitchen, too, now. He was shouting at me to snap out of it and rushing to attend to our daughter's leg, the lower half now sheathed in blood, which, let's be honest, looked much worse than it really was. When Kildare took a washcloth to it, the cut was tiny and unthreatening.

There is nothing more panic-inducing than the color red, is there?

Kildare admonished me: pay attention to the things that need attending to! Believe me, Professor, I was. In that moment, red was all I saw. The review of *The Colossus* cut up my insides, yet I could not bring myself to stop reading it any more than I'd been able to look away from the review of my book.

How Sylvia's review glowed! Motherhood hadn't wicked away her vitality. Rather, she had entered a period of manic productivity, and her collection brimmed with her newest offerings.

You used to say poetry's a zero-sum game, but you are wrong, Professor Lowell. Poetry is life, and life is a contest.

From the top shelf of the hallway closet, I removed a metal lockbox. It had belonged to my father and once held his ledgers and deeds to the company, as well as a loaded revolver. At the moment, it contained the most precious object in my arsenal—evidence.

I twisted the key into the eye of the lock. Maxine had told me to burn the photographs of Ted and the Mystery Woman. I cannot tell you why I'd kept them in the box instead, except that they'd always given me a kind of strength. *Go ahead, Sylvia,* I'd think, *present your perfect life to the world*. I knew better, even if no one else did.

I'd prove it to her now.

Oh, Professor! What you must think of me, to read these words, to see my anger so plainly stated on these pages. I need you to understand why I did what I did. Sylvia had stolen the workshop from me. She'd taken the Ring from me. She'd used my grief and ripped away the mantle of the confessional movement from me.

Truly, the act of addressing the envelope, and sealing the photographs within the envelope, and sending the envelope to Sylvia purged me of my indignant mood. I'd started to write a note to include with the photos, and paused. As you have said many times, confessional poetry can't be true unless it's *all* true. Neither can a confession.

But what does one say when one is presenting another with proof of a cheating spouse? *I'm sorry? Be well?*

In the end, I balled up the note I was going to send with the photos and tossed it. Anonymity, don't you know, is also a pen name.

I went from thinking about the photographs I sent Sylvia during much of my waking hours to hardly ever thinking about them at all as months passed and publicity for my poetry collection took up more of my attention, as well it should.

Despite Frost's attempted takedown, *To the Lip* sold quite well. Readers saw through his malicious scheme. He was but a little man who could not drown me out with his spiteful words any more than he could when he tried to shut you down with heckling and fire, Professor. Satisfaction is a warm blanket. For the first time in a long while, I slept quite well.

But then the phone rang in the middle of the night. Never a good thing.

Kildare did not stir. I sat up in our bed and took the call from the nightstand myself. Half-asleep, I heard Ted Hughes breathe my name into my ear.

"Rhodes . . ."

I was too scared to say anything back to Ted at first. While I'd pushed the thought of the photos to the back of my mind, they now came rushing back to the forefront, and I immediately wondered what Ted knew and if Sylvia had confronted him with the photographs. It was then that I recognized the folly of having sent the package anonymously. If Ted saw the photos, surely he'd recognized in the images the Athenæum where he'd confronted me on the steps the night these were taken. Uncovering the culprit in this scheme of mine would have been a matter of simple deduction.

The only thing I understood for sure at this moment, however, was that, by picking up the phone tonight, I'd made a terrible mistake.

"Ted—"

"She's gone. Sylvia. She's gone."

The hour was early, and my comprehension was thick. "Gone? Where'd she go?"

"Not gone. Dead . . ."

The news left me stunned and my head, bell-rung. Sylvia was dead? But of course she wasn't dead. She was alive, and she always would be alive. But then Ted said it again.

She's dead.

She's gone.

She's taken her life.

She's dead.

The question of how, and the question of why, both diminished under the question of what her death meant. The scope of such news can take an age to reveal itself, but the knowledge that I'd killed Sylvia struck me swiftly.

Rational thoughts prevailed. True, when Sylvia and I first met, I'd said to myself, *I feel the need to kill someone or something in order to live and thrive,* but it was all in the context of poetry.

Yet the venom voice, the one that had made me a Major Voice in poetry, spoke to me louder. By sending Sylvia these photographs, I'd walked her up a mountain, led her to the lip of a cliff, and given her all the reasons to jump from it.

But that wasn't true, I told myself. I'd sent the photos hoping to derail Sylvia's life, not drive her to kill herself.

People are always changing, and yet it can take so very little to return us to the person we once were, said the venom voice. *What did I think would happen once I tipped her back into madness?*

You might suggest that my agreeing to attend the funeral was a guilt response, but you'd be wrong. I did what any good friend would do, especially her closest American friend, as Ted said I was when he invited me to the memorial. Throughout the flight across the Atlantic, I was overcome by a feeling that I was unable to place. It was only when the border agent at Heathrow Airport asked me whether I was traveling for business or for pleasure that the duality of my emotions became clear. The truth was, burying Sylvia constituted a bit of both. Was I stricken by her loss? Yes, I was. Was I happy she was gone? More than I care to admit, though admit it I do.

Attention was the last thing I wanted to attract, so I quietly slipped into the transept of St. Thomas The Apostle Church in Heptonstall. I scaled the steps to the balcony and took a seat at the far back of the upper nave. There, I found myself inhaling the dense tang of musty fabrics, tapestries, and winter coats, smells seemingly lifted directly from my father's fabric factory.

Seeking Ted, I stared over the two hundred people below and eventually spied him. He was seated by the choir in a dark jacket and listening to the vicar.

Even though I'd been staring at the casket for a while, I hadn't noticed it at first. As soon as I was aware of the coffin just behind the vicar, all I could think was that life had reduced Sylvia to this, a pine hyphen. I was witnessing history write the first line of her obituary and the final sentence of her biography.

Eventually, the tears did come, and my breath grew shallow, but for the life of me I cannot tell you if these were apparatuses of grief or of liberation. If we are honest with ourselves, aren't the two one and the same?

The vicar related a few noteworthy occurrences of Sylvia's life, though the overall effect left me unmoved. He didn't know Sylvia. Candidly, neither did anyone else who was gathered in this stone temple—not friends, not family, not devotees.

Nobody knew Sylvia the way I did.

In the narthex after the ceremony, Ted thanked me for coming all this way. He said he wanted to talk more but not here.

From the periphery, a woman swooped over to him and, without so much as a word of warning, slapped Ted with such force that the sound reverberated across the church. Ted was stunned. He just stood there, absorbing the blow. Ushers rushed to intervene, but it was too late, and the damage was already done. Ted looked burned, bewildered, and shamed.

"Murderer!" The woman's voice sizzled. "Murderer! Murderer!"

The black cabs of London must come off an assembly line, replete with the same shoe-leather smell and the same cabbies, with their unnerving disregard for speed limits. The day after the funeral, my driver pulled over and let me out by a small park on Primrose Hill. Walking past storefronts on Fitzroy Road, I passed two women bundled in heavy coats and pushing strollers. A pack of dogs took interest in me. The dog walker passed without noticing.

Ted was drawing me into a confrontation. He knew I'd shot and sent the photos to Sylvia, that I'd set off this chain of events. The question for me was, was Ted dangerous? Any supposition about my role in Sylvia's death, intended or otherwise, might turn a man who was already capable of fucking a woman in the stacks of a library into a man capable of tapping far more animalistic, violent urges.

The first thing I noticed when Ted let me into the apartment in Chalcot Square was a lack of Ted's presence within it. There was no fancy pipe collection or pictures of Ted and Sylvia posing with famous writers and actors as there had been at their old place. The furniture was threadbare, the accoutrements throughout the flat quite basic. There was a small desk by a fireplace and a table with a simple sewing machine on it. To the side was a tiny room with a rocking chair and a rocking horse and a rocking crib inset with sunflowers on the foot-board. Beside the crib was a small cot. This was not merely a child's room, I saw, but a room for *children*. By dying, Sylvia had left two babes without a mother. This realization only added to an ever-deepening sense of absence I was getting from the home. What had happened here?

Ted had come to the door with his sleeves rolled to his elbows, his collar unbuttoned, his hair brushed forward and messy. There was a tense, hushed quality about him as he led me through the living room. He had me step over and around an expanding grid made up of two dozen piles of paper, journals, and books, a crude sorting system Ted was partway through devising. "Sivvy didn't throw away a scrap."

I settled into a chair in the kitchen and Ted brought me a cup of tea. His voice had no bite, only a subtle tremble beneath it. He moved a chair and sat across from me. When he raised his head and looked at me, he said rather plainly, "I don't know what rumors you've heard, but I'm sure there's a hint of truth to all of them."

I wanted to know more than a hint of truth, though. I'd come all this way to hear the *whole* truth about what had happened. Ted looked at me as though to say, *You already know the whole truth. Say it,* he dared me, so I did. "You were having an affair."

"Several."

I saw no shame in Ted as he revealed this, only a man fighting with his pride. What had begun as hidden liaisons had become more overt, and Sylvia had caught wise, because poets are detectives. *My Invisible Hand left a trail of evidence for Sylvia to follow,* intoned my venom voice. Sylvia had since left Ted behind, along with the richness of grand and expansive living, and brought the children here to these confined quarters with thumping radiators, and the smell of damp air, and thin wood floors, and pipes that thudded with the bass and meter of a miserable heartbeat.

"I invited you here to ask you a question."

I turned away from Ted, eying instead the display of papers along the ground in the next room, the crude sorting system of Sylvia's life in leaflet and notebooks. A life is messy, a death is even messier. I suddenly didn't want to hear Ted say what I'd come here to confirm. I'd taken and sent the photos, showing Sylvia that the world as she knew it was a duplicitous one. No matter who you are, when the truth is staring you down like that, there's only one thing left to do. Strike a match and light your world on fire.

"You and I, Rhodes, we've both been called the poets of our generation. We understand people better than they understand themselves. But in this competition of ours, there was always one thing you did better than I ever could. You understood Sylvia."

All too well, said the venom voice. If I tried in that moment, I could almost imagine Sylvia in this space of wood-tone countertops, cupboards, and shelves. In fact, I bet you can see her now, too, Professor, the old girl edging closer to the nadir of her grief. You can see her opening the gas supply with the twist of a black knob. You can see her taking in the poison air with slow inhalations, closing her eyes as she drifts to sleep with her cheek on the cool rack of the oven.

I wondered, had she gone through with it while the two children were in the home? Yes, she must have, just as I had tried to do years earlier when I'd filled a room of my own with carbon monoxide in my most desperate hour. Only, where I'd failed, Sylvia had succeeded.

"You and she were so similar that I believe you could climb into her head and tell me what she was thinking at the very end," Ted said.

I looked at him and made a clumsy attempt at a smile. "I'm sorry about what happened at the funeral yesterday. I really am. You didn't deserve that."

"Did Sylvia blame me?" His color changed. His eyes flickered. "Am I a murderer?"

In that moment, dear Professor, I felt a great weight lift, for three things became perfectly clear. The first was that the confrontation I'd anticipated with Ted was never going to happen; Sylvia had not shown Ted the photos I'd sent her. Just as plainly as I saw her final moments play out in this kitchen, I now saw Sylvia receiving my envelope from the mailbox, discovering what was inside the envelope, and keeping its contents to herself as she faced impossible choices. Given the option between staying with Ted and living a lie, or leaving Ted and forging out on her own, Sylvia had chosen to leave.

The second was that Ted believed he, and he alone, had led Sylvia to her breaking point. As long as he believed it, and everyone else did as well, then for all intents and purposes I was not culpable for Sylvia's death. In fact, from a certain rational point of view, Ted really was entirely to blame. Had he not perpetrated the act of shattering Sylvia's trust?

The third revelation I had was that I, like Sylvia, now had a choice to make.

I wish I could tell you that I eased Ted's burden and revealed my part in this sad series of events to him, or that I gave Ted what he was looking for and told him no, he didn't murder Sylvia, and that there was a fine line between what was possible and what was inevitable. But the truth is, I did not for even a moment consider saying any of this to him. Absolving Ted was not my place, you understand. And if Ted's belief in his lone culpability absolved all others' in his eyes, so be it. Instead, I touched Ted's hand as it lay on the kitchen table between us, and I chose to lie. For what is the *whole* truth, really?

"I don't know what she was thinking, Ted. I honestly don't."

I left Ted cleaning up from our tea in the kitchen and gathered my coat and hat from the sofa in the living room. I felt bad for the old boy. He'd invited me over so that I might bring him reassurance. As for me,

I'd come for absolution. I was leaving the flat with what I'd come for, and also something more . . .

As I looked around me, I found myself standing in Sylvia's living room among stacks of her poems that Ted had organized across the hardwood floor. I might as well have been a ship floating atop an ocean of Sylvia's past. The current was towing me into my inevitable future.

Later, at my hotel, I finished packing for my return home. As I folded my dresses, sweaters, and hats, I couldn't help but feel I was carrying home more than I came with. *Opportunity,* sang the venom voice.

An hour into the international flight that night, as the passengers around me settled in, I emptied my pocketbook. Having gathered what pages I could as quickly as I did from the floor of Sylvia's flat, with little time to discern poetry from prose, finished work from the work in progress, only now, safely over the ocean, I got my first look at what I'd seized. Would Ted, a grieving man, really even notice a few items missing? In the low, languid light of the cabin, I was looking at a stack of pages and three spiral notebooks.

Inspiration, whispered the venom voice.

21

Ruth, 1962–1963

APRIL 3—

What does it mean when a patient you haven't heard from in nearly a decade takes up her correspondence with you again? It is never promising. And yet, when Miss Plath's letter arrived last month at my home, I was happy to hear from her. She has been in my thoughts over the years.

She moved to England with her husband, she writes. (Yes, she is married!) Her husband is a kind, creative man and a poet of some renown, she reports, a ruthless force that draws from her a purity of winsomeness and passion like a well. She adores his warmth, his big mess of arms and hair, his sharp wit, his stories, his honesty, his groundedness, and how he helps direct her in her poetry. Moreover, he is a loving father. (Yes, Sylvia is a mother!) I am pleased by this news, and encouraged to learn that she came into marriage and family life on her own terms without abandoning the intellectual self. Where the institution of McLean Hospital reignited her creative energy, she had long fretted that the institution of marriage would do the opposite. Instead, she has achieved a fuller expression in art, she says. That she is married suggests an evolution in her thinking, and that she is a mother, a reconceptualization of what it means to search for a life of emotional fulfillment.

Miss Plath asked after me. She wanted to know if I am married, if I have a family, and if I am well. As psychiatrists, what do we divulge and what do we keep to ourselves to preserve the sanctity of a pure therapeutic dynamic? Was I to reveal that I am not married and no closer to desiring a family than relinquishing the memory of the family I lost? Was I to tell her that I am ashamed of how she last saw me, a broken-down woman? Remaining vague but honest, I told Miss Plath in my reply that the decade has seen me teaching as an adjunct professor in various college classrooms, and that I have maintained a private practice in the house I purchased some years ago, which has kept me engaged.

Miss Plath's next letter included several new poems, and an admonishment for my having never seen her read in public. "I hope someday you will," she wrote.

I'd never told her how, one evening in the spring of 1955, I was leaving the Grover Cronin store with a pair of new shoes when I passed an awning. Through a mic system, jacked into a series of poorly amplified speakers, I heard a singular voice reciting verse. The voice was sincere and came from a maestro of melodic cadence. Through the window of the darkened, crowded club I saw Miss Plath on a tall stage. She'd dyed her hair platinum blonde. If I hadn't recognized her voice, I might have kept walking and missed her entirely.

She concluded this letter with a simple request, that I write back again soon, and often. I have promised myself that, whenever I hear her voice, on some stage or by letter, I will not walk away without acknowledging her again.

MAY 10—

Why is it we always say that someone sounds good in a correspondence? Maybe it's because when we read a letter, we assign a voice to inanimate sentences. Subtext is everything, but we only really *hear* when we *listen*.

Another letter, with another poem, has arrived from Miss Plath, this one titled "The Rabbit Catcher." It is a short poem concerning a walk through a hollow, and the discovery of animal snares on the ground. The language she's chosen here is full of hopelessness. Wind-blown hair that gags her. A silencing of her voice. Plants surrounding her, both beautiful and dangerous. Yet the phrase that's most ensnared my attention like one of those traps is a line that closes the piece, the one in which she writes of a certain constriction that is killing her.

I am neither poet, critic, nor literary scholar, but these words are signals. Buried in them are traces of loneliness and dread.

Let me be perfectly clear, I have now come to believe that Miss Plath has, with her letters, plotted points of a map designed to draw my attention to the delight of her life, creating for its intended reader a scene of emotional fulfillment. Despite the bluster and buoyancy, I have grown accomplished at deciphering the Plath code. Although she puts on a good face, I fear for her state of mind, for I have come to believe Miss Plath is purely keeping up appearances for my benefit. While she presents me with a picture of a happy, full-bodied life, there is more to these correspondences than she lets on.

Indeed, I sense an undercurrent of that passive, anguished, and gloomy soul.

JULY 7

I regret to report that my conjectures about Miss Plath's mental state were correct. All has not been well.

Her husband has left her. Though she offers few details on the dissolution of the marriage, she admits to a depression that alternates with a manic, boundless fervor. Now each letter to me is full of mourning and melancholia. The impracticality of her life hangs all over her. Desperately lonely, she worries about money and putting food on the table. She is not living, she writes, but simply enduring, and loses comprehension in the difference between night and day. I am afraid for her well-being. In the aerograms that have gathered on my desk, she informs me that her writing has begun to suffer under renewed insecurity. Barricades stand between her and the twenty poems roosting in her mind. A sanctimonious self-doubt has settled within her. It tells her that her work is flat, far from vital, and lacking surprise. She is terrible. She is a failure. The world has cut its strings of her. She is unseen and put away.

And here, in this last letter, she ends with a plea. Will I take her on as a patient again?

"At Codman Manor, you freed the big black bird within my chest. You gave me permission to acknowledge it and let it go. You're like a shot of brandy, a sniff of cocaine that hits me where I live, and I am alive. You are better than shock treatment." Though I still maintain a private therapeutic practice, the length and depth of an ocean, two continents, three thousand miles, and a decade without contact hinders my ability to reach her on any meaningful level. Still, days pass, and I imagine the worst for her. I listen to her in her letters, and I hear a woman driven to the end of her tether.

In psychiatry, reality quickly squashes the belief that we can help everybody. On account of Superintendent Frisch, I learned this fact long ago. The goal, to open that window of reprieve from madness and keep it this way for as long as possible, is a noble but endless fight. "Helpless but hopeful" becomes the mantra. The first time I felt this was with my daughter. Powerless to heal her, my muscles turned to paper, my bones to ash. My voice became a hush.

I must think on her request.

SEPTEMBER 25—

Finally, after weeks of back-and-forth letter writing (for Miss Plath still has not connected a phone to her new London flat), a ray of hope for my patient.

She writes me of a dream she's recently had. She was back in Codman Manor and standing in the first-floor parlor room, where the women from group used to meet in a little circle of chairs. Only, the chairs around her were empty, and the room was on fire. The rug was burning at her shoes. Soon, the curtains were on fire, too, and the wall paintings bubbled in the heat, and flames licked the ceiling.

Occasionally these days, she will ruminate on her time in the haven of Codman Manor, she writes. She does not think about it often, and when she does there is not a lot to recall, only that it was like being in a dream. Yet she is writing about it now, as she was recently reminded of how I told her, long ago, to put down what she sees in front of her so that others will understand. For years, this task has rested on her mind like a fine mist clinging to the cold ground. So she keeps reporting, chronicling as though her memory is testimony. She has decided she will not let any detail she sees or perceives go to waste.

She tells me she is producing something new and worthy of my original charge: A novel. "Yes, a novel (!), which, as I sit in my borrowed study, is one-sixth completed, about fifty pages. I was seized by fear, and then the dikes broke. I saw how it should be done. I write about what I see before me, and the flow of my story takes me beyond this moment."

OCTOBER 20

Massachusetts looks wrong in the heat of second summer days. From my front porch, I watch people in their short sleeves and sundresses and summer hats with their dogs on leashes as they walk the sidewalks of Napoleon Street.

The boulevard's natural state is slick with coal-smudged snow piled on its brick curbs and grit that rain never fully washes away. Mercifully, the heat breaks with an afternoon thunderstorm. Silent flashes of lightning blazed across the deep silver-on-silver sky. The air in South Boston smells of the richness of a downpour.

Another letter from Miss Plath has arrived.

Her mood seems to have grown balanced. She reports that she has never felt so peaceful as she does writing seven hours a day, and finds fulfillment in reading Roethke's poems and stories by Jean Stafford and Eudora Welty. She can see that her writing is coming to fruition after years of work and study, as she continues to eschew the pain of keeping an orderly routine and the home clean, the near-impossible blockade of creativity, and that wariness that sent her away to Codman Manor in the first place. All the while, she has tried to infuse her new work with my stark demand for truth. She progresses satisfactorily with the novel, having worked through a rough version of chapters five through eight, and completed a total of a hundred and five pages. She has also outlined chapters nine through twelve and projected in detail the next lap of the book. A small press has agreed to distribute the novel, though she doubts *The Bell Jar* will ever make it across the Atlantic.

"You are beyond any doubt my sole confessor, Dr. Barnhouse. It is uncommon and therefore exceptional that I go into the process of my work in detail. Professor Lowell has said many times that one's work must be drawn by an Invisible Hand. With this novel, I have come to understand why. People ask, is there anything that I will not show of myself through my work? I am, as they say, an open book . . . or so I believed. But to show the process—the wrong turns in language, the wreckage of ideas I've abandoned along the way—I believe is to show *too much* of me. Consider for a minute, if my readers only knew that the poems I wrote under your care were created while I was in the throes of lunacy, they would focus on the madwoman behind the pen and think, *What a poor and sad creature; let us pity her!* They would not take seriously the poem itself. I fear that if I put my name on this book, people will not see the book for what it is. They will only see the Sylvia that you saved."

FEBRUARY 28—

Anticipating the arrival of the novel in the mail, instead I've received awful news. Like a letter without ink, I have no words for what's transpired.

Rain still falls in South Boston. It sounds like stones dropping from the sky. The air has chilled, and soon the rain will turn to somersaulting snow. Struggling to comprehend what I've learned, I have revisited Miss Plath's final letters to me. I pore through them, line by line, looking for clues. In them, her voice is alive. I see her dancing on the head of a pin.

But she has fallen off of it. I am crushed.

Only a few book reviews of Miss Plath's novel, apparently written under the surreptitious moniker of Victoria Lucas, have appeared since its limited publication in England. I've had each review pulled and earmarked for me by the personnel of the public library. As the librarian handed me the periodicals, I was most pleased to find that Sylvia had made her way into the *New York Times*, under her own name no less. When I came to the page, however, I saw I wasn't reading a book review at all, but an obituary.

Phrases leapt out from the article. They appeared to me without order and detached from logic. On the morning of February 11, a Monday, the poet Sylvia Plath was found in her flat, lying on the floor of the kitchen, unresponsive, and cold to the touch, the room filled with gas.

I have not left this house in days. I exist as an object among objects in here. When people are torn from us, all we have left are objects, the remains of what we have lost and given up.

For the first time in many years, I found myself searching for an object I had fought hard to lose.

Opening a bureau, I drew out a small brown bottle. At one time, this was the only way to silence the memories, to silence the ghosts. The law of parsimony was showing me the simplest solution, the right solution, to end the grief, an emotion impervious to negotiation.

It can take so little to return us to the person we once were. I rubbed the bottle under my thumb. Drawing two milliliters of an opium tincture into a glass dropper, I dangled it above my head like a star.

Then I squeezed the dropper into the bathtub, and turned the bottle upside down, where all its contents, like the life force of Miss Plath, drained away.

EIGHTH STANZA

The Notebooks

Poetry is a competition between logic and sound,
a war in which meaning and the dream state face off against one another.
For one to win, it must snuff out the other.

—Boston Rhodes, final letter to Robert Lowell, 1963

22

Estee, 2019

A concealed door, flush to the wall behind the front podium, opens. Junior curators–turned–stagehands cloaked in dark suits bring out the glass pedestal showcase, an ark containing the three Plath notebooks. The music in the room again rises. The stage lights are boosted. Scarlett grips the edge of the plexiglass podium. She says the bidding opens at three hundred thousand dollars and triggers a flurry of numbered panels rising like flamingo heads.

The bids come in fast. From his position, seated nearly dead center in the audience, Nicolas counters as many bids as he can. With each, a tiny red balloon of hope for him rises within my chest. When the offer jumps to seven hundred thousand dollars, and Nicolas raises it by another ten thousand, I question how much higher he can possibly go. *The university's budget can only be so large,* I think, unless Nicolas is not using the university's money, but his own.

I glance at my watch. It is ten thirty in the morning. If the auction ends soon, Nicolas will have a fighting chance. Fifteen minutes later, however, the momentum of the auction renders wrong all predictions of a swift sale. Scarlett, possessed by the spirit of a revival preacher, stirs the room and keeps the auction alive. To the side of her riser, the phone bank ignites with activity. A digital readout above it keeps track of the current offering, now at a million one. Nicolas can no longer afford to make another bid, though I find myself willing him to. I want him to have the notebooks. He deserves them as much as, if not more than, anyone.

Thanks to a man with a hair bun, the bid lands at a million five. The air grows warm and tense. For thirty seconds, the auction stalls. I see Elton's shoes tapping the floor, and I see Jay Jay struggling to open his mandarin collar.

At the last second, a numbered paddle rises, and the bidding once again staggers forward, picks up speed, transforms the sales floor of St. Ambrose into something far more unfamiliar than it's already become for me.

Forty minutes in, bidders are still facing off and thwarting one another. At one time employing practiced mechanisms of strategy, they now come after the Plath notebooks anxious and deranged. If intent had talons, this room would be pulling the notebooks apart with motions, repeated pleas, incoherent propositions.

A woman in a purple structured hat announces to Scarlett, "Two-point-five million."

A sharply dressed man with thick silvery hair and a handlebar mustache replies with a counteroffer. "Two-six."

The woman in the structured hat counters. "Two-seven."

The man ups the bid by another fifty thousand dollars.

Glaring at the man, the woman in the structured hat rises to her feet and shouts, "Two-million-nine!"

Like a plunging spear, a third voice comes between the two battling factions. It belongs to a younger man in a crimson Harvard hoodie. He offers three million dollars.

Elton has stopped tapping his foot. Jay Jay remains perfectly motionless, as though a floor of ice is cracking beneath his chair, and any sudden move might send him plunging into the cold, dark depths.

Quimby stops pacing at the back of the sales floor, his fingers kneading his forehead.

Sold.

Scarlett's tiny hammer smacks the podium. The entire building seems to tilt forty-five degrees under the force of its blow.

In the lobby after the auction, I tell Nicolas I'm sorry, that I really wanted him to be the successful bidder today. I knew the final bid was going to be large, but nobody imagined reaching three million dollars.

"You know what's truly crazy?" he says. "That someone spent three million on notebooks Sylvia *never* wanted people to see. Read her letters, her journals. She makes her thoughts abundantly clear. Sylvia wanted the process of her writing to be invisible. No one was supposed to witness her hand." Before he leaves St. Ambrose, Nicolas offers me a sad smile, a tacit acknowledgment of defeat. "Goodbye, Estee."

"So, the notebooks wound up in some random attic, and nobody knows how they got there?" the Harvard-hoodied man asks me when I return to the sales floor.

"We've looked into the matter extensively. The provenance of the items remains a mystery, though we suspect they originated among Sylvia Plath's personal items, enumerated just prior to her death."

"They're stolen?"

"Possibly, but our Department of Restitution has found no evidence of a prior claim."

There is no point in me saying my mother knew Sylvia Plath, or that my mother took the notebooks from her flat, or that my mother believed she'd murdered her. My mother's letter to Robert Lowell, available in his papers and read by scholars, has been deemed a confession from an unstable mind. It is inadmissible, valueless, doubtful, and has no bearing on this man's new prize.

"Rest assured, if it were ever to come to light that the items were stolen, St. Ambrose is obliged to refund the entire amount you paid."

The Harvard-hoodied man does not seem too concerned over matters of insurance at the moment, though. He approaches the glass case on the small riser. "Sounds like they've seen a lot." He places his hands on two corners and admires the notebooks inside of it. "No more attics for you three."

Nicolas might be right, that Sylvia never intended for anyone to see this nascent version of her book, but legacy dictates value, not the artist. Today's successful bidder has offered millions for the Plath notebooks, and he will give them a safe home and shower them with appreciation and respect.

Around us, St. Ambrose has adopted a celebratory mood. Scarlett pulls the Harvard-hoodied man in for publicity photos beside the glass pedestal showcase. Around me hands are shaking hands. More photos are snapped. Generally, master curators shy away from such ceremony, but after the sales floor clears, an exhibition of champagne flutes appears in my honor. There is a toast to my years at the auction house and a lifetime's dedication to the field of antiquities. The room asks me to say a few words, which I do. Afterward, a group of junior curators surrounds me. Unsure whether to offer me their sympathies or their congratulations, they ask me where I'm going next and what I'll be doing now that I won't be here. What marvelous questions. One's life beyond retirement is a kind of burial of a life that once was. We become memory, antiquity, legacy.

I watch two aides lift the glass pedestal showcase and carry it away, bound once again for the safe holdings room.

"How do we get our money?" Jay Jay asks me. It's a relatively simple process of transferring money into an escrow account and signing paperwork, I say. In twenty-four hours, the Dyce brothers will have their three million dollars.

Elton says no one told him they'd have to wait.

As the role of a master curator is to please and to appease, I return to my office to expedite the transfer of sale. In preparation for my retirement, I've taken down books from the shelves, bound small pieces of pottery in bubble wrap, unhooked framed photographs and the mounted parchments from the walls. Over the next few days, I will place the remainder of my files in cartons, these relics and remnants from auctions past. As good as I am about cataloging and organizing objects, I'm terrible at packing them. And as much as I relish the idea of discovering what's inside boxes, I cannot stand placing things in them. Each one is a coffin, emblematic of little deaths.

I put the banking paperwork aside and take the old Corona typewriter with the dented frame off of the bookshelf. I never use the typewriter anymore. For years, it has rested between rows of bound texts, the machine a once-functioning tool rendered to trinket status and a reminder to me of where I've come from. The keys are loose. The ribbon is dry. The heavy steel frame containing hundreds of moving parts is cool and still and silent. Once, my mother used the typewriter to produce her letter to Robert Lowell. We return to the places where we begin.

With two fingers, I slowly toggle between two keys. The hammers rise and fall as Quimby pokes his head in my doorway with the day's final participant count: four hundred and twenty-five bidders, St. Ambrose's largest. Of course, we blew way past the projected sales model. "Less our seven percent," he adds.

"You're angry it's not ten."

"You did what you needed to do. It was the right decision. There's not an outlet in the country that won't be talking about this sale tomorrow. Plath's put St. Ambrose back in play."

"You're not getting sentimental."

"Just appreciative."

I smile. If twenty-two years of enduring officious prickliness from this malcontent has occasioned a rare show of admiration, it will have almost been worth it.

From the security feed on my open laptop, I observe Quimby as he walks away from my office down the corridor. The cameras track him to the sales floor, where the party is still going on, and the caterers are serving my cake and refilling people's glasses with champagne. What better illustration of one's usefulness is there than watching a retirement party in your honor go on without you?

Before leaving St. Ambrose for the day, I take the elevator downstairs to visit the Plath notebooks one last time.

In the safe holdings room, Sylvia Plath's manuscript rests in its glass sarcophagus. *The Bell Jar* has no awareness that it has once again changed hands. Its legacy continues, even if my own has a sell-by date. Such is the existentialism of objects.

Using a small key from my pocket, I open the lock to the pedestal showcase. My fingers trace the initials on the green cover—V. L., Victoria Lucas—just as my mother's might have done decades ago. All objects carry a piece of those who have ever possessed them. In the end, we are really auctioning a fragment of ourselves. Sylvia Plath, Boston Rhodes, and me: we are each part of the kaleidoscope.

Lifting the green-covered notebook, I turn to the first page. Sylvia's handwriting is faint. I touch a line of print—

Suddenly, the page cracks. A web of fissures appears in the paper under the pressure of my index finger.

Calmly, I close the notebook and I slide it into my purse.

I feel the eyes of the twin ceiling-mounted security cameras on me. As an operative of St. Ambrose Auction House, I can get around the rule forbidding personal bags in the safe holdings room, and I can access the secured archive space, with its hundred million possible combinations, by punching in a code. The one thing operatives cannot do easily, however, is escape the closed-circuit surveillance system that tracks and records personnel coming and going from all areas of the building. Surveillance is monitored off-site, and it's not like there's a circuit breaker I can remove. But master curators, we are safe builders. We are vulnerability assessors.

And we also know quite a bit about archives.

I've spent my life organizing and digging through archives of antiquities. This afternoon following the auction, I created a new archive of old surveillance footage of all the corridors, rooms, and vaults of St. Ambrose. Scarlett can rule her online sales domain, but let's see her try and reset the security account to have full run of the system's hard drives, view and intercept the closed-circuit camera live feed, and push prerecorded video to the network, all from her laptop, as I have done. At this moment, the surveillance system is spewing ten minutes of my repurposed footage, set on a loop, to the off-site recording bank.

With the cameras blind to the present, my movements are concealed as I bend and work the black-covered notebook into my purse beside the green-covered notebook. The third notebook barely fits in my purse at all. I have to roll the sides using both hands and then push it into place, and when I do, its cover tears completely off of the spiral binding. The bag strains as I pull the its clasp shut.

In the lobby, the caterers are beginning to remove used-up food trays and disassemble the tables. Scarlett is taking selfies with her arm around the shoulders of the EDM musician, whom she'll probably go home with tonight. My pulse renders a thudding in my head so soft and distant that my heart might be running away from my body.

Elton and Jay Jay Dyce are standing on the sidewalk, smoking cigarettes out in the cold. I hug my purse close as Elton gets the door of my town car for me.

I tell the driver to take the long way.

As we pull away from St. Ambrose, I open my laptop and with a simple command shut down the prerecorded security feed, ending the loop.

Around me, the city becomes the ancillary glow of Five Guys,

Starbucks, and Burger King signs, the lights of Fenway Park in the distance, and the thrum of traffic on the 93. Gas stations and ATMs and all the modern glass buildings exist within a milieu of relics. Tear down a wall in Boston and you'll find nails cut from English slitting mills. The credit union? That's the location where Paul Revere slept. The Chinese takeout? It's where Samuel Adams coordinated the resistance against the British. The city is a vitrine filled with antiquities, a museum of human suppression and past revolutions. The one thing each exhibit has in common is an ancient voice that all objects secretly possess. Tonight, I hear Sylvia's. She tells me to keep going, that what I'm looking for, and what I've always looked for, isn't far now.

23

Boston Rhodes, 1963

The Ring gathered to honor Sylvia's life with toasts and readings in the retreat of our splendid hotel bar grotto. I knew something had changed because the acrimony that I'd held on to was finally gone. I felt a calmness that I imagine follows all momentous armistices.

That night, I stood and recited a new poem I'd written Sylvia for this occasion. The sonnet invoked imagery of London buried in winter and Sylvia, our duchess, crawling into a stone place, called there by a beat that rang in her ears like an old song. The music doubled as an echo of Death.

Obviously, this was not the first time Sylvia had inspired me to write. Despite what you might think, I did not take Sylvia's memos and notebooks with the intent of passing the material in them off as my own. I desired her work for a far more essential reason. The greatest rivalries in history motivated their players to build ever more spectacular toils. Without the enmity of Michelangelo to spur him, would Leonardo have created his most striking Florentine frescoes? My rival was no more, and a part of me missed the very thing that had kept me sharp. I needed Sylvia's words to maintain my focus and production.

You spoke next, and with your exaltations you revealed just how greatly you needed Sylvia's words, too.

"Most of all, I will miss her voice, her voice, her voice—igneous and genuine. With each syllable Sylvia scripted, she became herself. Every word was a signature. She was hardly a person at all, or a woman, and certainly not another poetess, but one of the super-real, hypnotic, great classical heroines. A racehorse, galloping relentlessly with risked, outstretched neck, death hurdle after death hurdle topped."

At Sam's turn, he said that Sylvia was a poet with virtuoso grace and style.

Maxine said Sylvia was the strongest of the most infirm prophets.

The venom voice in my head, by far the loudest voice that night, said that I knew that by sending the photos, I was bringing harm to Sylvia. I wanted harm to come to her. I let harm come to her. Regardless of what Ted Hughes believed, I killed her.

No, amended the venom voice, *I beat her.*

"Out of the ash, I rise with my red hair," Sylvia once wrote. Death was just another rebirth. And for me, Sylvia's death ushered in my own reawakening.

I produced dozens of new pieces, among them "The Lust of the Despised," "Shapes in the Dark," and "Love Is Where I Mourne." In your parlance, like Sylvia, I was becoming myself. Success lifted my moods, and I bathed in a glow of newly discovered self-assurance. Where at one time I saw my life as an ever-narrowing corridor that would have had me crawling on my hands and knees, now I saw my life as an ever-expanding vista.

This vision culminated in the spring when I opened my mailbox. The announcement inside arrived on letterhead of the Harvard women's college.

That I had won the Radcliffe literary prize was a thrill. I mean, Maxine had tried to win the prize for years, and Sylvia was never even nominated!

The award presentation was a magnificent event held in a Cambridge theater auditorium. In her remarks, the dean of the college said that I was already an accomplished poet, but with this award I was primed to be a lasting one.

Tearfully, from where I sat on the wide stage, I looked into the audience, and there you were, seated in the front row. Afterward, you put your hands on my shoulders. Do you remember what you said to me? I do. Your words are seared into the limestone of my memory. "I'm proud." How that simple verse mended every broken piece of me. The moment I had been waiting for all my life did not come from my father. It came from you.

With history sealing my status among its most revered contemporary poets, from time to time I thought about Sylvia and how she'd pushed me to be a better writer and a better woman—my own. I was finally positioned to surpass Sylvia's legacy and arrive at my own glimmering Gettysburg when Sylvia struck back from the grave.

Following a poetry reading from my collection before a hearty audience at Sanders Theatre, a woman in line for an autograph asked if I agreed with the recent criticism concerning me and Sylvia Plath. I admitted I was aware of no such criticism. "You know," said the woman, "that one of her poems is strikingly similar to one of yours."

The accusation left me staggered. Later, unearthing the source of such distasteful rumors wasn't difficult. My old friend M. L. Rosenthal, again writing for the *Saturday Review*, had conducted a side-by-side analysis of two poems, "The Competitor" by Boston Rhodes and Sylvia Plath's "The Rival," a lesser-known work she'd published in a minor literary journal some years earlier. Rosenthal highlighted analogous words, parallel structures, and imagery that was, he wrote, too close to be mere coincidence. This wasn't all that surprising, he argued, as Sylvia Plath and Boston Rhodes were cut from the same confessional cloth.

"It is not a stretch to imagine that these two contemporaries, who for a time were both members of an elite workshop under Robert Lowell, relied on each other for creative stimulation."

Still, the implication was damning. Rosenthal had all but called one of us a thief. With keen observation, his story unwound the path of "The Competitor." In uncanny detail, he chronicled the evening Kildare and I visited Sylvia and Ted's home for dinner, down to the food Sylvia served and the seating arrangements, and how, between the main course and dessert, I slipped away and discovered "The Rival" on Sylvia's workroom desk. Considering that only four people were present that night, and that one of the witnesses was currently deceased, Rosenthal's source was suspect. Kildare would never entertain the notion that I was a thief, let alone confirm details to a newsman whose goal was to paint me as such. That only left Ted . . .

Ted, who'd discovered pages and pages of work belonging to his late wife missing from her flat after her funeral.

Oh, prejudiced universe! For the second time, my face appeared on the cover of a magazine accompanying an article by M. L. Rosenthal, and comparing me with Sylvia Plath. Only this time, the magazine might as well have placed an asterisk by my chin.

**Thief!*

In spite of everything, the knowledge that a poet's body of work is so much more than a single poem, or a lone controversy, brought me comfort. I took stock in my fortunes of late. I was receiving invitations to join literary retreats and encouragement from my publisher, who was awaiting selections for my second collection of poetry. I told myself that the only way to move forward from this was to keep writing.

With the Radcliffe literary prize money, in the amount of five hundred dollars, I converted the loft above the detached garage into a proper private study. No longer relegated to working from the dining room table, I now had a real desk, my own shelves, a cabinet, a new transistor radio, and as many ashtrays as I wanted to fill. You'd have thought I was retreating from the world, hiding up in the loft for those hours-long stretches and coming down for briefer and briefer periods.

On my way back into the house one late afternoon, I saw an unfamiliar blue Impala sitting in the drive. I walked the porch steps as Kildare was showing out a group of men. They reminded me of movie G-men, all suited, stiff, and grim, and for a moment I thought maybe we were in trouble. Kildare waited at the screen door until they had driven away, and when I asked him who they were, because they'd looked important, he said slowly, dryly, "Standard Textile is pretty damn important."

I'd heard of Standard Textile before. Back when my father was still alive and Kildare was pounding on doors to land sales with Apparel Center and Sears, Roebuck and Company, Kildare lamented over Emperor Fine Fabrics' most accomplished competitor. Standard Textile had outsold and outmaneuvered Kildare at every turn.

"Isn't that rich," I crowed. With my father gone, Standard Textile was coming to Kildare for a piece of the business.

Kildare fixed himself a bourbon in a highball glass. "Not quite."

My husband had always been secretive about matters of my father's company, and though I didn't bother him with questions about his work, just as the magazines said, one would have been oblivious not to notice that the job was weighing on him.

"Your father died driving back from Norristown. Did you know what he was doing there?"

I knew even less about my father's business than my husband's. Kildare's eyes tightened. He was searching; he didn't believe me.

"The things you keep from me . . ."

He sat on the sofa, crossed his legs, and spilled his bourbon a little in the process. All of a sudden, I wanted nothing more than to staunch his arrogance.

"Your father was soliciting Standard Textile for a hundred thousand dollars in capital and business contacts in exchange for making them a silent partner," he said.

I told Kildare he didn't know what he was talking about.

"He lied and sold the company out from under us. We're broke, Agatha, and all you care about is fucking other men and . . . your *scribbling* . . ."

I seethed. "Take that back."

"Your father stole from his own flesh and blood."

I started laughing at Kildare. I was tearing up and cackling such that I couldn't bring myself to stop. He just stared at me, defenseless and confused.

"It's just," I said, "you really are a dupe."

"And you're selfish."

Our daughter was creeping downstairs, drawn by the arguing, and I was glad because I wanted her to finally see—I wanted her to remember—the fool that her father was. Her hands were at her ears. She was crying, and I was shouting, and the ice cubes in Kildare's glass clinked as he tilted the last of his bourbon into his mouth.

I left the house, slamming the screen door behind me. When I returned to the living room a few minutes later, I was holding my typewriter in both hands. Raising the Corona above my head, I was reminded how deceptively heavy this hunk of metal was.

Kildare's eyes met mine. I hurled the machine at him. The sound of our daughter's strident scream snapped Kildare from his trance just in time to see the typewriter careening toward his cranium, and he vaulted out of its way. The typewriter crashed into the wall, leaving an indentation with hundreds of little fractures around it. The margin bell rang out in a perfect E note.

What had I done?

For a long while, the typewriter lay there all dinged up and in pieces on the living room rug like a body left over from a crime scene. Without this machine, I was the one broken. My anger at Kildare turned into desperation. I needed to fix the Corona. Without it, I was missing my own fingers, my tongue, my ears. Without it, my roiling inner sea had nowhere to go but rise within me until I could no longer take it. I swept the levers, the ribbon spool, and key tops into a dustpan. What was left, I brought to a repair shop on Massachusetts Avenue that replaced the broken parts with shiny new parts.

When I picked it up the next week, the husband from the husband-and-wife couple who ran the store wanted to know what had happened to the typewriter, if it had fallen out of the back of a moving truck. That's exactly what happened, I said. Then the husband from the husband-and-wife couple apologized because, even with all of his tools and experience, he wasn't able to pull the large dent from the corner of the frame, which was fine by me. Why should the typewriter look any better than I felt?

On my way home, I stopped to look in the window of the Harvard Book Store, pausing there to admire a display copy of *To the Lip*. In the reflection, a picture of me came into view. My hair was windblown. My skin was wan. Dark circles cradled my lashes. *Dire,* I thought.

Beside the lone copy of my collection was a display for a new book. Squinting, I took a step closer to the window and nearly dropped the typewriter.

"It's not possible."

The typewriter awkward in my arms, I stumbled into the bookshop. Snapping up a copy of the novel from its display, I slapped it on the checkout counter and demanded the seller tell me how the store had come by it. The woman at the register was unsurprised that I hadn't heard of *The Bell Jar* before. An obscure novel, published overseas by a little-known writer called Victoria Lucas who'd recently died, no less, few had read the novel, let alone known of it. But then the oddest thing happened, said the bookseller. A monumental revelation came to light. The author of *The Bell Jar* was none other than Sylvia Plath all along. With Sylvia's name on the cover, now the book was flying off the shelves.

Was I, Boston Rhodes, big enough to put aside my scruples and read the final work of my rival? No, because one does not read a threat, rather one interprets and considers it, which I did thoroughly. Make no mistake, this book, full of references both veiled and plain, was aimed at a single reader. Me.

Just as Sylvia's poem, "The Colossus," had its roots with my father, so *The Bell Jar* referenced my work. You might suggest me unreasonable, submitting that the name of a psychiatrist in the novel, a Dr. Nolan, hews awfully close, phonetically speaking, to "A Visit to Doctor No." And a psychiatric patient in the novel called Miss Norris, is similar in phoneme to my poem, "A Death in Norristown."

Still have your doubts, Professor? Still shrug at my suppositions? Then consider this: Sylvia named the protagonist of her seminal opus Esther, after *my own daughter*!

But at this moment, as I stood at the store counter demanding an explanation for the inexplicable success of a novel by a deceased writer, the only name that landed was Sylvia's. The bookseller looked at me strangely. "It's the darnedest thing," she said, "but since her death, well, I guess Plath's become iconic."

Where does a person take refuge when her professional life and her home life both come under siege? George Starbuck came to mind.

The status of our affair was ongoing. George had suggested more than once that we leave our respective spouses and get married, not that I'd say yes or that he really wanted to marry me. He worried I wasn't going to need him anymore now that my collection was published and Sylvia was gone. George knew he was a means to an end.

Only, when I retreated into bed with George this time, I discovered no sanctuary.

I'd figured that the Rosenthal scandal was going to fade, but George said that in his estimation, one of the two poems was obviously copying the other. I shot him a look. "The Rival" and "The Competitor" were two distinct poems!

George backed off, but I knew he was thinking the same thing Sam and Maxine had been thinking: that Sylvia would never have stolen a poem.

Rosenthal's story might not fade away after all, and now that George had brought it up, I couldn't let it go. "The story's not true, not a word of it." My hand was stroking his chest. "You do believe me, don't you?"

"Sure." George said that if you put a hundred people with a hundred typewriters in a room, two would eventually write the same thing. He also said that there was only one way he saw me getting past this story. "Tell your readers you're sorry."

"Sorry?" I sneered. "Sorry for what?"

"Ask them to forgive you."

But what was a plea for forgiveness if it wasn't sincere? I'd known that my standing within the Ring was fragile, and that my readers would question the truth and choose sides, yet it wasn't until George's words sank into the soil of my psyche that I began to fret; the only person whose forgiveness I worried about capturing was yours, Professor.

Surely by now, you'd seen the Rosenthal article. I asked George if he'd spoken to you, or if you'd said anything to him about the exposé. "What did the professor say about it, George? Please tell me."

But George refused to say, even after I called him a feckless coward. An ineffectual chicken shit. An impotent milksop.

I got dressed in a tantrum, flinging George's clothes as I tore through the hotel room for my things. As I stormed out of the suite, I shouted that he and I were finished.

For his part, George didn't beg me to stay. He didn't chase after me into the hotel hallway. He didn't try to stop me from getting into the elevator.

Though you hadn't taught your workshop in months—you were on leave working on your own poetry collection—you still kept an office at the university. From a pay phone in the hotel lobby, I tried reaching you there. It was past eleven at night, but I had to try on the off chance you were working late, as you sometimes did when the mania took hold. I needed to explain myself to you. The article in the *Saturday Review* was full of lies. Couldn't you see they were trying to take down our revolution one piece at a time? Sylvia Plath, debatably the movement's most prominent champion, was gone. Next, the critics and the disparagers were all coming after me. You and I, we needed to stick together lest they bury this beautiful thing we'd created.

When you didn't pick up the phone, I dialed the operator and called you at your home. Your wife picked up. I tried to sound calm, but my tears were fresh, my voice so obviously raw. "Yes, is Professor Lowell available?" Your wife said it was nearly midnight. "I need to speak to him. I wouldn't be calling if it weren't a terrific emergency." But your bitch of a wife, she hung up on me. I screamed into the receiver, for I knew then that I'd indeed lost you. You'd forsaken me, and here I was, begging you to invite me home again like some banished mongrel.

I remained desperate to win back your affection, and so I decided to give you the one thing you said you wanted more than any other. It was an impossible thing, really. And luckily, no one else but I, your very own Boston Rhodes, currently possessed it.

I kept it in a lockbox.

Call it an offering. You'd said of Sylvia that, most of all, you would miss her voice, her voice, her voice. So in exchange for your approval, and with the hope that I might someday re-earn your love, I am giving you what remains of Sylvia's voice, *igneous and genuine*, her Major Voice, as it inhabits the last true pages of her work.

Will this be enough?

Did you know, Professor, the word for "room" in Italian is "stanza"? Like I said, I picture all my life in terms of rooms. The ones I've moved into. The ones I've moved through. Rooms define every scene in my memory. When you look at life as a series of rooms, suddenly all the good and bad and in-between starts to look like poetry.

As I began to write to you, this room was quiet and affected by a chill. Spooling sheets of paper into my typewriter, I conveyed the opening words of this letter to you. Once, I made the mistake not to include a letter with a gift full of evidence, and I will not make this mistake again.

The air in my loft has since grown warm, and here we are, together in this place, and finally at the end. With this letter, I want you to know that, for the first time, I feel at peace. I've accepted that to beat Sylvia, I must also share my final room with her. You were aware from the start that my story and Sylvia's were yoked in genius and madness, and so, I've determined, it will be, too, with my final maneuver to beat Sylvia once and for all. With *The Bell Jar*, I have watched America rediscover her. She is gone, but the spotlight on Sylvia has never shined brighter. Absence has not diminished her name but solidified it. A discovery of *The Bell Jar* enlightened me about the virtue of legacy; Sylvia's death has shown me the way to finally achieve it. I'm only indignant that she's reached this apocryphal status first! It's my lot, it seems, to always be following the old girl. Sylvia, you see, has played her last move with mastery.

I still have a move left, as well.

Will the full contents of this bottle of Nembutal bring about the same notoriety it has brought her? *It will*, promises the venom voice. *It must!* For how am I supposed to compete with Sylvia in your eyes when I am merely mortal?

When I'm gone, I do believe my death will coalesce around my legacy as it has Sylvia's and will lift it from the ashes. My words will take their rightful place in the world. People will eulogize me, but will you, my beloved Professor Lowell? I put this down plainly here so that you might understand, my rivalry with Sylvia began not over winning the Ring, but over winning your affection and satisfaction in me. I am not of this world, but an otherworldly poet, and you were the first person to see that. You were *my* Polaris. You invited me—and only me—to follow your guiding light.

In sending you a lockbox of Sylvia's final works, these loose pages and notebooks, I am gifting you her voice; with this letter, I am gifting you *my* voice, along with a closing thought. When I struggle to remember that I am a poet at all, I think of Sylvia not with hard-boiled contempt, but with gratitude. Yes, gratitude! You see, I needed her from the start. I could not have reached you, or these heights, without her. I believe she needed me, as well.

Sylvia taught me that it doesn't take much to tip one back into the person we have always been. With this confession, I want you to see me as I was, even as the world comes to see me as the poet of a generation. You will know me better than any of them. It's with this intention that I take my final step. Sometimes striking a match and lighting your world on fire is the only truly independent choice one can make. Sylvia taught me that, too.

I am going to go now. I hold out hope that you are capable of finding it in your heart to forgive me for the sins I proclaim here. Know that I've done them all for you, so that I might finally lead your revolution, like I promised you I would.

When I'm gone, read my poems aloud just as surely as you will Sylvia's. The voices of your winglets are forever in both.

Yours,
Agatha Rhodes

24

Ruth, 1963

JUNE 10—

Often those who play the listening game are those who also initiate it. Sometimes, however, those who need to be heard the most will seek out a listener, like a sinner desperate to confess.

Today, a man in a raincoat showed up at my home and rang the doorbell. Through the glass of the front door, I recognized the shape of his sloping shoulders and robust chin like a musical cue to a once-forgotten song. As he shook out his umbrella on my porch, a wave of affection moved through me. Mr. Lowell, the Mad Poet, was waiting at my threshold.

"Dr. Barnhouse, I'm sorry to show up like this. I haven't made an appointment."

"Nonsense," I said, and beckoned him to come in out of the rain. He stepped inside and put down his umbrella and a bag he was carrying, then removed his hat. There in my foyer he stood, raggedy and damp in a gaberdine suit, heat fogging the lenses of his glasses.

In between writing one-act plays and debuting new collections of poems to great commendation, he admitted to having taken refuge in the hospital several times over the years. A mild, disinhibiting quality of mania is like mineral spirits to an artist's oil paints; it loosens the imaginative thought, he said. The problem was, it came with violence. "It's the most awful feeling. I never know when I'm going to hurt the people I love."

He spoke all of this in a small, low voice. I tried my best to follow his thoughts, which seemed loose and tangential. Soon enough, Mr. Lowell was succumbing to the Mad Poet within him again, the manic essence that, at McLean Hospital, used to gobble up the man's thoughts and would have him spewing on the corruptible nature of his art. Here in my home study, he was talking about confessions of faith, of poetry, of crimes.

"Crimes?"

"Yes, crimes," he said.

"What sorts of crimes?"

"I'm responsible for her death."

I asked him whose death. "Sylvia's," he said. "And another's death, too."

Of course Mr. Lowell isn't responsible for Miss Plath's death, though in my study he repeated the claim with certitude. He said he'd killed Miss Plath through the instrumentation of another. "Another?" I asked.

"Another poet!" he said.

I told Mr. Lowell that I didn't understand what he was talking about, but that I saw he was hurting.

He took his head in his hands, his fingers bent and shaking. "I'm a monster, a darkly tinted tyrant."

"Take a compassionate view for the person beholden to disturbing forces. The rather scary power that drives you is governed by a good, merciful heart."

Mr. Lowell looked at me with a sad half smile. "You mean like Sylvia."

I nodded, then said that I was glad he'd thought well enough of our relationship throughout the years that he would seek me out when he was suffering so.

Mr. Lowell corrected me. "I'm not here for myself. No one can help me."

He brushed a knuckle under his lens to wipe his left eye, then rose to retrieve the paper grocery bag he'd arrived with. He carried it to my desk, where I joined him.

"I wanted to bring you this." He withdrew from the bag a metal lock-box. "It's the only thing I could think to do."

Again, I said I didn't understand.

Using a small key, Mr. Lowell opened the lid of the box. Inside were three spiral notebooks. I asked him what they were.

"They were hers. I believe Sylvia wrote them for you."

JUNE 12—

I was unable to bring myself to read Mr. Lowell's gift of the notebooks. I left them in my study, and I did not touch them until I woke this morning, having scrounged a touch of courage over the past thirty-six hours. I retreated to my sofa with the first notebook and recognized what it was the moment I began to study it.

I discovered that, although I was reading a draft of Miss Plath's novel for the first time, this wasn't the first time I'd *listened* to it. I'd heard *The Bell Jar* once before when it was but the spark of some greater work to come, as Miss Plath recited it aloud in front of the hospital committee at my competency hearing a decade ago.

Undeniably, there are differences in the statement Miss Plath read before the panel and the draft of her novel resting in my hands today. She's changed names, added flair, eliminated other moments that did not serve her story. It's immaterial that she calls me "Dr. Nolan" in it, or Miss Drake "Miss Norris," or herself "Esther Greenwood." I'd recognize Codman Manor in the "Caplan Ward" any day.

The thing that remains true is that, when I read the words, I'm listening to *our story.*

The Bell Jar is a confession.

It is a letter of exoneration.

It is a chronicle of my failed intervention and my inability to save her in time.

I do not want these notebooks, nor the story within them. I reject Mr. Lowell's gift. The pages bring me pain and anguish. Miss Plath is gone. How cruel it is that these words have outlasted her. One might suggest the novel provides a view through a keyhole into the way Miss Plath had observed life, relayed through the mind of a raconteur whose memories had more than a passing resemblance to our experiences together. Let me just say, insight does not get you far in this world. Insight only keeps you locked in the past, with memories and with ghosts.

I will discard these notebooks. I will put them away. I will deny them life within my life. They belong hidden high up in a dark space.

JUNE 25—

The way to Codman Manor is etched into my memory. I believe that it always will be. Blindfold me and spin me around and I will find my path.

I took the outbound number 73 bus from Boston along the parkway to the turnpike. Around three o'clock, just past Concord, the bus exited onto a narrow lane. The woods on either side were dark and dense. Soon, I began to see signs for Trapelo Road again.

The bus stopped at a small theater to take on passengers for Juniper Hill and beyond, but this was where I grabbed my handbag and coat from the overhead rack and got off. I stood still on the sidewalk and watched the bus pull away, then zipped up my jacket and walked the half mile to the familiar arched stone gateway of the hospital.

Closing in on Proctor House, I saw that the road was newly repaved. The view from the top of the hill offered a vista of new buildings, bulldozers, and brick manors under heavy scaffolding. When Dr. Beuscher phoned me last week, inviting me to come to the hospital and see him, he'd said I'd hardly recognize the grounds, what with all the new construction, something unheard-of in the days when Superintendent Frisch was still in charge. I hadn't been back to McLean Hospital since my dismissal. That, and the memory of Miss Drake, had both kept me away. I used to think that, after everything that's happened, revisiting the grounds would have been unthinkable. But Dr. Beuscher pressed, and eventually I agreed. The time that's passed between the inquiry and his call is just barely enough to pacify my averse inclinations and replace them with nerve.

It's a wonder how the addition of crow's-feet lends to a perception of a man's decency. Of course, Dr. Beuscher has always been a compassionate soul. These days, he wears his silver-white hair longer than before. It was, I admit, good to see him.

"Are you up for a walk?" he asked.

We left Proctor House together and wandered through the orchard fields. We approached an acre of young apple trees. I saw that the rows were busy with patients plunking fruit into baskets. Farther ahead, Dr Beuscher pointed out patients playing tennis and badminton on newly fashioned courts. Beyond them, in a small yard, was a group of women engaged in a game of croquet.

"Alternative treatments, Ruth. The simplest solution is the right solution. Let the patients tell us what they need."

I said I'd never expected to see these kinds of changes, and he explained that this was just phase one, that the hospital was replacing the old conventions with the programs I'd once introduced.

"You wanted to change the way we practice? Well, you changed it. All of it."

"I did no such thing."

"We picked up where you left off."

But where I left off was nowhere at all, I thought. We were approaching Codman Manor.

"There's still a place for you here. You'd have your pick of posts. You could be in charge of modernizing the protocols. Heck, you could finally run your own lab."

I reproached him as he led us inside. "Dr. Beuscher, you didn't really bring me all the way out just to offer me a job."

The furniture in the lounges was new. The dusty smell throughout the mansion was not. Dr. Beuscher's smile came with the spectacle of those wonderful crow's-feet. "Even if I had, you're too smart to accept one."

"It has nothing to do with intelligence. There's nothing left for me here."

"I don't know about that."

I'd followed Dr. Beuscher to the first-floor dormitory wing. We were standing outside of room nineteen, the room Miss Plath had briefly occupied. An anxious and dreadful feeling was settling within me.

I took in Miss Plath's old bed, old desk, old closet, and old wicker rocking chair. After all this time, the configuration was still the same, these objects as firmly rooted in place as they are in my dreams.

"There's no need for me to see this."

"I believe there is," Dr. Beuscher said gently. "Think of it as a kind of treatment. This was where Miss Plath got better."

The notebooks Mr. Lowell recently gave me rose in my mind, items too personal to throw away, and too heartbreaking not to keep, now stowed in my attic so that I will someday disremember them.

"It's where I failed her."

"I didn't call to offer you a job. I needed you to see all the good that you did."

"I let her die."

"You saved her."

"She tried to tell me something. I missed it."

"You heard her in a way no one else did, or could."

"You're an idiot."

"I am, but it doesn't change the fact that there are dozens of little miracles that happened in this manor every single day, and you were the only one who was able to see them."

I clenched my teeth. "I was responsible for her!"

"You showed her how to be self-directed."

"Where did it all lead?"

"Away from this place."

And then I thought, as I stood at the entry to Miss Plath's old room, about how when people left Codman Manor, a part of them always stayed behind. Not so much the madness, but the past. It lingered like the dead.

The dead, I have no use for. The living, I do.

"Ruth, she lived!" he said. "She lived! She lived!"

As I stepped past the narrow bed, my legs went weak. I caught myself against the mattress. Miss Plath once said she believed we had the same problem. Our hearts were too big. They let in too much. We couldn't help but feel everything. At the time, I'd thought she couldn't have been more wrong about me. I'd denied myself the ability to feel anything, let alone everything. Only now, in what had been her room, did I finally understand how right she was.

Dr. Beuscher sat on the edge of the bed with me. He took me in his arms. I turned away. He pulled me closer. I cried into his chest.

I cried for Miss Plath. I cried for Miss Drake, too, and for my daughter, and for Superintendent Frisch, and for Nurse Edme, and for the dogs that died on the hill. I wept for all those no longer around, and who, in the long and sober nights ahead, will continue to visit and speak to me. I will listen to them all.

THE LAST STANZA

Invisible Hand

Every one of us must try to be human BEINGS, not simply human OBJECTS moving through time and circumstance. By that I mean we all have the ability to mask the events of pain and sorrow, but the human BEING peels back the mystery, asks why and how, and does not hide behind her own hands. Life must be examined. OBJECTS exist, sightless and without agency, and are doomed to crumble like the Colossus of Rhodes. Human BEINGS endure.

—Robert Lowell,
foreword to the tenth-anniversary edition of *To the Lip*

The depth of history has nothing on the depth of regret.

—Boston Rhodes, "A Visit to Dr. No."

EPILOGUE

Estee, 2019

The path of a master curator's life can be as circuitous as the path of any object. In the midnineties, after my first years in Barcelona, I spend a year curating special collections at the Museum of Marrakech, followed by two years amassing works for the Museum of Czech Literature, and eight months at the National Museum in Rio de Janeiro when Turkey's Ministry of Culture sends for me. This is how I find myself curating the works of an early eighteenth-century writer known as Ari the Poet.

Ari the Poet is known to have produced a hundred volumes of romantic poems, all dedicated to his muse and lover, Bal the Beauty. Preserved in these volumes are vast descriptors of Bal's splendor and kindnesses, though Bal is mostly remembered as a cold-blooded murderer who poisoned the poet and was later hanged for the crime.

Taking into account the rate and severity of paper deterioration, the poet's works, preserved for generations in chests, dresser drawers, pillowcases, and cardboard boxes, are in astonishingly good condition when I examine them. As my translator and I identify and tag the items, I come across a piece of parchment the color of Jerusalem stone. The translator reads it for me. This find is not a poem at all, I realize, but a suicide note written in Ari the Poet's hand. In a single moment, the find both exonerates Bal the Beauty and finishes the story of Ari the Poet.

The role of a master curator is to fill in the missing pieces. A single letter can change the meaning of a life and a legacy.

The morning after the auction of the Plath notebooks, I wait for my friend Nicolas on the front stoop when his Civic pulls up to my apartment building. The wind carries and turns a mist of winter snow. The car is breathing, the street is breathing, the rooftops are breathing. Nicolas loads my suitcases into his back seat and arranges them with enough precision so that if we stop fast, nothing will budge.

We are driving toward Logan airport, and I have Nicolas take a detour. I direct him through the winding streets of Harvard Square to Alewife Parkway. From beyond the earflaps of his fur-trapper winter hat, Nicolas gives me the side-eye. When I said "detour," he figured I meant stop for coffee.

I tell him that we're getting closer, but ten miles along the Concord Turnpike, Nicolas says that if I don't explain where he's going, then he's pulling off the road, and I'm not getting to the airport today. So I reach behind me for my duffel bag and bring it to my lap, unzip the bag, and take out a New Balance shoebox.

I remove the lid, exposing the Plath notebooks to daylight. The car swerves sharply. The tires screech, and Nicolas cries out, "What the—? Are those—?"

"Keep driving. Just watch the highway."

"You've lost your mind!"

Nicolas is pulling off of the turnpike to a barren farm road. He brakes hard on the shoulder and gets out of the car. For a bit, he paces in front of the hood. Behind him rise gray haystacks and low hills. The winter morning sky is so blue that it just might be made of glass.

I roll down my window. "Please come back in."

Nicolas returns to the driver's seat and sits at the wheel.

"Just tell me what you were thinking."

"You said it yourself, Nicolas. Some things don't belong to people."

"I watched a man pay three million dollars for these notebooks yesterday. Trust me, they belong to somebody."

"I've focused on understanding what others wanted from Sylvia, never once stopping to understand what *Sylvia* wanted."

"She wanted none of this."

"So you said. Given that, I've been thinking about the likelihood of having come across the Plath notebooks. What are the odds that the manuscript my mother took would find its way back to me? The Dyce brothers could have brought it to any curator at any auction house in the city. Things this improbable don't happen. It leads me to believe that maybe it shouldn't have happened. But it did happen. I have to assume, on some level, that Sylvia *wanted* me to find these notebooks for her, to set things right."

Nicolas looks worried. Whatever I'm thinking about doing with the notebooks, it's not worth throwing my career away for, or going to prison over, he says. "The Dyce brothers? St. Ambrose? They're all going to come after you."

How can I explain to Nicolas that there has been no crime? Our successful bidder has yet to deliver the money, and the Dyce brothers have yet to sign a transfer of sale. Once the insurance policy St. Ambrose takes out on its objects pays Elton and Jay Jay the final sales value of the manuscript, tax- and fee-free, they'll be satisfied. Sure, St. Ambrose, the insurance company, and the Dyce brothers can always sue me, and they are welcome to if they find me.

But they won't find me.

In fact, as far as I'm concerned, the only crimes here are those committed against Sylvia. It's these crimes I'm determined to rectify.

I pass Nicolas the shoebox. He once again holds the manuscript in his hands. I'm asking him to trust me. "You were right before. I can't sell the notebooks."

"I said you can't *sell* them; I never said *take* them."

"My mother took the notebooks. If I sell them, I'm perpetuating her transgression."

Nicolas holds the box in his lap. He takes my fingers in his, a despairing act to appeal to my better senses. "By keeping the notebooks, you're no better than Boston Rhodes."

"I'm not keeping them or selling them," I say. "I'm returning them."

Nicolas is driving again. Our expedition carries us through the countryside of Eastern Massachusetts. The road to the hospital traverses a land of weatherworn silos and barns. At a rushing creek just off Trapelo Road, Nicolas drives through an open-arched stone gateway with a small metal plaque on one side that reads MCLEAN HOSPITAL.

To our right I take in a tidy cemetery and, in the distance, a water tower that glints rust-red in the sun. Snowplowed walkways cut through scrubby New England pines, offset by blue-tinged peaks that rise into piles of pristine white clouds. Brick mansions and cottages come into view.

Nicolas parks in a lot by the child-care center under a bald and sprawling spruce tree. Bundled in coats and winter gloves, we walk the grounds, which might as well be the grounds of any other New England university, fortified in red brick and busy with people who can pass for students and professors on their way to classes. With the shoebox in the crook of Nicolas's right arm, we pass a research center built into a blocky manor and an outpatient service building with a short green tower topped with a rooster weather vane. The sun hovers just above the rooftops and shines in between the buildings.

Determining that there are too many people around, we decide to walk north on Mill Street, away from the cluster of mansions. I feel a tingle originating from some untouchable region of my body: This is where *The Bell Jar* began. Right here, in this place. I sense a turn of the kaleidoscope, a coming together of past, present, and legacy.

At the end of Mill Street, near a Colony gas station—also steepled—the hospital buildings come to an end. To the left of the road is a forested thicket and a small path that feeds into a clearing. For a few minutes, Nicolas and I stand at its edge. We look across the field of bluish-white ice and snow. The cold burrows into my coat and jeans. Nicolas adjusts his fur hat.

We follow the footpath down into the field, eventually coming to a pitched-roof stone cottage overgrown with ivy. Nicolas stops and opens the shoebox.

I take a notebook, the first of the three, and flip through it with a rough shuffle. Sunlight glints against the paper. With each turn, a page crumbles against the pad of my thumb. The sheets give little resistance. Each disintegrates as though made of dry earth.

Beside me, Nicolas fingers the second notebook. He tears pages from its coil and balls them in his fist. The wind carries the flecks of paper that lift from our hands. Nicolas finds himself lifted with wonder at the sight.

Nicolas then tears the third notebook into halves. The pages pull apart at the spiral binding without effort, as though they have been waiting for this moment. One second they are whole; an instant later they break into fine chips. He passes a half to me.

I crumble one sheet of it at a time. The paper fragments at this precise combination of air and cold and light and age, and the wind gusts gain strength.

Just ahead, on a north-lilting rise and spreading across the land, I've spotted a grouping of bee boxes. Each pine tower within the colony is four drawers high and set among a jumble of footprints in snow. The insects, relatively dormant, slowly become aware of our presence, of our heat and our smells, and eventually, shadows of the swarms undulate against the snow like water reflecting off of stones.

"You think people will ever forgive us for this?" Nicolas asks.

I gaze at the ground and notice a blanket of ash-like flecks covering the tops of my boots. The breeze picks at it. The pieces drift and tumble, stir and spread.

"I don't think so."

I expect that by now, a curator at St. Ambrose has likely discovered the notebooks are no longer in the safe holdings room. Quimby, no doubt, has started asking questions. It won't take long for the auction house to note that I have not come into work. When I don't answer my phone, Quimby will call the Boston Police Department. By the end of the day, detectives and agents from the FBI Art Crime Division will transform St. Ambrose into a command center worthy of a hostage negotiation. Jay Jay and Elton Dyce will be livid. They had every reason to believe I was going to make good on my promises to them, that I'd sell the three notebooks of *The Bell Jar* and they'd grow rich. The Harvard-hoodied man would have given the notebooks a decently proper home. A person willing to pay three million dollars for a rare manuscript is a person who would have taken care of it and seen to its upkeep. As for Moses Quimby, I envision the man struggling to come to grips with what the loss means for his auction house, putting his hands up to his face, and weeping. And yes, I feel bad, because I don't want to hurt any of them. And yes, I'm lousy with guilt for what I'm doing. And yes, I'm the Sistine Chapel of remorse, a masterpiece of culpability. They'll all wonder if I took the notebooks to sell them to another buyer willing to pay more to own them. They'll want to know where the notebooks are and if they are safe.

If they are to ever find me, if they are to ever ask me why, I will tell them I did this to give the notebooks back to Sylvia and redeem my mother. I will tell them that some things you can't own; they belong to the world. I will tell them I destroyed them to honor the wishes of Sylvia, who wanted the process of her writing to be invisible. I will tell them stories from the life of a master curator: the pilfered Bruegel Ten, the mishandled matchbook, the stolen Bible, the exploited final chapter of a famed novel, the busted typewriter, the poet's lost note, and the stolen notebooks of *The Bell Jar*—disparate objects, each one solely possessing the power to absolve us of our unforgivable sins against them.

Like Esther Greenwood says, I shut my eyes and all the world drops dead; I lift my eyes and all is born again. I hope she's right. I believe that she is.

For a moment, I take in the distance Nicolas and I have crossed and the small red buildings of the hospital at the top of the hill. It's getting late in the day.

"Let's get you to the airport," Nicolas says. "You've got a flight to catch."

ACKNOWLEDGMENTS

Every name here belongs on the cover, mad poets each.

From Inkwell Management, thank you to Richard Pine, who, with vision, uniform kindness, and aplomb, saw a novel in this piece from the beginning; as well as Eliza Rothstein, Alexis Hurley, Naomi Eisenbeiss, Nathaniel Jacks, Claire Friedman, and Kristin van Ogtrop.

From Harper, thank you to Gail Winston and Jonathan Burnham, along with Hayley Salmon, Jane Beirn, Becca Putman, Andy LeCount, Gabriel Barillas, Doug Jones, Leah Wasielewski, Christopher Connolly, Katie O'Callaghan, Amelia Beckerman, and Robin Bilardello (for an iconic cover design).

Thank you to my readers and supporters Karen Rinaldi, Paul Harding, Adam Johnson, Dana Spiotta, Christina Clancy, Scott James, Shana Mahaffey, Janis Cooke Newman, Julie Lythcott-Haims, Jane Ciabattari, Susanne Pari, Anita Amirrezvani, Jeanne Carstensen, Karen Bjorneby, Emily Cooke, Mona Kerby, Janice Shiffler, and Miriam Landis.

Thank you to my family, a wellspring of patience, love, and support: Mimi, Alec, Chloe, Carin, Paul, Terri, and Jim.

I'm grateful to be a part of supportive writing communities including the Lit Camp Writers Conference, the San Francisco Writers Grotto, the Castro Writers Cooperative, and the Wellstone Center in the Redwoods.

Thank you to Praveen Madan, Christin Evans, and Elaine Petrocelli of Kepler's Books & Magazines, The Booksmith, and Book Passage respectively, and to independent booksellers everywhere, the conduits and compasses leading us to the world of words and ideas.

Thank you to these works, my roadmaps: Sylvia Plath's *The Bell Jar,* Linda W. Wagner-Martin's *Sylvia Plath: A Biography,* Diana Wood Middlebrook's *Anne Sexton: A Biography, Anne Sexton: A Self-Portrait in Letters,* edited by Linda Gray Sexton and Lois Ames, Alex Beam's *Gracefully Insane,* Enoch Callaway's *Asylum,* Peter K. Steinberg and Karen V. Kukil's *The Letters of Sylvia Plath,* Kay Redfield Jamison's *Robert Lowell: Setting the River on Fire,* and Matthew Zapruder's *Why Poetry.*

And finally, thank you to Sylvia Plath, Ruth Barnhouse, William Beuscher, Anne Sexton, Robert Lowell, Maxine Kumin, George Starbuck, Ted Hughes, W. D. Snodgrass, Marianne Moore, and Aurelia Plath for making appearances in spirit and in name.

ABOUT THE AUTHOR

LEE KRAVETZ is the author of acclaimed nonfiction, including *Strange Contagion* and *SuperSurvivors.* His work has appeared in the *New York Times, Psychology Today,* the *Daily Beast,* the *San Francisco Chronicle,* and on PBS. He lives in the San Francisco Bay Area. *The Last Confessions of Sylvia P.* is his debut novel.